The Dark Frigate

Charles Boardman Hawes

Illustrated by

Warren Chappell

DOVER PUBLICATIONS, INC.
Mineola, New York

Bibliographical Note

This Dover edition, first published in 2018, is an unabridged republication of the work originally published in 1924 by Little, Brown and Company, New York.

Library of Congress Cataloging-in-Publication Data

Names: Hawes, Charles Boardman, 1889-1923, author. | Chappell, Warren, 1904-1991, illustrator.
Title: The dark frigate / Charles Boardman Hawes ; illustrated by Warren Chappell.
Description: Mineola, New York : Dover Publications, Inc., 2018. | "This Dover edition, first published in 2018, is an unabridged republication of the work originally published in 1924 by Little, Brown and Company, New York"—Title page verso. | Summary: In seventeenth-century England, orphaned Philip Marsham, forced to flee London after a terrible accident, finds himself in an even more difficult situation when his ship is taken over by pirates and he is forced to become a member of their crew.
Identifiers: LCCN 2017046935| ISBN 9780486823928 (paperback) | ISBN 048682392X (paperback)
Subjects: | CYAC: Orphans-Fiction. | Pirates-Fiction. | Sea stories. | BISAC: JUVENILE FICTION / Action & Adventure / Pirates.
Classification: LCC PZ7.H312 Dar 2018 | DDC [Fic] —dc23
LC record available at https://lccn.loc.gov/2017046935

Manufactured in the United States by LSC Communications
82392X01   2018
www.doverpublications.com

TO

George W. Cable

WITH WARM ADMIRATION

AND

FILIAL AFFECTION

Contents

FROM curious old books, many of them forgotten save by students of archaic days at sea, I have taken words and phrases and incidents. The words and phrases I have put into the talk of the men of the Rose of Devon; *the incidents I have shaped and fitted anew to serve my purpose.*

C. B. H.

CHAPTER I

Flight

PHILIP MARSHAM was bred to the sea as far back as the days when he was cutting his milk teeth, and he never thought he should leave it; but leave it he did, once and again, as I shall tell you.

His father was master of a London ketch, and they say that before the boy could stand unaided on his two feet he would lean himself, as a child does, against the waist in a seaway, and never pipe a whimper when she thrust her bows down and shipped enough water to douse him from head to heels. He lost his mother before he went into breeches and he was climbing the rigging before he could walk alone. He spent two years at school to the good Dr. Josiah Arber at Roehampton, for his father, being a clergyman's son who had run wild in his youth, hoped to do better by the lad than he had done by himself, and was of a mind to send Philip home

1

a scholar to make peace with the grandparents, in the vicarage at Little Grimsby, whom Tom Marsham had not seen in
twenty years. But the boy was his father over again, and taking to books with an ill grace, he endured them only until he
had learned to read and write and had laid such foundation
of mathematics as he hoped would serve his purpose when
he came to study navigation. Then, running away by night
from his master's house, he joined his father on board the
Sarah ketch, who laughed mightily to see how his son took
after him, do what he would to make a scholar of the lad.
And but for the mercy of God, which laid Philip Marsham on
his back with a fever in the spring of his nineteenth year, he
had gone down with his father in the ketch *Sarah,* the night
she foundered off the North Foreland.

Moll Stevens kept him, while he lay ill with the fever, in
her alehouse in High Street, in the borough of Southwark,
and she was good to him after her fashion, for her heart was
set on marrying his father. But though she had brought Tom
Marsham to heel and had named the day, nothing is sure till
the words are said.

When they had news which there was no doubting that
Tom Marsham was lost at sea, she was of a mind to send the
boy out of her house the hour he was able to walk thence;
and so she would have done, if God's providence had not
found means to renew his strength before the time and send
him packing in wonderful haste, with Moll Stevens and certain others after him in full cry.

For the third day he had come down from his chamber
and had taken the great chair by the fire, when there entered
a huge-bellied countryman who carried a gun of a kind not
familiar to those in the house.

"Ah," Phil heard them whispering, as he sat in the great
chair, "here's Jamie Barwick come back again." Then they
called out, "Welcome, Jamie, and good morrow!"

Philip Marsham would have liked well to see the gun himself, since a taste for such gear was born in him; but he had

been long bedridden, and though he could easily have walked over to look at it, he let well enough alone and stayed where he was.

They passed it from one to another and marvelled at the craftsmanship, and when they let the butt fall on the floor, the pots rang and the cans tinkled. And now one cried, "Have care which way you point the muzzle." But the countryman who brought it laughed and declared there was no danger, for though it was charged he had spent all his powder and had not primed it.

At last he took it from them all and, spying Moll Stevens, who had heard the bustle and had come to learn the cause, he called for a can of ale. There was no place at hand to set down his gun so he turned to the lad in the chair and cried, "Here, whiteface with the great eyes, take my piece and keep it for me. I am dry—Oh, so dry! Keep it till I have drunk, and gramercy. A can of ale, I say! Hostess! Moll! Moll! Where art thou? A can of ale!"

He flung himself down on a bench and mopped his forehead with his sleeve. He was a huge great man with a vast belly and a deep voice and a fat red face that was smiling one minute and frowning the next.

"Ho! Hostess!" he roared again. "Ale, ale! A can of ale! Moll, I say! A can of ale!"

A hush had fallen upon the room at his first summons, for he had been quiet so long after entering that his clamour amazed all who were present, unless they had known him before, and they now stole glances at him and at one another and at Moll Stevens, who came bustling in again, her face as red as his own, for she was his match in girth and temper.

"Here then!" she snapped, and thumped the can down before him on the great oaken table.

He blew off the topmost foam and thrust his hot face into the ale, but not so deep that he could not send Phil Marsham a wink over the rim.

This Moll perceived and in turn shot at the lad a glance so ill-tempered that any one who saw it must know she rued the day she had taken him under her roof in his illness. He had got many such a glance since word came that his father was lost, and more than glances, too, for as soon as Moll knew there was nothing to gain by keeping his good will she had berated him like the vixen she was at heart, although he was then too ill to raise his head from the sheet.

It was a sad plight for a lad whose grandfather was a gentleman (although he had never seen the old man), and there had been times when he would almost have gone back to school and have swallowed without a whimper the Latin and Greek. But he was stronger now and nearer able to fend for himself and it was in his mind, as he sat in the great chair with the gun, that after a few days at longest he would pay the score in silver from his chest upstairs, and take leave forever of Moll Stevens and her alehouse. So now, giving her no heed, he began fondling the fat countryman's piece.

The stock was of walnut, polished until a man could see his face in it, and the barrel was of steel chased from breech to muzzle and inlaid with gold and silver. Small wonder that all had been eager to handle it, the lad thought. He saw others in the room furtively observing the gun, and he knew there were men not a hundred leagues away who would have killed the owner to take it. He even bethought himself, having no lack of conceit in such matters, that the man had done well to pick Phil Marsham to keep it while he drank his ale.

The fellow had gone to the opposite corner of the room and had taken a deep seat just beneath the three long shelves on which stood the three rows of fine platters that were the pride of Moll Stevens's heart.

The platters caught the lad's eye and, raising the gun, he presented it at the uppermost row. Supposing it were loaded and primed, he thought, what a stir and clatter it would make to fire the charge! He smiled, cocked the gun, and rested his finger on the trigger; but he was over weak to hold the gun steady. As he let the muzzle fall, his hand slipped. His throat tightened like a cramp. His hair, he verily believed, rose on end. The gun—primed or no—went off.

He had so far lowered the muzzle that not a shot struck the topmost row of platters, but of the second lower row, not one platter was left standing. The splinters flew in a shower over the whole room, and a dozen stray shots—for the gun was charged to shoot small birds—peppered the fat man about the face and ear. Worst of all, by far, to make good measure of the clatter and clamour, the great mass of the charge, which by grace of God avoided the fat man's head although the wind of it raised his hair, struck fairly a butt of Moll Stevens's richest sack, which six men had raised on a frame to make easier the labour of drawing from it, and shattered a stave so that the goodly wine poured out as if a greater than Moses had smitten a rock with his staff.

Of all in the room, mind you, none was more amazed than Philip Marsham, and indeed for a moment his wits were quite numb. He sat with the gun in his hands, which was still smoking to show who had done the wicked deed, and stared at the splintered platters and at the countryman's furious face, on which rivulets of blood were trickling down, and at the gurgling flood of wine that was belching out on Moll Stevens's dirty floor.

Then in rushed Moll herself with such a face that he hoped never to see the like again. She swept the room at a single glance and bawling, "As I live, 'tis that tike, Philip Marsham! Paddock! Hound! Devil's imp!"—at him she came, a billet of Flanders brick in her hand.

He was of no mind to try the quality of her scouring, for although she knew not the meaning of a clean house, she was a brawny wench and her hand and her brick were as rough as her tongue. Further, he perceived that there were others to reckon with, for the countryman was on his feet with a murderous look in his eye and there were six besides him who had started up. Although Phil had little wish to play hare to their hounds, since the fever had left him fit for neither fighting nor running, there was urgent need that he act soon and to a purpose, for Moll and her Flanders brick were upon him.

Warmed by the smell of the good wine run to waste, and marvellously strengthened by the danger of bodily harm if once they laid hands on him, he got out of the great chair as nimbly as if he had not spent three weeks in bed, and, turning like a fox, slipped through the door.

God was good to Philip Marsham, for the gun, as he dropped it, tripped Moll Stevens and sent her sprawling on the threshold; the fat countryman, thinking more of his property than his injury, stooped for the gun; and those two so filled the door that the six were stoppered in the alehouse until with the whoo-bub ringing in his ears Phil had got him out of sight. He had the craft, though they then came after him like hounds let slip, to turn aside and take to earth in a trench hard by, and to lie in hiding there until the hue and cry had come and gone. In faith, he had neither the wind nor the strength to run farther.

It was "Stop thief!"—"Murders done!"—"Attach the knave!"—"Help! Help!"

Who had dug the trench that was his hiding-place he never knew, but it lay not a furlong from the alehouse door, and as he tumbled into it and sprawled flat on the wet earth he gave the man an orphan's blessing. The hue and cry passed him and went racing down the river; and when the yells had grown fainter, and at last had died quite away, he got up out of the trench and walked as fast as he could in the opposite direction, stopping often to rest, until he had left Moll Stevens's alehouse a good mile behind him. He passed a parish beadle, but the fellow gave him not a single glance;

he passed the crier calling for sale the household goods of a man who desired to take his fortune and depart for New England, and the crier (who, one would suppose, knew everything of the public weal) brushed his coat but hindered him not. In the space of a single furlong he met two Puritans on foot, without enough hair to cover their ears, and two fine gentlemen on horseback whose curls flowed to their shoulders; but neither one nor other gave him let. The rabble of higglers and waggoners from the alehouse, headed by the countryman, Jamie Barwick, and by Moll Stevens herself, had raced far down the river, and Phil Marsham was free to go wherever else his discretion bade him.

Now it would have been his second nature to have fled to the docks, for he was bred a sailor and could haul and reef and steer with any man; but they whom he had no wish to meet had gone that way and in his weakness it had been worse than folly to beard them. His patrimony was forfeit, for although his father had left him a bag of silver, it lay in his chest in Moll Stevens's alehouse, and for fear of hanging he dared not go back after it. She was a vindictive shrew and would have taken his heart's blood to pay him for his blunder. His father was gone and the ketch with him, and, save for a handful of silver the lad had about him, he was penniless. So what would a sailor do, think you, orphaned and penniless and cut off from the sea, but set himself up for a farmer? Phil clapped his hand on his thigh and quietly laughed. That a man needed money and skill for husbandry never entered his foolish head. Were not husbandmen all fond fellows whom a lively sailor man might fleer as he pleased? Nay, they knew not so much as one rope from another. Why, then, he would go into the country and set him up as a kind of prince among husbandmen, who had, by all reports, plenty of good nappy liquor to drink and bread and cheese and meat to eat.

With that he turned his back on the sea and London and on Moll Stevens, whom he never saw again. His trafficking with her was well ended, and as well ended his father's affair, in my belief; for the woman had a bitter temper and a sharp tongue, and there are worse things for a free-hearted, jovial man such as Tom Marsham was, than drowning. The son owed her nought that the bag in his chest would not repay many times over, so he set out with all good courage and with the handful of silver that chanced to be in his pocket and, though his legs were weak and he must stop often to rest, by nightfall he had gone miles upon his way.

CHAPTER II

A Leal Man and a Fool

CLOUDS OBSCURED the sun and a gusty wind set the road-side grasses nodding and rustled the leaves of oak and ash. Phil passed between green fields into a neat village, where men and women turned to look after him as he went, and on into open country, where he came at last to a great estate and a porter's lodge and sat him down and rested. There was a hoarse clamour from a distant rookery, and the wind whispered in two pine trees that grew beside the lodge where a gentleman of curious tastes had planted them. A few drops of rain, beating on the road and rattling on the leaves of a great oak, increased the loneliness that beset him. Where he should lie the night he had no notion, or whence his supper was to come; but the shower blew past and he pressed on till he came to a little hamlet on the border of a heath, where there was a smithy, with a silent man standing by the door.

As he passed the smithy the lad stumbled.

The man looked hard at him as if suspecting some trick-ery; but when Phil was about to press on without a word the man asked in a low voice, "Who the de'il gaed yonder on sic like e'en and at sic like hoddin' gait?"

At this Phil sat down on a stone, for his weakness had grown on him sorely, and replied that whither he was going he neither knew nor cared. Whereupon the man, whom he knew by his tongue to be a Scot, cried out, "Hech! The lad's falling!" And catching the youth by the arm, he lifted him off the stone and led him into the smithy.

Phil found himself in a chair with straight back and sides, but with seat and backing woven of broad, loose straps, which seemed as easy as the best goose-feathers. "It is nought," he said. "A spell of faintness caught me. I'll be going; I must find an inn; I'll be going now."

"Be still. Ye'll na be off sae soon."

The man thrust a splinter of wood into the coals, and light-ing therewith a candle in a lanthorn, he began rummaging in a cupboard behind the forge, whence he drew out a quarter loaf, a plate of cheese, a jug, and a deep dish in which there was the half of a meat pie. Placing before his guest a table of rough boards blackened with smoke, a great spoon, and a pint pot, he poured from the jug a brimming potful of cider, boiled with good spices and fermented with yeast.

"A wee healsome drappy," said he, "an' then the guid vit-tle. Dinna be laithfu'."

Raising the pot to his lips the lad drank deep and became aware he was famished for food, although he had not until then thought of hunger. As he ate, the quarter loaf, the cheese, and the half of a meat pie fell victims to his tren-chering, and though his host plied the jug to fill his cup, when at last he leaned back he had left no morsel of food nor drop of drink.

Now, for the first time, he looked about him and gave heed to the smoking lanthorn, the dull glow of the dying sea-coals in the forge, the stern face of the smith who sat opposite him, and the dark recesses of the smithy. Outside was a driving rain and the screech of a gusty wind.

It was strange, he thought, that after all his doubts, he was well fed and dry and warm. The rain rattled against the walls of the smithy and the wind howled. Only to hear the storm was enough to make a man shiver, but warmed by the fire in the forge the lad smiled and nodded. In a moment he was asleep.

"Cam' ye far?" his host asked in a rough voice.

The lad woke with a start. "From London," he said and again he nodded.

The man ran his fingers through his red beard. "God forgie us!" he whispered. "The laddie ha grapit a' the way frae Lon'on."

He got up from his chair and led Phil to a kind of bed in the darkest corner, behind the forge, and covered him and left him there. Going to the door he looked out into the rain and stood so for a long time.

Two boys, scurrying past in the rain, saw him standing there against the dim light of the lanthorn, and hooted in derision. The wind swept away their voices so that the words were lost, but one stooped and, picking up a stone, flung it at the smithy. It struck the lintel above the man's head and the boys with a squeal of glee vanished into the rain and darkness. The blood rushed to the man's face and his hand slipped under the great leathern apron that he wore.

By morning the storm was gone. The air was clean and cool, and though puddles of water stood by the way, the road had so far dried as to give good footing. All this Philip Marsham saw through the smithy door, upon waking, as he raised himself on his elbow.

He had slept that night with his head behind the cupboard and with his feet under the great bellows of the forge, so narrow was the space in which the smith had built the cot; and where his host had himself slept there was no sign.

The smith now stood in the door. "Na, na," he was saying, "'tis pitch an' pay—siller or nought. For the ance ye hae very foully deceived me. Ye shall henceforth hae my wark for siller; or, an ye like—"

A volley of rough laughter came booming into the smithy, and then a clatter of hoofs as the man without rode away; but the face of the smith was hot as flame when he turned to the forge, and, as he thrust his fingers through his red beard, an angry light was in his eyes. Reaching for the handle of the bellows, he blew the fire so fiercely that the rockstaff and the whole frame swayed and creaked. He then took up a bar of metal and, breaking it on the anvil with a great blow of the up-hand sledge, studied the grey surface and smiled. He thrust the bar into the white coals and with the slicer he clapped the coals about it.

Now drawing out the bar a little way to see how it was taking its heat, and now thrusting it quickly back again, he brought it to the colour of white flame, and, snatching it out with his pliers and laying it on the face of the anvil, he shaped it with blow after blow of the hand hammer, thrust it again into the coals and blew up the fire, again laid it on the anvil, and, smiting it until the sparks flew in showers, worked it, with a deftness marvellous in the eyes of the lad, who sat agape at the fury of his strokes, into the shape of a dagger or dirk.

At last, heating it in the coals to the redness of blood and throwing it on the floor to cool, he paced the smithy, muttering to himself. After a time he took it up again and with the files in their order—the rough, the bastard, the fine and the smooth—worked it down, now trying the surface with fingertips, now plying his file as if the Devil were at his elbow and his soul's salvation depended upon haste, until the shape and surface pleased him.

He then thrust it again into the coals and blew up the fire softly, watching the metal with great care till it came to blood-red heat, when he quenched it in a butt of water and, laying it on the bench, rubbed it with a whetstone until the black scurf was gone and the metal was bright. Again he laid it in the coals and slowly heated it, watching with even greater care while the steel turned to the colour of light gold and to the colour of dark gold; then with a deft turn of the pliers he snatched it out and thrust it deep into the water.

As he had worked, his angry haste had subsided and now, drawing out the metal, he studied it closely and smiled. Then he looked up and meeting the eyes of Philip Marsham, who had sat for an hour watching him, he gave a great start and cried, "God forgie us! I hae clean forgot the lad!"

Laying aside his work he pushed before the chair the smoke-stained table he had used the night before, placed on it a bowl and a spoon, and, setting a small kettle on the forge, blew up the fire until the kettle steamed. He then poured porridge from the kettle into the bowl, and bringing from the cupboard a second quarter-loaf, nodded at the lad and, as an afterthought, remarked, "There's a barrel o' water ahint the smiddy, an ye'd wash."

Rising, Phil went out and found the barrel, into which he thrust head and hands to his great refreshment; and returning, he sat down to the bread and porridge.

While Phil ate, the smith worked at a bit of bone which he shaped to his desire as a handle for the dirk.

With light taps of the riveting-hammer he drove it into place and bound it fast with ferules chosen from a box under the cot. He then sat looking a long time at Phil, nodded, smiled, ran his fingers through his beard, smiled again and, with a fine tool, fell to working on the ferules. There had been a friendly look in the lad's eyes, and of friendly looks the smith had got few in England. People bought his work because he was a master craftsman, but the country folk of England had little love for the Scots who came south in King James's time and after, and a man had need to look sharp lest he fall victim to theft or worse than theft. He stopped and again looked at his guest, ran his fingers through his beard and demanded suddenly, "Thy name, laddie?"

"Philip Marsham."

"Ye'll spell it out for me?"

This Phil did.

After working a while longer he said as if in afterthought, "Ye'll bide wi' me a while?"

"No, I must be on my way."

The man sighed heavily but said only, "I hae ta'en a likin' to ye."

Rising, the lad thrust his hand into his bosom and stood as if to take his leave.

"Na, na! Dinna haste! I'll ask ye to gie me help wi' a bit that's yet to be done."

The smith turned his work over and over. He had made a dirk with a handle of bone bound with silver, and, as he turned it, he examined it with utmost care. "'Twill do," he said at last, "and noo for the wark that takes twa pair o' hands."

He pointed to a great grindstone.

> *He that will a guid edge win,*
> *Maun forge thick an' grind thin.*

Sitting down at the grindstone, the lad began to turn it while the smith, now dashing water over it, now putting both hands to the work, ground the dirk. An hour passed, and a second, with no sound save the whir of steel on stone and now and again the muttered words:

He that will a guid edge win,
Maun forge thick an' grind thin.

Leaning back at last, he said, "'Tis done! An' such wark is better suited to a man o' speerit than priggin' farriery."

He tried the edge with his thumb and smiled. From a chip he sliced a thin circular shaving that went with and across and against the grain. Laying a bit of iron on a board, he cut it clean in two with the dirk and the edge showed neither nick nor mark.

Phil rose now, and drew from inside his shirt his small pouch of silver. "I'll pay the score," he said.

The Scot stared at him as if he would not believe his ears, then got up as if to thrust the dirk between the lad's ribs.

"Those are very foul words," he said thickly. "Nae penny nor plack will I take, and were ye a man bearded, I'd leave ye a pudding for the hoodie-craw."

The lad reddened and stammered, "I—I—why, I give you thanks and ask your pardon."

The smith drew himself up and was about to speak harshly, but he saw the lad's eyes filling and knew no harm was intended. He caught his breath and bit his beard. "'Tis forgi'en an' forgot," he cried. "I hae ta'en a likin' to ye an' here's my hand on't. I hae made ye the dirk for a gift an' sin ye maun be on your way, ye shall hae my ane sheath, for I've no the time to mak' ye the mate to it e'er ye'll be leavin' me."

With that he drew out his dirk, sheath and all, and placing the new blade in the old leather, handed it to the lad, saying, "'Tis wrought o' Damascus steel and there's not twa smiths in England could gi'e ye the like."

So with few words but with warm friendliness they parted, and Philip Marsham went away over the heath, wondering how a Scottish smith came to be dwelling so many long leagues south of the border. In those days there were many Scots to be found in England, who had sought long since to better their fortunes by following at the heels of their royal countryman; but he had chanced to meet with few of them.

Not until he had gone miles did he draw the dirk and read, cut in fine old script on the silver ferule, the legend, *Wrought by Colin Samson for Philip Marsham*. There are those who would say it was a miracle out of Bible times, but neither Philip Marsham nor I ever saw a Scot yet who would not share his supper with a poorer man than himself.

At the end of the day he bought food at a cottage where the wife did not scruple to charge him three times the worth of the meal, and that night he lay under a hedge; the day thereafter he chanced upon a shepherd with whom he passed the night on the hills, and the third day he came to an inn where the reckoning took all but a few pence of his silver. So as he set out upon his way in the morning, he knew not whence his supper was to come or what roof should cover his head.

It was a fine day, with white clouds blowing across a blue sky and all the colours as bright as in a painted picture, and there was much for a sailor to marvel at. The grass in the meadows waved in the great wind like running water. The river in the valley was so small and clear and still that, to a man bred at sea, it appeared to be no water at all but a toy laid between hills, with toy villages for children on its banks. Climbing with light quick steps a knoll from which there was a broader prospect, Phil came unawares upon a great thick adder, which lay sunning its tawny flanks and black-marked back but which slipped away into a thicket at the jar of footsteps. The reptile gave him a lively start, but it was soon gone, and from the knoll he saw the valley spread before him for miles.

It was a day to be alive and, though Philip Marsham was adrift in a strange world, with neither chart nor compass to show the way, his strength had at last come back to him and he had the blithe spirit that seasons a journey well. His purse was light but he was no lad to be stayed for lack of wind, and seeing now a man far ahead of him on the road, and perceiving an opportunity to get sailing directions for the future, he leaped down from the knoll and set off after the fellow as hard as he could post.

The man had gone another mile before Phil overhauled him and by then Phil was puffing so loudly that the fellow, who carried a huge book under his arm and bore himself very loftily, turned to see what manner of creature was at his heels. Although he had the air of a great man, his coat was now revealed as worn and spotted and his wristbands were dirty. He frowned, bent his head, and pursued his journey in silence.

"Good morrow to you!" Phil cried and fell into step beside him.

The man answered not a word but frowned and hugged his book and walked the faster.

At that Phil bustled up and laid hand on his dirk. "Good morrow, I say. Hast no tongue between thy teeth?"

The fellow hugged his book the tighter and frowned the darker and fiercely shook his head. "Never," he cried, "was a man assaulted with such diversity of thoughts! Yet here must come a lobcock lapwing and cry 'Good morrow!' I will have you know I am one to bite sooner than to bark."

Already he was striding at a furious gait, yet now, giving a hitch to his mighty book, he made shift to lengthen his stride and go yet faster.

Unhindered by any such load, Phil pressed at his heels.

"'A lobcock'? 'A lapwing'?" he cried. "Thou puddling quacksalver—"

Stopping short and giving him a look of dark resentment, the fellow sadly shook his head. "That was a secret and most venomous blow."

"I gave you good morrow and you returned me nought but ill words."

"The shoe must be made for the foot. I have no desire to go posting about the country with a roystering coxcomb but—well—as I say, I have no liking for thy company, which consorts ill with the pressure of many thoughts; but since you know what you know (and the Devil take him who learned you it!), like it or not, I must even keep thy company with such grace as may be. Yea, though thou clappest hand to thy weapon with such facility that I believe thee sunk to thy neck in the Devil's quagmire, bogged in thy sin, and thy hands red with blood."

With that, he set out again but at an ordinary pace, and Phil, wonderfully perplexed by his words, fell into his step.

Again the fellow shook his head very sadly. "A secret and most venomous blow! Th' art a Devon man?"

"Nay, I never saw Devon."

The fellow shot him a strange glance and shifted the book from one arm to the other.

"And have never seen Devon? Never laid foot in Bideford, I'll venture." There was a cunning look in his eyes and again he shifted the book.

"'Tis even so."

"A most venomous blow! This wonderfully poseth me." After a time he said in a very low voice, "There is only one other way. Either you have told me a most wicked lie or Jamie Barwick told you."

The fellow, watching like a cat at a rat-hole, saw Phil start at the sound of Jamie Barwick's name.

"I knew it!" he cried. "He'd tell, he'd tell! He's told before—'twas he took the tale to Devon. He's a tall fellow but I'll hox him yet. It was no fault of mine—though I suppose you'll not believe that."

Upon the mind of Philip Marsham there descended a baffling array of memories. The name of the big countryman with the gun carried him back to that afternoon in Moll Stevens's alehouse, whence with good cause he had fled for his life. And now this stray wight, with a great folio volume under his arm, out of a conglomeration of meaningless words had suddenly thrown at the lad's head the name of Jamie Barwick.

"We must have this out between us," the fellow said at last, breathing hard, "I'll not bear the shadow longer. Come, let us sit while we talk, for thereby we may rest from our travels. You see, 'twas thus and so. Jamie Barwick and I came out of Devon and took service with Sir John—Jamie in the stables, for he has a way with horses, and I was under-steward till my wits should be appreciated, which I made sure, I'd have you know, would be soon, for there are few scholars that can match my curious knowledge of the moon's phases and when to plant corn or of the influence of the planets on all manner of husbandry; and further, I have kept the covenant of the living God, which should make all the devils in hell to tremble; and if England keeps it she shall be saved from burning. So when I made shift to get the ear of Sir John, who hath a sharp nose in all affairs of his estate, said I—and it took a stout heart, I would have you know, for he is a man of hot temper—said I, if he would engage a hundred pounds at my direction I would return him in a year's time a gain of a fourth again as much as all he would engage.

"'Aha!'" quoth he, "'this is speech after mine own heart. A hundred pounds, sayest thou? 'Tis thine to draw upon, and the man who can turn his talents thus shall be steward of all mine estates. But mind'—and here he put his finger to his nose, for he hath keen scent for a jest—'thou shalt go elsewhere to try the meat on the dog, for I'll be no laughing-stock; and if thou fail'st then shalt thou go packing, bag and baggage, with the dogs at thy heels. Is't a bargain?'

"Now there was that in his way of speech which liked me little, for I am used to dealing with quieter men and always I have given my wits to booklearning and to Holy Writ rather than to bickering. But I could not then say him nay, for he held his staff thus and so and laughed in his throat in a way that I have a misliking of. So I said him yea, and took in my own name fifty acres of marsh land, and paid down more than thirty pound sterling, and expended all of eight pound sterling for the ploughing and twice that for the burning, and sowed it with rape-seed at ninepence the acre, and paid twelve pound for the second ploughing and eleven pound for the fencing—all this did I draw from Sir John, who, to pay the Devil his due, gave it me with a free hand; and if God had been pleased to send the ordinary blessing upon mine acres I should have got from it at harvest three hundred or four hundred or even five hundred quarters of good rape-seed. And what with reaping and threshing and all, at four and twenty shillings the quarter I should have repaid him his hundred pounds, threefold or fourfold. All this by the blessing of God should I have done but for some little bugs that came upon mine acres in armies, and the fowls of the air that came in clouds and ate up my rape-seed and my tender young rape, so that I lost all that I laid out. And Sir John would not see that in another year I ought, God favouring me, to get him back his silver I had lost, even as the book says. He is a man of his word and, crying that the jest was worth the money, he sent me out the gate with the dogs at my heels and with Jamie Barwick laughing till his fat belly shook, to see me go; for I was always in terror of the dogs, which are great tall beasts that delight to bark and snap at me. And the last word to greet my ears, ere I thought they would have torn me limb from limb, was Sir John bawling at me, 'Thou puddling quacksalver!' which Jamie Barwick hath told in Bideford, making thereby such mirth that I can no longer abide there but must needs flit about the country. And lo! even thou, who by speech and coat are not of this country at all, dost challenge me by the very words he used."

Phil lay meditating on the queer fate that had placed those words in his mouth. "Who," he said at last, "is this Sir John?"

"'Who is Sir John?'" The fellow turned and looked at him. "You have come from farther than I thought, not to know Sir John Bristol."

"Sir John Bristol? I cannot say I have heard that name."

"Hast never heard of Sir John Bristol? In faith, thou art indeed a stranger hereabouts. He is a harsh man withal, and doubtless my ill harvest was the judgment of God upon me for hiring myself to serve a cruel, blasphemous knight who upholdeth episcopacy and the Common Prayer book."

"And whom," asked the lad, "do you serve now?"

"Ah! I, who would make a skillful, faithful, careful steward, am teaching a school of small children, and erecting horoscopes for country bumpkins, so low has that harsh knight's ill-considered jest cast me. 'Twas worth the money,' quoth he; but it had paid him in golden guineas had he had the wit and patience to wait another year." The fellow closed his eyes, tossed back his long hair, and pressed his hands on his forehead. "Never, never," he cried, "was a man assaulted with such diversity of thoughts!"

Philip Marsham contemplated him as if from a distance and thought that never was there a long-haired scarecrow better suited for the butt of a thousand jests.

There were people passing on the road, an old man in a cart, a woman, and two men carrying a jug between them, but Phil was scarcely aware of them, or even of the lank man beside him, so absorbing were his thoughts, until the man rose, clasping his book in both hands and running his tongue over his lips.

His mouth worked nervously. "I must be off, I must be off. There they are again, and the last time I thought I should perish ere I got free of them. O well-beloved, O well-beloved! they have spied me already. If I go by the road, they'll have me; I must go by wood and field."

Turning abruptly, he plunged through a copse and over a hill, whence, his very gait showing his fear, he speedily disappeared.

And the two men, having set their jug down beside the road, were laughing till they reeled against each other, to see him go.

CHAPTER III

Two Sailors on Foot

AS THE two men roared with laughter by the wayside so that the noise of it made people a quarter-mile away turn round to see what was the matter, those who passed eyed them askance and gave them the width of the road. But to the few passers the two paid no heed at all. Pointing whither the lank fellow with the book had gone, they roared till they choked; then they fell on each other's necks, and embracing, whispered together.

Separating somewhat unsteadily, they now looked hard at Philip Marsham who knew their kind and feared them not at all. Shifting his dirk within easy reach of his hand, and so drawing his knees together that he could spring instantly to one side or the other, he coolly waited for them to come nearer, which they did.

The foremost was a fat, impudent scoundrel with very red cheeks and a very crafty squint. The other was thin and dark, less forward, but if one were to judge by his eyes, by far the braver. Both had put on long faces, which consorted ill with their recent laughter, and both, it was plain, were considerably the worse for strong drink.

The first glanced back over his shoulder at the second, who gave him a nudge and pushed him forward.

"Ahem," he began huskily. "You see before you, my kind young gentleman, two shipwrecked mariners who have lost at sea all they possess and are now forced to beg their way from London into Devon Port where, God willing, they will find a berth waiting for them. They—ahem—ahem—" He scratched his head and shut his eyes, then turning, hoarsely whispered, "Yea, yea! So far is well enough, but what came next?"

The other scowled blackly. "Bear on," he whispered. "Hast forgot the tale of calamities and wrecks and sharks?"

"Yea, yea! Troubles, my kind young gentleman, have somewhat be-puzzled my weary wits. As I was about to say, we have journeyed into those far seas where the hot sun besetteth a poor sailor with calentures, and nasty rains come with thunder and flash, and the wind stormeth outrageously and the poor sailor, if he is spared falling from the shrouds into the merciless waves—for he must abide the brunt of those infectious rains upon the decks to hand in the sails—goeth wet to his hammock and taketh aches and burning fevers and scurvy. Yea, we have seen the ravenous shark or dogfish (which keepeth a little pilot-fish scudding to and fro to bring it intelligence of its prey) devour a shipmate with its double row of venomous teeth. Surely, then, young gentleman, kind young gentleman, you for whom we have brought home curious dainties from that strange and fearful sea, will give us a golden guinea to speed us on our way; or if a guinea be not at hand, a crown; or sparing a crown, a shilling; or if not a shilling, sixpence. Nought will come amiss—nay, even a groat will, by the so much, help two poor sailors on their way."

As the two looked down at Philip Marsham, a score of old tales he had heard of worthless sailors who left the sea and went a-begging through the kingdom came to his mind. It was a manner of life he had never thought of for himself, nor had he a mind to it now. But he knew their game and, which was more, he knew that he held a higher trump than they. He leaned back and looked up at them and very calmly smiled.

"How now!" the spokesman blustered. "Dost laugh at a tale so sad as mine? I ha' killed an Italian fencing-master in my time. I ha' fought prizes at half the fairs in England."

His companion laid a hand on his arm and whispered in his ear.

"Nay," he retorted angrily, "'tis nought but a country fellow. I'll soon overbear him."

Again Phil smiled. "Hast thou never," he said in a quiet voice, "heard the man at the mainmast cry, 'A liar, a liar!' and for a week kept clean the beakhead and chains? Nay, I'll be bound thou hast sat in bilbowes or been hauled under the keel. The marshal doubtless knew thee well."

The faces of the two men changed. The fat man who had been the spokesman opened his mouth and was at loss for words, but the thin, dark man began to laugh and kept on laughing till he could hardly stand.

"We ha' reached for a pheasant and seized a hawk," he cried. "Whence came you, my gay young gallant, and what are you doing here?"

"Why, I am here to set myself up for a farmer. I had a reason for leaving London—"

Again the thin man burst out laughing. "Why, then," quoth he, "we are three men of like minds. So had Martin and I a reason for leaving London, too. And you are one who hath smelt salt water in your time. Nay, deny it not. Martin's sails are still a-flutter for wind, so sorely did you take him aback. 'Twas a shrewd thrust and it scored. Why, now, as for

farming"—he spread his hands and lifted his brows—"come
with us. There's a certain vessel to sail from Bideford on a
certain day, and for any such tall lad as thou I'll warrant
there'll be a berth."

Leaning back against a little hill, the lad looked from the
red, impudent face of the fat man to the amused, lean, daring face of his companion and away at the hills and meadows,
the green trees and ploughed fields, and the long brown road
that would lead the man who followed its windings and turn-
ings, however far afield they might wander, all the way across
England from the Channel to the Severn. He had made port,
once upon a time, in Bristol and he remembered lifting
Lundy's Island through the fog. A fair countryside lay before
him, with the faint scent of flowered meadows and the fra-
grance of blossoming fruit-trees on the wind, but the sea was
his home and the half-witted creature with the book and the
ranting talk of ploughing and planting had made the lad feel
the more his ignorance of country matters, a suspicion of
which had been growing on him since first he left the town
and port behind him. These were not men he would have
chosen, but he had known as bad and he was lost in a wilder-
ness of roads and lanes and never-ending hills and meadows
and woods, with villages one after another. Any port in a
storm—any pilot who knew his bearings! And for the matter
of that, he had seen rough company before. Though his
grandparents were gentlefolk, his father had led a rough life
and the son had learned from childhood to bear with low
humour and harsh talk.

The lean man still smiled, and though Martin was angry
still, neither the lad nor the man heeded him.

"I could bear you company, but—" A doubt crept on him:
when sober they might be of quite another mind.

"Nay, say us no buts."

"I have neither money nor gear for a journey."

"Nor we—come!—Nay, I am not so deep in my cups that I do not know my own mind." The man chuckled, perceiving that his intuition had fathomed the lad's hesitation.

Rising, Phil looked at the two again. He was as tall as they, if not so broad. After all, it was only Martin whose head was humming with liquor; the lean man, it now appeared, was as sober as he pleased to be.

"And if I have no money?"

"We are the better matched."

They returned to the highway, where Martin and the thin man took up the jug between them, each holding by his fore-finger one of its two handles, and together all three set out. But the jug was heavy and they progressed slowly.

"In faith, the day's warm and the road is dusty and I must drink again," said Martin at last.

They stopped and set the jug down in the road.

"You must pay," said the thin man.

Taking from his pocket a penny, Martin handed it to his companion and filling a great cup, drained it to the bottom. He then shook the jug, which showed by the sound that there was little left.

They walked on a while; then the thin man stopped. "I'll take a bit of something myself," he said. He took the penny out of his pocket, handed it to Martin, filled the cup and drained it.

Both then looked at Phil. "It is tuppence a quantum," said the thin man. "Have you tuppence?"

Phil shook his head, and the three went on together.

Three times more they stopped. The penny changed hands and one or the other drank. Martin's speech grew thicker and his companion's face flushed.

"Neither one of us nor the other," said the thin man, with a flourish of his hand, "is often seen in drink. There is a rea-son for it this time, though. 'If any chuff,' say I, 'can buy good wine for a half crown the jug and sell it at profit for tuppence the can, why cannot we?' So we ha' laid down our half crown and set out upon the road to peddle our goods, when Martin must needs drink for his thirst, which, as the Scripture hath it, endureth forever. 'But,' quoth I, 'for every pot a penny to him and a penny to me.' 'Why,' quoth he"—lowering his voice, the thin man whispered to Phil, "he is a rare fool at times," then resumed in his ordinary voice—"'Why,' quoth he, 'here's thy penny for thee.' So, presently, I to him: his penny for the wine that I drink. Before we have gone far it comes upon me as a wondrous thrifty thought, that the more we drink the more we earn."—Again he whispered to Phil, drawing him aside, "When I had drunk a few cans, which much enlivened my wits, I saw he was not so great a fool as I had thought"; and resumed his ordinary voice—"'Tis little wonder that all the world desires to keep an alehouse or a tavern!"

Never was there plainer example of befuddled wits! Passing back and forth, from one to the other, the single penny, the two had consumed their stock in trade, believing that they were earning great profit on their investment. Perceiving that the jug was nearly empty, Phil waited with quiet interest for the outcome.

They stopped again in the road. Martin handed the penny to the thin man and poured from the jug into the cup. There was a gurgle or two and the jug was empty. The cup was but half full.

"'Tis not full measure," he muttered, "but let it be." He emptied the cup and wiped his lips.

"Now," said the thin man, his face by this time fully as red as his fellow's, "where's thy store of silver? Count and share, count and share."

"Thou hast it, pence and pounds."

Martin's eyes half closed and his head nodded. Breathing hard, he sat down beside the road.

"Nay, th' art drunk. Come, now, thy purse and a just division." Out of a fog of wild notions the befuddled thin man had pitched upon this alone, that Martin withheld from him their common profit from their adventure into trade. He had keen mind and strong will, and his head had long resisted the assaults of the wine; but wine is a cunning, powerful foe and not easily discouraged, which by sapping and mining can accomplish the fall of the tallest citadel; and now, although steadier on his feet, the fellow was nearly as drunk as his mate and in no condition to perceive the flaw in his own logic.

To all this Martin gave no heed at all. He covered his eyes with his hands and uttering a prolonged groan, cried thickly—apparently to Phil—"And did you ever see a man dance on air! Ah, a hanging is a sight to catch the breath in your throat and make an emptiness in a man's belly!"

"Tush!" the thin man cried. Leaning over Martin he thrust his hands into pocket, pouch and bosom. "Where hast thou hid it?" he fiercely whispered.

Martin tried to stand and fell weakly back, but slapped the thin man across the face as he did so.

In an instant the thin man had out a knife and was pressing the point firmly against Martin's ribs.

Over Martin's florid face there came a ghastly pallor. "Let me go!" he yelled. "Take away thy knife, thou black-hearted, thrice accurst old goat! I've nought of thine. O Tom, to use me thus basely!" And sprawling on his back, he wriggled under the knife like a great, helpless hog.

The thin man smiled. To Phil Marsham his face seemed to have grown like pictures of the Devil in old books. He held the knife against the shrieking fat man's breast and pressed it the harder when Martin clutched at his wrist, then with a fierce "Pfaw!" of disgust released his victim and stood erect. "Pig!" he whispered. "See!" The point of the knife was red with blood. "Th' art not worth killing. Thy thin blood would quench the fire of a fleshed blade."

With that, he deliberately spat in the man's face, and turning, went off alone.

They were two sober men that watched him go, for the fumes of liquor had fled from the fat man's brain as he lay with the knife at his heart, and of their wine Phil Marsham had taken not a drop. Striding away, the thin man never looked behind him; and still showing them only his back, he passed out of sight.

Martin remained as pale as before he had been red. He rubbed his sore breast where the knife had pricked him, and gulped three or four times. "Ah-h-h!" he breathed. "God be praised, he's gone!" He made the sign of the cross, then cast a sharp glance at Phil to see if he had noticed. "God be praised, he's gone! He hath a cruel humour. He will kill for a word, when the mood is on him. I thought I was a dead man. Ah-h-h!"

The colour returned to his round face and the sly, crafty look returned to his eyes. "We'll find him at Bideford, though, and all will go well again. He'll kill for a word—nay, for a thought! But he never bears a grudge—against a friend. We'll lie tonight, my lad, with a roof over our heads, and by dawn we'll take the road."

CHAPTER IV

The Girl at the Inn

A s THEY came at nightfall to the inn whither Martin had been determined they should find their way, a coach drawn by two horses clattered down the village street and drew up at the inn gate before them. There was calling and shouting. Hostlers came running from the stables and stood by the horses' heads. The landlord himself stood by the coach door to welcome his guests, and servants unloaded their boxes. The coachman in livery sat high above the tumult, his arms folded in lofty pride, and out of the coach into the light from the inn door there stepped an old gentleman who gallantly handed down his lady. The hostlers leaped away from the bridles, the coachman resumed the reins, and when the procession of guests, host, and servants had moved into the great room where a fire blazed on the hearth, the horses, tossing their heads, proceeded to the stable.

All this the two foot-weary travellers saw, as unobserved in the bustle and stir, they made their way quietly toward the rear of the building. When they passed a dimly lighted window Martin glanced slyly around and with quick steps ran over to it and peeped in. Whatever he sought, he failed to find it, and he returned with a scowl. The two had chosen the opposite side of the house from the stable and no one perceived their cautious progress. Martin repeated his act at a second window and at a third, but he got small satisfaction, as his steadily darkening frown indicated.

They came at last to a brighter window than any of the others, and this he approached with greater caution. He crouched under it and raised his great head slowly from the very corner until one eye saw into the room, which was filled with light and gave forth the clatter and hum of a great domestic bustling. Here he remained a long time, now ducking his head and now bobbing it up again, and when he came away a smile had replaced his frown. "She's here," he whispered. "From now on we've a plain course to sail, without rock or sandbar."

They retraced their steps and went boldly round the inn to the kitchen door. There were lights in the stable and men talking loudly of one thing and another. From the kitchen door, which stood ajar, came the rattle of dishes and the smell of food and a great bawling and clamouring as the mistress directed and the maids ran.

With a jaunty air and an ingratiating smile, Martin boldly stepped to the door. He knocked and waited but no one heeded his summons. A scowl replaced his smile and he knocked with redoubled vigour. The sound rang out clearly in the inn yard. Several men came to the door of the stable to see what was the matter and the clamour in the kitchen ceased. Steps approached, a firm hand threw wide the door, and a woman cried with harsh voice, "Well, then, what'll you have, who come to the back when honest folk go to the front?"

There was for a moment a disagreeable cast in Martin's eyes, but his facile mouth resumed its easy smile. "An it please you, mistress, there are two gentlemen here would have a word with Nell Entick."

"Gentlemen!" she cried with a great guffaw. "Gentry of the road, I make no doubt, who would steal away all the girl has—it's little enough, God knows."

A couple of men came sauntering out of the stable and the kitchen maids stood a-titter.

Martin sputtered and stammered and grew redder than before, which she perceiving, bawled in a great voice that rang through the kitchen and far into the house, "Nell Entick, Nell Entick! Devil take the wench, is she deaf as an adder? Nell Entick, here's a 'gentleman' come to the kitchen door to see thee, his face as red as a reeky coal to kindle a pipe of tobacco with."

A shrill chorus of women's laughter came from the kitchen, echoed by a chorus of bass from the stable, and Phil Marsham stepped back in the dark, unwilling to be companioned with the man who had drawn such ridicule upon himself. But as Martin thrust himself forward with a show of bluster and bravado, the click of light footsteps came down the passage, and through the kitchen walked a girl whose flush of anger wondrously became her handsome face.

"Where is the wretch," she cried, and stepping on the doorstone, stood face to face with Martin.

"So, 'tis thou," she sneered. "I thought as much. Well—" she suddenly stopped, perceiving Phil, who stood nearly out of sight in the shadow. "Who is that?" she asked.

The mistress had returned to the kitchen, the girls to their work, the men to the stable.

"Th' art the same wench," Martin cried in anger, seizing at her hand. "Hard words for old acquaintance, and a warm glance for a strange face."

She snatched her hand away and cuffed him on the ear with a force that sent him staggering.

Though he liked it little, he swallowed his wrath.

"Come, chuck," he coaxed her, "let bygones lie. Tell me, will he turn his hand to help his brother?"

She laughed curtly. "The last time he spoke your name, he said he would put his hand in his pocket to pay the sexton that dug your grave and would find pleasure in so doing; but that he'd then let you lie with never a stone to mark the place, and if the world forgot you as soon as he, the better for him."

"But sure he could not mean it?"

"He did."

Martin swore vilely under his breath.

From the kitchen came the landlady's voice. "Nell Entick, Nell, I say! Gad-about! Good-for-nought!"

"Go to the stable," she whispered, "and tell them I sent you to wait there. She'll be in better humour in an hour's time. It may be I can even bring you in here."

She shot another glance over Martin's shoulder at the slim form of Phil Marsham and went away smiling.

Few in the stable looked twice at the two strangers in worn coats and dusty shoes who entered and sat on a bench by the wall, for there is as much pride of place in a stable as in a palace. There was talk of racing and hunting and fairs, and the beasts champed their oats, and everywhere was the smell of horses and harness. Presently there came from the inn a coachman in livery and him they greeted with nods and good morrows, for he was sleek and well fed and, after a manner, haughty, which commanded their respect. He sat down among them affably, as one conscious of his place in the world but desiring—provided they recognized him as a

man of position—to be magnanimous to all; and after inquir-
ing into the welfare of his horses he spoke of the weather and
the roads.

"Hast come far?" a wrinkled old man asked.

"Aye, from Larwood."

"The horses stood the day's travel well?"

"Aye, they are good beasts. But much depends on proper
handling. It makes a deal of difference who holds the reins."
He looked about with an air of generous patronage. "That,
and their meat." He nodded toward one of the men. "'Tis
well, though, when at night they are well fed, to fill the rack
with barley-straw or wheat ere leaving them, as I showed
thee, that perceiving it is not pleasant they may lie down and
take their rest, which is in itself as good as meat for the next
day's work."

A general murmur of assent greeted this observation.

"Goest far?" another asked.

"Aye, to Lincoln."

A rumble of surprise ran about the stable and the defer-
ence of the stablemen visibly increased.

"Hast been long away?"

"Aye, six weeks to the day."

"It do take a deal of silver to travel thus."

"Aye, aye." He condescended to smile. "But there are few
of the clergy in England can better afford a journey to the
Isle o' Wight than the good Dr. Marsham, and he is one who
grudges nought when his lady hath been ill. 'Tis wonderful
what travel will do for the ailing. Aye, he hath visited in many
great houses and I have seen good company while we have
been on the road."

Phil had looked up. "Where is this Doctor Marsham's
home?" he asked.

All frowned at the rash young man's temerity in thus famil-
iarly accosting the powerful personage in livery, and none
more accusingly than the personage himself; but with a

scornful lift of his brows he replied in a manner to tell all who were present that such as he were above mere arrogance. "Why, young man, he comes from a place you doubtless never heard of, keeping as you doubtless do, so close at home: from Little Grimsby."

Martin glanced at Phil. "The name, it seems, is thine own. Hast ever been at Little Grimsby?"

"Never."

And with that they forgot Philip Marsham, or at all events treated him as if he had never existed.

"'Tis few o' the clergy ride in their own coaches," someone said, with an obsequiousness that went far to conciliate the magnificent coachman.

"Aye, very few," he said smiling, "but Dr. Marsham is well connected and a distant relation some years since left him a very comfortable fortune—not to mention that in all England there are few better livings than his. There is no better blood in the country than runs in his veins. You'd be surprised if I was to tell you of families he's connected with."

So the talk ran.

Presently a little boy appeared from the darkness beyond the door and hunting out Martin, touched his shoulder and beckoned. Martin, having long nursed his ill temper, rose. "It is time," he said, "yea, more than time." With swagger and toss he elbowed his way out past the liveried coachman; but missing Phil he turned and saw him still sitting on the bench, his eyes fixed on the harness hanging on the opposite wall.

"Come, come," he called loudly. "Come, make haste! Where are thy wits? Phil, I say!"

Starting suddenly awake from his revery, Phil got up and followed Martin out of the stable, seeing no one, and so blindly pressed at his heels, so little heeded what went on about him, that the sudden burst of laughter his absence of mind had occasioned passed unheard over his head.

In the kitchen, whither the boy led them, they found places laid at one end of a great table and Nell Entick waiting to serve them, who gave Martin cold glances but looked long and curiously at Phil Marsham. The mistress and the other girls were gone. The boy sat in the corner, by the great fireplace where the roast had been turning on the now empty spit. Nell set before them a pitcher of beer and all that was left of a venison pasty.

Martin ate greedily and whispered to her and talked in a mumbling undertone, but she gave him short answers till his temper flew beyond his grasp and he knocked over his beer in reaching for her. "Witch!" he snarled. "Yea, look him in the eye! His wits are a-wandering again."

Looking up, Phil met her eyes staring boldly into his. He leaned back and smiled, for she was a comely lass.

"Have the two guests who came tonight in a coach gone yet to bed?" he asked.

"How should I know that?"

His question baffled her and she looked at him from under her long lashes, half, perhaps, in search of some hidden meaning in his words, but certainly a full half because she knew that her eyes were her best weapons and that the stroke was a telling one. She made little of his meaning but her thrust scored.

He looked at her again and marked the poise of her shapely head, the curves of neck and shoulders, the full bosom, the bare arms. But his mind was still set on that other matter and he persisted in his design. "I want," he said slowly, "to see them—to see them without their knowing or any one's knowing—except you and me." Here he met her at her own game, and he was not so far carried away but that he could inwardly smile to see his own shot tell.

"They have supped in the little parlor and are sitting there by the fire," she whispered. "It may cost me my place—but—"

Again she looked at him under her long lashes. He gave her as good as she sent, and she whispered, "Come, then— come."

Martin gave an angry snort over his beer, but she returned a hot glance and an impatient gesture. With Phil pressing close at her heels she led the way out of the kitchen and down a long passage. Stopping with her finger on her lips, she very quietly opened a door and motioned him forward. Again her finger at her lips! With her eyes she implored silence.

Without so much as the creaking of a board he stepped through the door. A second door, which stood ajar, led into the little parlor and through the crack he saw an old man with long white hair and beard—an old man with a kindly face mellowed by years of study, perhaps by years of disappointment and anxiety. The old man's eyes were shut, for he was dozing. In a chair on the other side of the hearth a lady sat, but only the rich border of her gown showed through the partly open door.

The lad stood there with a lump in his throat and a curious mingling of emotions in his heart and head. It had happened so suddenly, so strangely, he felt that baffling sense of unreality which comes sometimes to all of us. He touched the wall to make sure he was not dreaming. Had he but stayed in school, as his father had desired, and gone back to Little Grimsby, who knew what might have come of it? But no! He was a penniless vagabond, a waif astray on the highroads of England. He was now of a mind to speak out; now of a mind to slip like a fox to earth. His gay, gallant ne'er-do-well of a father was gone. He was alone in the world save for his chance acquaintance of the road, which was perhaps worse than being entirely alone. What madness—he wondered as he looked at the kindly face of the drowsy old man—had led Tom Marsham away from his home? Or was it more than a mere mad prank? Had the manners of a country vicarage so stifled him that he became desperate? As Phil thought of Martin drinking in the kitchen, a wave of revulsion swept over him; but after all, his father had kept such company in his own life, and though he had brought up the boy to better things, the father's reckless and adventurous nature, in spite of his best intentions, had drawn the son into wild ways. Something rose in Phil's throat and choked him, but the hot pride that came straightly and honestly from his father now flamed high. He knew well enough that Tom Marsham had had his faults, and of a kind to close upon him the doors of such a home as the vicarage at Little Grimsby; but he had been a lovable man none the less and Tom Marsham's son was loyal.

The girl, daring not speak, was tugging at Phil's coat in an agony of misgivings. He stepped softly back, closed the door on a world he might have entered, and carried away with him the secret that would have brought peace—if a sad, almost bitter peace—to two lonely souls.

He paused in the passage and the girl stopped beside him. There was no one in sight or hearing, and he kissed her. Such is the curious complexity with which impressions and emotions crowd upon one, that even while the vicarage at Little Grimsby and his dead father were uppermost in his thoughts, he was of a mind then and for many a long day thereafter to come back and marry her. Since he had closed the door through which he might have passed, this was a golden dream to cling to in hard times and glad, he thought. For he had caught her fancy as well as she his and she kissed him full on the lips; and being in all ways his father's son, he fell victim to a kitchen wench's bright eyes at the very moment when Little Grimsby was within his reach, as his father had done before him. Then they walked out into the kitchen, trying to appear as if nothing had happened, and Martin, perceiving their red cheeks, only sneered.

"You must sleep on the hay," she whispered; and to Martin, "I'll send him word before morning and give you his reply."

So they again followed the little boy through the darkness to the stable by a back way, and climbed a ladder to the great mow and crawled behind a mountain of hay, and lay with their thoughts to bear them company while men far below talked of country affairs, horses were trampling uneasily in their stalls, and the little boy was off through the night with a message.

CHAPTER V

Sir John Bristol

THERE WAS not a cloud in the sky at dawn. Cocks crowed lustily, near and loud or far and faint. The blue light grew stronger and revealed the sleeping village and the rambling old inn and the great stable, where the horses stood in their stalls and pulled at the hay and pease in the racks or moved uneasily about. The stars became dim and disappeared. The rosy east turned to gold and the dark hills turned to blue and the village stirred from its sleep.

The master of the inn came down, rubbing his eyes and yawning, to the great room where one of the maids, bedraggled with sleep, was brushing the hearth and another was clearing a table at which two village roysterers had sat late. The master was in an evil temper, but for the moment there was no fault to be found with the maids, so he left them without a word and went through the long passage to the kitchen.

Seeing there a candle, which had burned to a pool of tallow, still guttering faintly in its socket, he cried out at the waste and reached to douse the feeble flame, then stopped in anger, for in a chair by the table, on which he had rested his head and arms, the little boy sat fast asleep.

"Hollo!" the master bawled.

Up started the little boy, awake on the instant and his eyes wide with fear.

"What in the fiend's name hast thou been up to, this night?" quoth the master in a fierce bellow.

The little boy burst into tears. "He'll have nought to do with him," he wailed. "'Twas a long way and fearful dark but I went it, every step, and ferreted him out and gave him the message; and he swore most wickedly and bade me tell the man go to a place I don't like to name, and bade me tell Nell Entick he took it ill of her to traffic with such as that brother of his."

"Ah-ha!" cried the host, belting his breeches tighter. "Most shrewdly do I suspect there have been strange doings hereabouts. Where's Nell Entick? Nell Entick, I say, Nell Entick!" His voice went through the house like thunder. The sashes rattled and the little boy quaked.

Down came the hostess and in came the maids—all but Nell Entick.

"Nell Entick! Where's Nell Entick, I say! Fiend take the wench—where's Nell Entick?"

Then in came the sleepy hostlers, and the coachman, his livery all awry from his haste—but not Nell Entick. For Nell Entick, a-tremble with well-founded apprehensions, having gone late to bed and slept heavily, had risen just after the host, had followed him down the passage and, after listening at the door until she made sure her worst fears were realized, had darted back along the passage and out through the inn yard to the stable where as loudly as she dared, but not loudly enough to rouse the weary sleepers above, she was calling, "Martin! Martin! Awake, I say, or they'll all be upon thee! Martin, awake!"

The host in fury seized the little boy by the ear and dragged him shrieking across the table. "Now, sirrah," quoth he, "of whom mak'st thou this squalling and squealing? A stick laid to thy bum will doubtless go far to keep thy soul from burning."

"Unhand me!" he squalled. "She'll kill me, an I tell."

"An thou tellest not, thou slubbering noddy, I'll slice thee into collops of veal." And still holding the unhappy child by the ear, the host, making a ferocious face, reached for a long and sharp knife.

"I'll tell—I'll tell—'Tis the two men that slept in the hay."

"Ha! The hounds are in cry."

And with that the host released his victim and dashed, knife in hand, out the kitchen door. The household trailed at his heels. The sleeping guests woke in their chambers and faces appeared at curtained windows.

Nell Entick fled from the stable as he came roaring, but seeing her not, he mounted the ladder and plunged into the hay with wild thrusts of his knife in all directions. "Hollo! Hollo!" he yelled. "At 'em, dogs, at 'em!" And the two sleepers in the far corner of the mow, as the household had done before them, started wide awake.

For the second time since they had met, Martin, crouching in the hay, crossed himself, then shot a scared glance at Phil. Martin was white round the lips and his hands were shaking like the palsy. "Said he aught of hanging?" he whispered. But Philip Marsham was then in no mood to heed his chance companion, whose bubble of bluster he had seen pricked three times.

What had occurred was plain enough and the two were cornered like rats; but Phil got up on his toes, shielded from sight by a mound of hay, and squatting low, got in his arms as much of the hay as he could grasp.

Bawling curses and thrusting this way and that with his knife, the host came steadily nearer. He passed the mound. He saw the two. Knife in hand he plunged at them over the hay, with a yell of triumph. But his footing was none of the best, and as he came, Phil rose with a great armful of hay to receive the knife-thrust and sprang at him.

Thus thrown off his balance, the man fell and the lad, catching his wrist and dexterously twisting it, removed the knife from his hand and flung it into the darkest corner of the great mow.

"Help! Treason! Murder! Thieves!"

With his hand on the host's throat, Phil shoved him deeper in the hay and held him at his mercy, but Martin was already scrambling over the mow, and with a last thrust Phil left the blinded and choking host to dig himself out at his leisure and followed, dirk in hand. As the two leaped down on the stable floor, the flashing dirk bought them passage to the rear, whither they fled apace, and out the door and away.

They passed Nell Entick at the gate, her hands clasped in terror, who cried to Martin, "He'll have nought of you. Hard words were all he sent."

To Phil she said nothing but her glance held him, and he whispered, "I will come back and marry you."

She smiled.

"You will wait for me?" he whispered, and kissed her.

She nodded and he kissed her again ere he fled after Martin.

When they had left the village behind them they stopped to breathe and rest.

Leaning against a tree, Martin mopped the sweat from his brow. "Had I but a sword," he cried, "I'd ha' given them theme for thought, the scurvy knaves!"

"It seems thy brother, of whom we were to have got so much, bears thee little love." And Phil smiled.

For this Martin returned him an oath, and sat upon a stone.

On the left lay the village whence they had come, and, though the sun was not yet up, the spire of the church and the thatched roofs of the cottages were very clearly to be seen in the pure morning air. Smoke was rising from chimneys and small sounds of awakening life came out to the vagabonds on the lonely road, as from the woods at their back came the shrill, loud laugh of the yaffle, and from the marsh before them, the croaking of many frogs.

Martin's shifty eyes ranged from the cows standing about the straw rack in a distant barton in the east to a great wooded park on a hill in the west. "I will not go hungry," he cried with an oath, "because it is his humour to deny me. We shall see what we shall see."

He rose and turned west and with Phil at his heels he came presently to the great park they had seen from a distance.

"We shall see what we shall see."

With that he left the road and following a copse beside a meadow entered the wood, where the two buried themselves deep in the shade of the great trees. The sun was up now and the birds were fluttering and clamouring high overhead, but to the motion and clamour of small birds they gave no heed. From his pocket Martin drew a bit of strong thread, then, looking about, he wagged his head and pushed through the undergrowth. "Hare or pheasant, I care not which. Here we shall spread our net—here—and here." Whereupon he pulled down a twig and knotted the thread and formed a noose with his fingers. "Here puss shall run," he continued, "and here, God willing, we shall eat."

Having thus set his snare, he left it, and sulkily, for the sun was getting up in the sky and they had come far without breaking their fast. So Phil followed him and they lay on a bank, with an open vale before them where yellow daffodils were in full bloom, and nursed their hunger.

After a while Martin slipped away deftly but returned with a face darker than he took, and though he went three times to the snare and scarcely stirred a leaf—which spoke more of experience in such lawless sports than some books might have told—each time his face, when he returned, was longer than before.

"A man must eat," he said at last, "and here in his own bailiwick and warren will I eat to spite him. Yea, and leave guts and fur to puzzle him. But there's another way, quicker and surer, though not so safe."

So they went together over a hill and down a glade to a meadow.

"Do thou," he whispered, "lie here in wait."

With a club in his hand and a few stones in his pocket he circled through the thicket, and having in his manner of knowing his business and of commanding the hunt, resumed his old bravado, he now made a great show of courage and resourcefulness; but Phil, having flung himself down at full length by the meadow, smiled to hear him puffing through the wood.

Off in the wood wings fluttered and Martin murmured under his breath. Presently a stone rapped against a tree-trunk and again there was the sound of wings.

Then the lad by the meadow heard a stone rip through the leaves and strike with a soft thud, whereupon something fell heavily and thrashed about in the undergrowth, and Martin cried out joyously.

He had no more than appeared, holding high a fine cock-pheasant, with the cry, "Here's meat that will eat well," when there was a great noise of heavy feet in the copse behind him, and whirling about in exceeding haste, he flung the pheasant full in the face of the keeper and bolted like a startled filly. Thereupon scrambling to his feet, Phil must needs burst out laughing at the wild look of terror Martin wore, though the keeper was even then upon him and though he himself was of no mind to run. He lightly stepped aside as the keeper rushed at him, and darting back to where Martin had dropped his cudgel, snatched it up and turned, cudgel in hand. He was aware of a flash of colour in the wood, and the sound of voices, but he had no leisure to look ere the keeper was again at him, when for the first time he saw that the keeper was the selfsame red-faced countryman who had brought the gun to Moll Stevens's alehouse by the Thames—that it was Jamie Barwick.

Now the keeper Barwick was at the same moment aware of something familiar about his antagonist, but not until he was at him a second time in full tilt did he recollect where and when he had last seen him. He then stopped short, so great was his amazement, but resumed his attack with redoubled fury. His stick crashed against the cudgel and broke, and ducking a smart rap he dived at Phil's knees.

To this, Phil made effective reply by dropping the cudgel and dodging past the keeper to catch him round the waist from behind (for his arms, exceeding long though they were, were just long enough to encompass comfortably the man's great belly), and the lad's iron clutch about the fellow's middle sorely distressed him. As they swayed back and forth the keeper suddenly seized Phil's head over his own shoulder and rose and bent forward, lifting Phil from the ground bodily; then he flung himself upon his back and might have killed the lad by the fall, had Phil not barely wriggled from under him.

Both were on their feet in haste, but though the keeper was breathing the harder, Philip Marsham, having come far without food, was the weaker, and as Barwick charged again, Phil laid hands on his dirk, but thought better of it. Then Barwick struck from the shoulder and Phil, seizing his wrist, lightly turned and crouched and drew the man just beyond his balance so that his own great weight pitched him over the lad's head. It is a deft throw and gives a heavy fall, but Phil had not the strength to rise at the moment of pitching his antagonist—which will send a man flying twice his length—so Barwick, instead of taking such a tumble as breaks bones, landed on his face and scraped his nose on the ground.

He rose with blood and mud smearing his face and with his drawn knife in his hand; and Philip Marsham, his eyes showing like black coals set in his stark white face, yielded not a step, but snatched out his dirk to give as good as he got.

Then, as they shifted ground and fenced for an opening, a booming "Holla! Holla!" came down to them.

They stopped and looked toward the source of the summons, but Phil, a shade the slower to return to his antagonist, saw out of the corner of his eye that Barwick was coming at him. He leaped back and with his arm knocked aside Barwick's blow.

"Holla, I say! Ha' done, ha' done! That, Barwick, was a foul trick. Another like that, and I'll turn you out."

A crestfallen man was Barwick then, who made out to stammer, "Yea, Sir John—yea, Sir John, but a poacher—'e's a poacher, Sir John, and a poacher—"

"A foul trick is a foul trick."

The speaker wore a scarlet cloak overlaid with silver lace, and his iron-grey hair crept in curls from under a broad hat. His face, when he looked at Barwick, was such that Barwick stepped quietly back and held his tongue. The man had Martin by the collar (his sleek impudence had melted into a vast melancholy), and there stood behind them a little way up the bank, Phil now saw, a lady no older than Phil himself, who watched the group with calm, dark eyes and stood above them all like a queen.

"Throw down those knives," the knight ordered, for it took no divining to perceive that here was Sir John Bristol in the flesh. "Thrust them, points into the ground. Good! Now have on, and God speed the better man."

To Philip Marsham, who could have expected prison at the very least, this fair chance to fight his own battle came as a reprieve; and though he very well knew that he must win the fight at once or go down from sheer weakness and want of food, his eyes danced.

The knight's frown darkened, observing that Barwick appeared to have got his fill, and he smote the ground with his staff. Then Barwick turned and Philip Marsham went in upon him like a ray of light. Three times he threw the big man, by sheer skill and knowledge, for the other by his own weight hindered himself, but after the third time the world went white and the lad fell.

He sat up shortly and looked into Sir John's face.

"'Tis the lack of food," he stammered, "or I'd outlast him as well as out-wrestle him."

Sir John was laughing mightily. "You gave him full measure, and thank God you are fresh from a fast or I'd ha' lost a keeper. As for food, we shall remedy that lack. Two things I have to say: one to you, Barwick. You attempted a foul trick. I'll have none such in my service. If it happens again, you go. And as for you, you white-livered cur, that would leave a boy to a beating and never turn a hand to save him, I'll even take you in hand myself."

And with that, Sir John flung back his cloak and raising his staff with one hand while with the other he kept hold of Martin's coat-collar, he thrashed the man till he bellowed and blubbered—till his coat was split and his shirt was bloody and his head was broken and his legs were all welts and bruises.

"Help! Help! O Holy Mary! Saints in Heaven! Help! O Jamie, Jamie, Jamie! O sir! Kind sir! Let me go! Let me go!"

Sir John flung him away with a last whistling stroke of the great staff. "That," said he, "for cowardice."

And Jamie Barwick, having already forgotten his own rebuke, was broadly smiling.

Sir John turned then and looked Philip Marsham in the eye. "It was a good fight," he said, and smiled. "Courage and honour will carry a man far."

He then looked away across his wide acres to the distant village. For a while he was lost in revery and the others waited for him, but he came to himself with a start and turned brusquely, though not unkindly, to Philip Marsham.

"Come now, begone, you vagabond cockerel! If a farm is robbed from here to the Channel, or a hundred miles the other way, I'll rear the county upon your track and scour the countryside from the Severn to the Thames. I'll publish the tale of you the country over and see you hanged when they net you."

He stood there looking very fierce as he spoke, but there was a laugh in his eyes, and when Phil turned to go, he flung the lad a silver coin.

Phil saw the gesture and picked the money from the air, for he was quick with his fingers, but before he caught it Sir John seemed to have forgotten him; for he bent his head and walked away with his eyes on the ground. There was something in the knight's manner that stung the lad, who looked at the coin in his hand and almost as quick as thought hurled it back at Sir John.

"How now?" cried Sir John, turning about.

"I'll take no money that is thrown me," Phil replied.

"So!" Sir John stood looking at him. "I have a liking for thee," he said, and smiled. But he then, it seemed, again forgot that there was such a lad, for he once more bent his head and walked away with the lady who had stood above them in the wood.

As for Phil, he did not so lightly forget Sir John. He watched him until he had fixed in his mind every line of his tall, broad figure, every gesture of his hand and every toss of his head. He then walked off, and when he turned to look back a last time Sir John was gone.

"What was that he said of hanging?" Martin whispered.

The fellow's face was so white and his lips and his bruises were so blue that Phil laughed at him before his eyes, who thereupon lost his temper and snarled, "It's all well enough to take things lightly, you who got no beating; but hanging is no laughing matter."

He then looked cautiously around and ran back the way they had come. When he returned he held between thumb and forefinger the silver coin Phil had thrown back at the burly knight. Martin bought food with it and Phil, though he thought it would have choked him, helped him eat it; and so they survived the day.

"That keeper, Barwick," Martin said that evening as the two tramped west along the highway, "is my brother, and an ungrateful wretch he is."

"I knew he was your brother," Phil said. But he was not thinking of Martin or his brother. He was thinking of the old knight in the scarlet cloak so bravely decked with silver lace. There was only one man Philip Marsham had ever known, who had such a rough, just, heavy-handed humour as Sir John Bristol or any such indomitable sense of fair play, and that man was Phil's dead father.

CHAPTER VI

The *Rose of Devon*

THEY CAME to Bristol over the hills that lie to the south of the town. They had lost time on the way and had grown weary and sore of foot; and finding at last that there was little hope of overtaking at Bideford the thin man with whom they had parted on the road, they had turned north in Somerset at the end of Polton Hill. They passed first across a lonely waste where for miles the only human being they saw was an aged man gathering faggots; then over the Mendip Hills and through rough valleys and rougher uplands, and so at last to the height whence Bristol and Avon Valley and Bristol Channel in the east lie spread in a vast panorama.

Far away in Hungroad and Kingroad ships were anchored, but the vessels at the wharves of Bristol lay with their keels in mud, for the tide was out and the tides of Bristol, as all know, have a wonderful great flow and ebb.

The two went on into the town, where there were seafaring men standing about and talking of ships, which gave Phil Marsham a feeling of being once more at home after his inland travels; and passing this one tavern and another, they came to a square where there was a whipping-post and a stocks, and a man in the stocks.

Now a man in stocks was a pleasing sight to Phil, for he was not so old that he missed the humour of it, and he paused to grin at the unlucky wight who bore with ill grace the jeers of the urchins that had assembled to do him honour; but when Martin saw the fellow he looked a second time and turned very hastily round. Straightway seizing Phil by the arm he whispered hoarsely, "Come now, we must hie us away again, and that speedily."

"Why in so great haste?" Phil returned. "Here is a pleasant jest. Let us stay a while. Who knows but some day we may ourselves sit in the bilboes and yonder ballad-maker may take his fill of pleasure at our misfortune. Why, then, turn about is fair play. Let us enjoy his while there's time." And he waited with quiet glee for Martin's angry reply.

"Fool!" Martin whispered. "Stay and be hanged, an thou wilt."

Thereupon Martin posted in all haste back the way he had come and Phil, of no mind to be left now, since they had journeyed together thus far, followed at his heels with a curiosity that he was intent on satisfying.

"'Sin,' according to the proverb," he called after Martin, "'begins with an itch and ends with a scar,' but me-thinks thy scars, which are numerous, are all an-itch."

"Hist, fool," Martin snarled. "Be still! For ha'pence I'd slit thy throat to still thy tongue. I swear I can already feel the hemp at my neck. It burns and spreads like a fire." And he made haste up out of the town till despite his great weight and short wind he had Phil puffing at his heels.

"This is queer talk of ropes and hangings. It buzzeth through thy noddle like bees in clover. In faith, though thy folly be great, yet it sorely presses upon thee, for I have seldom seen a man walk faster. Yet at thine ordinary gait a tinpedlar's broken-down jade can set a pace too fast for thee to follow."

"Yea, laugh at me! Wouldst thou stay for sugared pills of pleasure with the hangman at thy heels?"

"What has a poor devil in stocks to do with the hangman, prithee? And why this fierce haste?"

"Th'art no better than a gooseling—fit for tavern quarrels. And did you never see a man dance on air? 'Tis a sight to catch the breath in the throat and make an emptiness in a man's belly."

"There be no hangings without reason."

"Reason? Law, logic, and the Switzers can be hired to fight for any man, they say. 'Tis true, in any event, of the law. I've seen the learned men in wigs wringing a poor man's withers and shaping the halter to his neck."

They had talked breathlessly at long intervals in their hasty flight, and thus talking they had come out of the town and up from the valley; nor would Martin stay to rest till from the southern hill that had given them their first prospect of Bristol city they looked back upon the houses and the river and the ships. Martin breathed more easily then and mopped his forehead and sat down until his wildly beating heart was quieter.

"To Bideford we must go, after all," said he, "and 'twere better by far had we never turned from the straight road."

"I am of no mind to go farther," Phil replied, looking back. "There will be more vessels sailing out of Bristol than out of Bideford. A man can choose in which to go."

Martin gulped and rubbed his throat. "Nay, I'll not hear to it. Daniel went but once into the lion's den."

He sighed mightily as he thought of begging his long way through Somerset and Devon, for he was a big heavy man and lazy and short of wind; but he would not go back, though he refused to speak further of his reason for it; and Phil, though in truth he liked Martin little, was too easy-going to part thus with his companion of the road. The lad was young, and the world was wide, and it was still spring in England.

So they turned toward the hills, which were blue and purple in the setting sun—a shepherd, did he but know it, lives in halls more splendid than a king's—and set forth upon their journey through the rough lands of Somerset. They went astray among the mines but found their way to Wells where, as they came out from the town, they passed a gallows, which gave Martin such a start that he stopped for neither breath nor speech until he had left that significant emblem of the law a mile behind him. They went through Glastonbury, where report has it that Joseph of Arimathea and King Arthur and King Edgar lie buried, and through Bridgewater, where to their wonder there was a ship of a hundred tons riding in the Parret. They went through Dulverton on a market day, and crossed the Dunsbrook by the stone bridge and so passed into Devon. They went on over heath and hill and through woods and green valleys until at the end of seven days from Bristol—for time and again they had lost their way, and a sailor on shore is at best like a lame horse on a rough road—they crossed the Taw at Barnstaple. Again going astray, they went nearly to Torrington before they learned their blunder and turned down the valley of the Torridge. But all things come to an end at last, and one pleasant evening they crossed the ancient bridge built on stately Gothic arches into the populous town of Bideford.

At the river front there lay a street the better part of a mile long, in which were the custom house and a great quay, and there they saw ships of good burden loading and unloading in the very bosom of the town, as the scribe hath it. Thither Phil would have gone straightly but Martin shook his head. So turning up from the river, they passed another long street, where the houses of wealthy merchants stood, and this, too, Martin hastened quickly by. He shot glances to one side and the other as if fearing lest he see faces that he knew, and led his companion by an obscure way, as night was falling, to a cottage whence a dim light shone through a casement window.

Standing on the rough doorstone under the outcropping thatch, which projected beyond the line of the eaves to shield the door from rain, he softly knocked. There was no answer, no sound, but the door presently moved ajar as if by its own will.

"Who knocks?" an old woman whispered. "'Tis that dark I cannot see thy face."

"'Tis thine eyes are ailing. Come, open the door and bid us enter."

"Thy voice hath a familiar ring but I know thee not. Who art thou?"

"We be two honest men."

"Ah, two honest men? And what, prithee, are two honest men doing here?"

"Yea, 'tis a fair thrust and bites both ways! Thou old shrew, dost bar the door to Martin Barwick?"

"So 'tis thou. I believe it even is. Enter then, ere the watch spy thee. Th'art a plain fool to stand here quibbling thus, though 'tis to be expected, since thou wert ever quicker of thy tongue than thy wit. But who's thy fellow?"

"Nay, thou old shrew, open to us. He is to be one of us, though a London man by birth."

"One of us, say'st thou? Enter and welcome, then, young sir. Mother Taylor bids thee welcome. One of us? 'Tis the more pity so few of the gentlemen are left in port."

"The Old One?"

"He hath sailed long since." She closed the door behind them, and the three stood together in the dark passage. "Hast money?"

"Not a groat."

She sighed heavily. "I shall be ruined. Seven o' the gentle-men ha' sailed owing me."

"Yea, thou old shrew, had I a half—nay, had I the tenth part of the gold thou hast taken from us and laid away wher-ever thy hiding-places are, I'd go no more to sea. But thou know'st what thou know'st, and there's not one among us but will pay his score. The wonder is that of them thou could'st hang by a word none has slit thy scrawny throat."

"Aye, they pay, they pay. And the gentlemen bear Mother Taylor nought but love. How else could they do their busi-ness but for good Mother Taylor?" She led them into a little back room where there was a fire and a singing kettle; and as she scuttled with a crooked, nimble gait from one window to another to make sure that every shutter was fast closed, in her cracked old voice she bade them sit.

To his prudent companion, whose quick glance was mark-ing every door and window—for who knows when a man shall have need to leave in haste a sailor's inn?—quoth Martin, "The old witch is a rare hand to sell a cargo got—thou can'st guess well enough how; and the man who would bring a waggon-load of spirits past the customs on a dark night or would bargain with a Dartmoor shepherd for wool secretly sheared, can lay the matter before her and go his way, knowing she will do his business better than he could do it himself. Yea, a man's honour and life are safer with her than with any lord in England."

She showed by a grunt that she had heard him but other-wise paid no attention to what he said. She brought food from a cupboard and laid the table by the fire, and going into a back room, she drew a foaming pitcher of beer.

"No wine?" cried Martin. "Mother Taylor has no wine? Come, thou old beldame, serve us a stronger tipple."

She laughed shrilly. "The beer," said she, "is from Frome-Selwood."

"Why, then, I must needs drink and say nought, since it is common report that the gentry choose it, when well aged, rather than the wine of Portugal or France. But my heart was set on good wine or stronger spirits."

"He who sails on the morning tide must go sober to bed else he may rue his choice. Aye, an' 'tis rare fine beer."

Her old bent back fitted into her bent old chair. Her face settled into a myriad wrinkles from which her crooked nose projected like a fish in a bulging net. She was very old and very shrewd, and though there was something unspeakably hard in her small, cold eyes, Martin trusted her as thus far he had trusted no one they had met. Even to Phil she gave an odd sense of confidence in her complete loyalty.

At Phil she cast many glances, quick and sharp like a bird's, but she never spoke to him nor he to her.

It was Martin who again spoke up, having blunted the edge of his hunger. "And now, you old witch, who's in port and where shall we find the softest berths? For you've made it plain that since trust us you must, you will trust us little—that is to say, it is not in thy head that our score shall mount high."

She chuckled down in her skinny old crop. "Let us see. The Old One has gone and that's done. You were late."

"'Tis a long road and we went astray."

"There's the *Nestor* and the *Essay*. They will be off soon; the one to Liverpool for salt, t'other to Ireland for wool."

Martin thereupon set down his pot of beer and sigficantly rubbed his throat, at which the old woman cackled with shrill laughter. "Aye, th'art o'er well known in Liverpool. Well, let us consider again. There's the *Rose of Devon*, new come from Plymouth. I hear she's never touched at Bideford before and her master hails from Dorset."

"His name?"

"'Tis Candle."

Martin laughed boisterously. "A bright and shining name! But I know him not and will chance a singeing. What voyage does she make?"

"She goeth to fetch cod from Newfoundland." The old woman saw him hesitate. "A barren voyage, think'st thou? Nay, 'twere well for one of the gentlemen to look into that trade. Who knows?"

"True, old mother witch, who knows?" Martin tapped the table. "Can'st arrange it?"

"Nay. But I can start the wedge."

"We'll go," said Martin at last. "But now for bed. We've been a weary while on the road."

It was a great bed in a small room under the thatch; and as they lay there on the good goose-feathers in the dark, Martin said, "We'll sail in this *Rose of Devon,* lad."

Phil, already nearly asleep, stirred and roused up. "Any port in a storm," he mumbled. Then, becoming wider awake, he asked, "What is all this talk of 'the gentlemen' and who, prithee, is the Old One?"

"Ah, a natural question." Though the room was dark as Egypt, Phil knew by Martin's voice—for he could recognize every inflection and change in tone—that the sly, crafty look was creeping over his fat, red face. "Well," Martin continued after a moment of silence, "by 'the gentlemen' she means a few seafaring men that keep company together by custom and stop here when ashore—all fine, honest fellows as a man may be proud to know. I have hopes that some day you'll be one of us, Phil my lad, and some day I'll tell you more. As for the Old One, it very curiously happens that you have met with him. Do you recall to mind the thin man I quarrelled with, that first day?"

"Yea."

"That is the Old One, and Tom Jordan is his proper name."

It was Martin, after all, who fell asleep first, for Phil lay in the great bed in the small room, thinking of all that had happened since the day he fled from Moll Stevens's alehouse. There was Colin Samson, whose dirk he wore; there was the wild-eyed, black-haired man with the great book and the woeful tale; there were Martin, and Tom Jordan, "the Old One"; there were the inn and the old lady and gentleman—it all seemed so utterly unreal!—and Nell Entick, and Sir John Bristol. He fell asleep thinking of Nell and Sir John and dreamed of marrying Nell and keeping a tavern, to which the bluff old knight came in the guise of a very aged gentleman from Little Grimsby with a coachman who went poaching pheasants in the tavern yard.

It was early morning when Mother Taylor called them down to breakfast at a table burdened with good food such as they had not eaten for many long days. She sat by the fire, a bent old woman in a round-backed little chair, watching them with keen small eyes while they ate, and smiling in a way that set her wrinkles all a-quiver to see them empty dish after dish.

"Th'art a good old witch, Mother Taylor, though the Devil cry nay," said Martin. "Though thy score be high never did'st thou grudge a man the meat he ate."

"'Tis not for nought the gentlemen love Mother Taylor," she quavered. "What can a woman do when her beauty's gone but hold a man by the food she sets before him? 'Tis the secret of blessed marriage, Martin, and heaven send thee a wife as knows it like I!"

"Beauty, thou old beldame! What did'st thou ever know of beauty? But beauty is a matter of little moment. Hast thou prepared the way for us?"

She laughed in shrill delight at his rough jesting. "Aye, I ha' sent a messenger. Seek out the *Rose of Devon* and do thy part, and all shall be well."

"And whence does good Captain Candle expect his men?"

"Say to Captain Candle that thou and this handsome young gentleman who says so little are come from the Mersey, where thy vessel, the *Pride o' Lancashire,* lies to be repaired, and that Master Stephen Gangley sent thee."

She looked at Phil, who had learned long before to hold his tongue in strange places, and he smiled; but Martin laughed hoarsely. "Th'art the Devil's own daughter. And does this Master Stephen Gangley in all truth dwell in Liverpool?"

"Dost think my wits are wandering, Martin? Nay, I be old, but not so old as that. Go hastily through the town lest thou be seen and known. Thou, of all the gentlemen, most needs make haste."

The two stopped just inside the door. "You have chalked down the score against us?"

She laughed in her skinny throat. "I be old, but not so old as to forget the score. The gentlemen always pay."

She pushed Martin out and shut the door behind him, then, seizing Phil by the arm, she whispered, "Leave him."

Martin angrily thrust the door open again and she gave Phil a shove that sent him stumbling over the threshold. The door slammed shut and they heard the bolt slide.

"They pay," Martin muttered. "Yea, they pay in full and the old witch hath got rich thereby, for 'tis pay or hang. So much does she know of all that goes on at sea! In faith, I sorely mistrust she is a witch in all earnest; but even be it so, a most useful witch."

As the two came into the town they saw at a distance a crowd gathering. Dogs barked and boys shouted and men came running and laughing, which seemed to give promise of rare sport of one kind or another.

"See!" cried Phil, catching Martin by the arm. "Here's a game. Come, let us join the cry."

"Thou art a very pattern of blockishness," quoth Martin. "Would'st see us in pillory, egged, turnipped, nay, beaten at the post?"

"Come, old frog, I for one will run the hazard."

"Old frog, is it?" Martin's face flamed redder than before. "An we loiter there'll be sharp eyes upon us. My very throat is itching at the thought. Justice is swift. Who knows but we'll swing by sundown? Hast never considered the pains of hanging? The way they dance and twitch is enough to take the sap out of a man's legs."

Martin's fears were an old story and the lad heeded them so little, save when he would make game of them, that he never even smiled. "See!" he cried. "There's a man in their midst. Stay! Who is he? He is—yea, he is the very one, come back to Bideford despite his fears. And it seems the townsfolk know him well."

The jeering mob parted and revealed a lank man with a great book. His voice rose above their clamour, "O well beloved, O well beloved, never was a man perplexed with such diversity of thoughts!"

But Martin was gone, and Phil hastening after him saw a face in a window, which was watching Martin hurry through the town. And when Phil pursued Martin the eyes in the window scanned the lad from head to foot.

They found lying at the quay the vessel they sought, and a brave frigate she was, with high poop and nobly carved fiddlehead and sharp, deep cutwater. The gun-deck ports were closed, but on the main deck was a great show of ordnance with new carriages and new yellow breechings. There were swivel-guns on the forecastle and the quarter-deck and there was a finely wrought lantern of bronze and glass at the stern. But as they came up to her, a cloud hid the sun and the gilded carving ceased to shine and the bright colours lost their brilliance and her black, high sides loomed up sombrely, and to Phil she seemed for the moment very dark and forbidding.

Of this Martin appeared to have no perception, for he smiled and whispered, "Mother Taylor hath done well by us.

This *Rose of Devon* is a tall ship and by all the signs she will be well found."

There were men standing about the capstan on the main deck and voices came from the forecastle; but on the poop there leaned against the rail to watch the two come down the quay a single man, of an age in the middle-thirties, with a keen, strong face, who wore a good coat on his back and had the manner of a king in a small island.

They stepped under the poop and Martin doffed his hat, having assumed his most ingratiating smile. "An' it please you, sir," said he, "have I the honour to address Captain Candle of the *Rose of Devon* frigate?"

"I am Captain Candle."

"Good morrow to thee, sir, and Master Stephen Gangley of Liverpool sent us—"

"Yea, I received his letter. I know him not, but it seems he knows friends of mine. You are over heavy for a good seaman but your fellow takes my eye."

Martin stammered and flamed up with anger, and perceiving this, the captain smiled.

"Let it be," he said. "I can make room for the two, and to judge by your looks, if you are slow aloft at handling and hauling, we can use you to excellent purpose as a cook. Of good food and plenty it is plain you know the secret."

He watched policy contend with anger in Martin's face and his own expression gave no hint of what went on in his mind; but there was that about him which made Phil believe he was inwardly laughing, and Phil had an instant liking for the man, which, if one might judge by the captain's glance or two, was returned.

"You may sign the articles in the tavern yonder," he said. "You are none too early, for we sail in an hour's time to get the tide."

As Phil followed Martin into the tavern he saw a bustle and flurry in the street, but it passed and while they waited by the fire for the captain and the agent to come with the articles he thought no more of it.

They came at last, and other seamen with them, and spread the articles on the oaken table where one man might sign after another. And when Martin's turn was come, he tried to speak of wages, but the captain named the figure and bade him sign, and before he thought, he had done so. He stood back, cursing under his breath, and when the captain named a higher wage for Phil, Martin's cursing became an audible mumble, which drew from master and agent a sharp glance. Though Martin smiled and looked about as if to see whence the sound came, he deceived no one.

Then men filed out of the tavern, walking soberly behind the master, and proceeded down the quay to their ship. Their feet clattered on the cobbles and they swung along at a rolling gait. Some were sober and some were drunk; and some were merry and some were sad. Some eyed one another with the curiosity that a man feels if he must sit, for months to come, at cheek and jowl with strangers; and some bent their eyes on the ground as if ill at ease and uncertain of their own discretion in thus committing themselves to no one knew what adventures in distant seas and lands.

Thus they came to the ship, following at the master's heels, and thus they filed on board, while Captain Candle stood at one side and looked them over as they passed.

To a young fellow leaning over the waist one of the men called, "Well met, Will Canty!"

Looking up, Phil himself then caught the eye of a lad of his own years who was returning the hail of a former ship-mate, and since each of the youths found something to his taste in the appearance of the other, on the deck of the ship they joined company.

"You come late," said the one who had answered to the name of Will Canty. "Unless I am much mistaken, you were not on board yesterday."

He was tall and slender and very straight, and he carried his head with an erectness that seemed at first glance to savour of vanity. His face, too, was of a sober cast and his expression restrained. Yet he seemed a likable fellow, withal, and one whom a man could trust.

"I have not until now set foot on this deck," Phil replied. "But having seen many vessels in my time, I venture that the *Rose of Devon* is a staunch ship, as Captain Candle, it is plain to see, is a proper master."

"Yea, both sayings are true. I know, for I have sailed before in this ship with Captain Candle."

An order bawled from the quarter-deck caused a great stir, and for the moment put an end to their talk, but they were to see more of each other.

Casting off the moorings in answer to the word of command, the men sprang to the capstan. It was "Heave, my bullies!" and "Pull, my hearts of gold!" Some, in a boat, carried out an anchor and others laboured at the capstan. The old frigate stirred uneasily and slipped away from the wharf, rolling slightly with the motion of the sea, and thus they kedged her into the tide.

"Bend your passeree to the mainsail!"

Back came a roaring chorus, "Yea, yea!"

"Get your sails to the yards there—about your gear on all hands!"

"Yea, yea!" men here and there replied.

"Hoist sails half-mast high—make ready to set sail!"

"Yea, yea!"

"Cross your yards!"

"Yea, yea!"

"Bring the cable to the capstan—Boatswain, fetch the anchor aboard!—Break ground!—Up there, a hand to the foretop and loose the foretopsail!"

"Yea, yea!" And the first man to set foot on the ratlines was running up the rigging.

It was Philip Marsham, for to him the sea was home and there was no night so dark he could not find his way about a ship. Nor did his promptness escape the sharp eye of Captain Candle.

Now, while the captain stood with folded arms at the poop, his mate cried, "Come, my hearts, heave up your anchor! Come one and all! Who says *Amen?* O brave hearts, the anchor a-peak!"

"Yea, yea!"

"Heave out your topsails!—Haul your sheets!—Let fall your foresail!—You at the helm, there, steer steady before the wind!"

On all the vessels in the harbour, and all along the quay and the streets, men had stopped their work to see the *Rose of Devon* sail. But though most of them stood idle and silent, there was a sudden flurry on the quay where but now she had been lying, and two men burst out, calling after her and waving their arms.

"'Tis the beadle and the constable," the men muttered. "Who of us hath got to sea to escape the law?"

The mate turned to the master, but the master firmly shook his head. "Come, seize the tide," he called. "We will stay for no man."

"Heave out the foretopsail—heave out the main topsail—haul home your topsail sheets!"

The men aloft let the lesser sails fall; the men on deck sheeted them home and hoisted them up. The mate kept bawling a multitude of orders: "Haul in the cable there and coil it in small fakes! Haul the cat! A bitter! Belay! Luff, my man, luff! You, there, with the shank painter, make fast your anchor!"

Then came the voice of the master, which always his mate echoed, "Let fall your mainsail!"

And the echo, "Let fall your mainsail!"

"Yea, yea!"

"On with your bonnets and drabblers!"

And again came the echo from the mate, "On with your bonnets and drabblers!"

"Yea, yea!"

The great guns ranged along the deck—each bound fast by its new breechings—with their linstocks and sponges and ladles and rammers, made no idle show of warlike strength. There was too often need to let their grim voices sound at bay, for those were wild, lawless days.

Such a ship as the *Rose of Devon* frigate, standing out for the open sea, is a sight the world no longer affords. Those ships are "gone, gone, gone with lost Atlantis." Their lofty poops, their little bonaventure masts, their lateen sails aft, their high forecastles and tall bowsprits with the square spritsail flaunted before the fiddlehead, came down from an even earlier day; for the *Rose of Devon* had been an ancient craft when King James died and King Charles succeeded to the throne. But she was a fine tall ship and staunch notwithstanding her years, and there was newly gilded carving on bow and stern and a new band of crimson ran her length. With her great sails spread she thrust her nose into the heavy swell that went rolling up the Bristol Channel, and nodding and curtseying to old Neptune, she entered upon his dominions.

She was, as I have said, a brave tall ship, yet, despite her gilded carving and her band of crimson, her towering sides which were painted black gave her a singularly dark appearance, and she put to sea like a shadow out of older days.

CHAPTER VII

The Ship's Liar

DEATH BY land is a sobering thing and works many changes; but to my thought death at sea is more terrible, for there is a vast loneliness, with only a single ship in the midst of it, and an empty hammock for days and weeks and even months, to keep a man in mind of what has happened; and death at sea may work as many changes as death by land.

Now the *Rose of Devon* was a week from England when a footrope parted and the boatswain pitched down, clutching at the great belly of the sail, and plunged out of sight. And what could a man do to save him? They never saw him after that first wild plunge. There, aloft, was the parted rope, its ends frayed out and hanging. Below decks was the empty berth. The blustering old boatswain, with his great roaring voice and his quick ear for a tune, had gone upon the ultimate adventure which all must face, each man for himself; but they only said, "Did you see the wild look in his eyes

when he fell?" And, "I fear we shall hear his pipe of nights."
And, "'Tis a queer thought that Neddie Hart is to lie in old
Davy Jones's palace, with the queer sea-women all about
him, a-waiting for his old shipmates."

Presently the master's boy came forward into the forecastle, where the men off duty were sitting and talking of the
one who had fallen so far, had sunk so deep, had gone on a
journey so long that they should never see him again; and
quietly—for the boy was much bedevilled and trembled with
fright to think of putting his head, as it were, into the mouth
of the lion—he crept behind Philip Marsham and whispered
in his ear, "The master would see thee in the great cabin."

They sat at close quarters in the forecastle of the *Rose of
Devon*, and the boy had barely room to pass the table and the
benches, for the men had crowded in and put their heads
together; but for once they were too intent on their own
thoughts to heed his coming or his going, which gave him
vast comfort. (Little enough comfort the poor devil got,
between the men forward and the officers aft!)

So Phil rose and followed.

The great cabin, when he entered, was empty. He stood at
loss, waiting, but curiously observed meanwhile the rich
hangings and the deep chairs and the cupboards filled with
porcelain ware. There was plate on the cabin table and a rich
cloak lay thrown loosely over a chair; and he thought to himself that those deep-sea captains lived like princes, as indeed
they did.

He shifted his weight from foot to foot in growing uneasi-
ness. The boy had disappeared. There was no sound of voice
or step. Then, as the ship rolled and Phil put out a foot to
brace himself, a door swung open and revealed on the old-
fashioned walk that ran across the stern under the poop, the
lean, big-boned figure of Captain Francis Candle.

The master of the *Rose of Devon* stood with folded arms
and bent head, but though his head was bent, his eyes, the

lad could see, were peering from under his heavy brows at the horizon. He swayed as the ship rolled, and remained intent on his thoughts, which so absorbed him that he had quite forgotten sending the boy for Philip Marsham.

So Phil waited; and the broad hat that hung on the bulkhead scraped backward and forward as the ship plunged into the trough and rose on the swell; and Captain Candle remained intent on his thoughts; and a sea bird circled over the wake of the ship.

After a long time the master turned about and walked into the cabin and, there espying Philip Marsham, he smiled and said, "I was remiss. I had forgotten you." He threw aside the cloak that lay on the chair and sat down.

"Sit you down," he said with a nod. "You are a practised seaman, no lame, decrepit fellow who serves for under-wages. Have you mastered the theory?"

"Why, sir, I am not unacquainted with astrolabe and quadrant, and on scales and tables I have spent much labour."

"So!" And his manner showed surprise. Then, "Inkpot and quill are before you. Choose a fair sheet and put down thereon the problem I shall set you."

The captain leaned back and half closed his eyes while Phil spread the paper and dipped the quill.

"Let us say," he finally continued, "that two ships sail from one port. The first sails south-south-west a certain distance; then altering her course, she sails due west ninety-two leagues. The second ship, having sailed six-score leagues, meets with the first ship. I demand the second ship's course and rhomb, and how many leagues the first ship sailed south-south-west. Now, my man, how go you to work?"

Phil studied the problem as he had set it down, and wrinkled his brows over it, while Captain Candle lay back with a flicker of a smile on his lips and watched the lad struggle with his thoughts.

After a time Phil raised his head. "First, sir," said he, "I shall draw the first ship's rhomb thus, from A unto E, which shall be south-south-west. Then I shall lay a line from A unto C as the ninety leagues that she sailed west. Next I shall lay my line from C to D, and further, as her south-west course. Then I shall lay from A a line that shall correspond to the six-score leagues the second ship sailed, which cuts at D the line I drew before." As he talked, he worked with his pen, and the master, rising as if in surprise, bent over the table and watched every motion.

The pen drew lines and arcs and lettered them and wrote out a problem in proportions. Hesitating, the point crawled over columns of figures.

"The rhomb of the second ship," said Phil at last, "is degrees sixty-seven, and minutes thirty-six. Her course is near west-south-west. And the first ship sailed forty-nine leagues."

Tapping the table, as one does who meditates, Captain Candle looked more sharply at the lad. "You are clever with your pen."

"'Tis owing to the good Dr. Arber at Roehampton," Phil replied. "Had I abode with him longer, I had been cleverer still, for he was an able scholar; but there was much in school I had no taste for."

The captain's eyes searched his face. "I sent for you," he said, "because I was minded to make you my boatswain. But now, if my mate were lost, I swear I'd seat you at mine own table."

Phil rose.

"Go then, Master Boatswain. But stay! You and your comerado make a strange pair. How came you bedfellows?"

"Why, sir, we met upon the road—"

"Yea, not at sea! Not at sea! Enough is said. Begone, Master Boatswain, begone!"

"How now," cried Martin when Phil passed him on the deck. "Art thou called before the mast?" And he laughed till he shook.

"Nay, he hath made me his boatswain."

"Thou?"

"Yea, comerado."

"Thou? A mere gooseling? The master's on the road to Bedlam! Why here am I—" Martin's red face flamed hot.

"Yea, he spoke of thee."

"Ah!"

"Quoth he, thou art a fine fellow, but hot-tempered, Martin, and overbold."

"Ah!" The crafty, sly look came upon Martin's face and he puffed with pride; but Phil, delighting to see the jest take effect, laughed before his eyes, which sorely perplexed him.

"A fine fellow, but overbold," Martin muttered, as he coiled the cable in neat fakes. "Yea, I did not believe he thought so well of me. From the glances he hath bestowed upon me, it was in my mind he was a narrow man—" Martin smiled and dallied over his work—"one with no eye for a mariner of parts and skill. 'A fine fellow, but overbold!' Nay, that is fair speech and it seems he hath a very searching observation."

Standing erect, Martin folded his arms and swelled like a turkey-cock. His eyes being on the horizon and his back toward the watchful mate, he remained unaware that he had attracted the mate's attention.

"A fine fellow, but overbold," he repeated and smiled with a very haughty air.

The mate, casting his eyes about the deck, picked up a handy end of rope and made a knot in it. One man and another and another became aware of the play that the mate and Martin were about to set and, grinning hugely, they paused in their work to watch, even though they risked getting themselves into such a plight as Martin's. The captain came to the break of the quarter-deck and, perceiving the fun afoot, leaned on the swivel-gun. Slowly his humour mastered his dignity and a smile twitched at his lips.

"A fine fellow, but overbold," Martin was murmuring for the fourth time, when the rope whistled and wound about his ribs and the knot fetched up on his belly with a thump that knocked his wind clean out.

He made a horrible face, gasping for breath, and his ruddy colour darkened to purple. Reaching for his knife he whirled round and drew steel.

"What rakehell muckworm, what base stinkard, what—" He met the cold eye of the mate and for a moment flinched, then, burning with his own folly, he cried, "Thou villain, to strike thus a man the captain himself called a fine fellow but overbold!"

A snicker grew in the silence and swelled into a rumble of laughter; then, by the forecastle bulkhead, a man began to bawl, "A liar! A liar!"

The mate stopped short and his hand fell.

A score of voices took up the cry—"A liar! A liar!"—and Martin turned pale.

Captain Candle on the quarter-deck was laughing softly and the mate in glee slapped his thigh. "Thou yerking, firking, jerking tinker," said he, "dost hear the cry? 'Tis a Monday morning and they are crying thee at the mainmast."

"A liar! A liar!" the men bawled, crowding close about.

"But 'tis no lie. Or this foully deceitful comerado, this half-fledged boatswain—" It came suddenly upon Martin that he had been sorely gulled, and that to reveal the truth would fix upon him the lasting ridicule of his shipmates. He swelled in fury and gave them angry glances but they only laughed the louder, then, rope in hand, the mate stepped toward him.

Though he made a motion as if to stand his ground, at sight of the rope Martin's hand shook in his haste to thrust his knife back into the sheath.

It was the old custom of the sea that they should hail as a liar the man first caught in a lie on a Monday morning and proclaim him thus from the mainmast, and unhappy was the man thus hailed, for thereby he became for a week the "ship's liar" and held his place under the swabber.

"For seven days, thou old cozzener," said the mate, "thou shalt keep clean the beakhead and the chains, and lucky art thou to be at sea. Ashore they would have whipped thee through the streets at the cart's tail."

Again a great wave of laughter swept the deck and by his face Martin showed his anger. But though he was "a fine fellow" and "overbold," he kept his tongue between his teeth; and whatever he suspected of Philip Marsham, he held his peace and went over the bow with ill grace and fell to scraping the chains, which was a task to humble the tallest pride. There was that in the laughter of the crew which had taught discretion to even bolder men than Martin Barwick.

"I have seen his kind before," a voice said low in Phil's ear. "But though there be much of the calf in him, beware lest you rouse him to such a pitch that he will draw and strike."

It was Will Canty, the youth who had already won the young boatswain's liking, spoke thus. He was a comerado more to Phil's taste than was the luckless Martin; but fate is not given to consulting tastes, and necessity forces upon a traveller such bedfellows as he meets by the way.

CHAPTER VIII

Storm

THE STORM brewed long in grey banks of cloud that hung in the west and north. It drew around the *Rose of Devon* from north to east with a slow, immutable force, as yet perceived rather than felt, till she sailed in the midst of a circle of haze. At night the moon was ringed. The sun rose in a bank of flaming red and the small sea-birds that by their presence, mariners say, tell of coming gales, played over the wake.

Captain Candle from the poop sniffed at the damp air; and studying the winds as they veered and rose in brisk flourishes and fell to the merest whisper of a breeze, he puckered his lips, which was his way when thoughts crowded upon him. Martin on the beakhead pursued his noisome task of cleaning it under the watchful eye of the swabber (who took unkind joy in exacting from him the utmost pains) and cast

furtive glances at the grey swell that came shouldering up
from the east.

"Holla, boatswain," the captain cried.

"Yea, yea!"

"Our foresail is old and hath lost its goodness. Look to thy
stores and see if there be not another. Have it ready, then, to
bend in haste if there be need."

"Yea, yea!"

"And lay out thy cordage, boatswain, that if sheet or hal-
yard or tackling shall part, we may be ready to bend another
in its place."

Descending thereupon into the forehold with his boatswain's mate to fetch and carry, Boatswain Marsham fell to
work overhauling the bolts of sail-cloth and the hanks of
cordage and the coils of rope, till he had found a new foresail
and laid it under the hatch, and had placed great ropes and
such cordage as headlines and marlines and sennets so that
a man could lay hands on them in a time of haste and confusion. For the *Rose of Devon* was heavily pitching and the seas
crashed on her three-inch planks with a noise like thunder-
claps; and when she lifted on the swell, the water rumbled
against her bilge and gurgled away past her run.

Very faintly he heard a sailor's voice, "The pump is
choked." There was shouting above for a time, then the cry
arose, which brought reassurance to all, "Now she sucks,"
and again there was quiet.

Climbing through the hatch and passing aft along the
main deck, he heard for himself the *suck-suck* from the
pump well, then the rattle of tiller and creak of pintle as the
helmsmen eased her off and brought her on to meet a rising
sea.

"Holla, master!"

"Holla, is all laid ready below?"

"Yea! Ropes and cordage and sail are laid ready upon the
main deck and secured against the storm."

"And seemeth she staunch to one in the hold?"

"Yea, master."

"Then, boatswain, call up the men to prayer and breakfast, for we shall doubtless have need of both ere the day is done. Boy, fetch my cellar of bottles, for I would drink a health to all, fore and aft, and I would have the men served out each a little sack."

By midday the veering winds had settled in the east and the overcast sky had still further darkened. The ship, labouring heavily, held her course; but as the wind blew up a fresh gale, the after sails took the wind from the sails forward, which began to beat and thresh. Swarming aloft, the younkers handed the fore-topsail-steering-sail, the fore and main topsails, and the main-topsail-staysail. But as they manned the foreyard, the ship yawed in such a manner that the full force of the wind struck the old foresail and split it under their fingers.

Philip Marsham on the weather yard-arm, with the grey seas breaking in foam beneath him at one minute and with the forecastle itself seeming to rise up at him the next minute, so heavily did the old ship roll, was reaching for the sail at the moment it tore to ribands; and a billow of grey canvas striking him in the face knocked him off the yard; but as he fell, he locked his legs round the spar and got finger hold on the earing, and crawled back to the mast as the sailors stood by the ropes to strike the yard and get in the threshing tatters of the sail.

The mate, going aft, was caught in the waist when the ship gave a mighty lurch, and went tumbling to leeward where the scupper-holes were spouting like so many fountains all a-row. The fall might well have ended his days, had he not bumped into the capstan where he clung fast with both arms, and twice lucky he was to stay his fall thus, for a sea came roaring over the waist and drowned the fountains in the scuppers and in a trice the decks were a-wash from forecastle to poop. But the old ship shook her head and righted and Captain Francis Candle, leaning against the wind, his cloak flapping in the gale and his hat hauled hard down over his eyes, descended from the poop and braced himself in its lee.

"The wind blows frisking," the mate cried, scrambling up the ladder and joining the master.

"Yea, it is like to over-blow. She took a shrewd plunge but now. We shall further our voyage by striking every sail. Go thou, mate, and have them secure the spritsailyard, then take thy station on the forecastle."

For an hour or two the old *Rose of Devon* went plunging through the seas; and there was much loosing and lowering of sails. For a while, then, the wind scanted so that there was hope the storm had passed, and during the lull they bent and set the new foresail and must needs brace and veer and haul aft. But ere long the gale blew up amain, and in the late afternoon Captain Candle, sniffing the breeze, called upon all to stand by and once more to hand both foresail and mainsail.

"Cast off the topsail sheets, clew garnets, leechlines and buntlines!" The order came thinly through the roar of the wind.

"Yea, yea!" a shrill voice piped.

"Stand by the sheet and brace—come lower the yard and furl the sail—see that your main halyards be clear and all the rest of your gear clear and cast off."

"It is all clear."

"Lower the main yard—haul down upon your downhaul." As the yard swayed down and the men belayed the halyards, one minute staggering to keep their feet, the next minute slipping and sliding across the decks, the captain's sharp voice, holding them at their work, cut through the gale, "Haul up the clew garnets, lifts, leechlines and buntlines!

Come, furl the sail fast and secure the yard lest it traverse and gall!"

"'Twas a fierce gust," an old sailor cried to Phil, who had reached for the rigging and saved himself from going down to the lee scuppers. "We best look the guns be all fast. I mind, in the *Grace and Mary*, my second Guinea voyage, a gun burst its breechings—"

"Belay the fore down-haul!" the mate thundered, and leaving his tale untold, the old man went crawling forward.

The men heard faintly the orders to the helmsman, "Hard a-weather!—Right your helm!—Now port, port hard! More hands! He cannot put up the helm!"

Then out of the turmoil and confusion a great voice cried, "A sail! A sail!"

"Where?"

"Fair by us."

"How stands she?"

"To the north'ard."

She lay close hauled by the wind and as the *Rose of Devon*, scudding before the sea, bore down the wind and upon her, she hove out signs to speak; but though Captain Candle passed under her lee as near as he dared venture and learned by lusty shouting that she was an English ship from the East Indies, which begged the *Rose of Devon* for God's sake to spare them some provisions, since they were eighty persons on board who were ready to perish for food and water, the seas ran so high that neither the one vessel nor the other dared hoist out a boat; and parting, the men of the *Rose of Devon* lost sight of her in the gathering dusk.

Still more and more the storm increased. Darkness came, but there was no rest at sea that night.

Thanks to the storm, and the labour and anxiety it brought all hands, Martin, the latter part of that day, escaped the duties of ship's liar, and glad was he of the chance to slip unobserved about the deck with no reminder of his late humiliation. But by night he was blue with the cold, and drenching wet and so hungry that he gnawed at a bit of biscuit when he needed both hands to haul on a rope.

Finding Phil Marsham at his shoulder and still resenting bitterly the jest to which he had fallen victim, he shot at him an ill-tempered glance and in sullen silence turned his back.

"Belay!"

A line of struggling men tripped and stumbled as they secured the rope and went swaying and staggering across the deck when the ship rolled; for the weight of her towering superstructure and her cannon would set her wallowing fearfully in the merest seaway. One caught up the rope's end in loose coils; another, having fallen, got clumsily on his feet and staunched his bleeding nose; the rest shivered as the icy wind struck through their wet shirts.

Martin again turned his back on the boatswain and hugged himself, but to little profit, although his fat arms covered a goodly area. Phil laughed softly at Martin's show of spleen and was about to warm the man's temper further by a thrust well calculated to stir him to fury, when the ship rose with a queer lurch and descended into a veritable gulf.

They saw above them a sea looming like a black cloud. It mounted slowly up, hung over them, curled down a dark tongue of water and, before the *Rose of Devon* had righted from her plunge into the trough, broke upon the ship and overwhelmed her. The waist was flooded from the head of the forecastle to the break of the poop. Water, licking across the quarter-deck, rose in a great wave that drenched the captain to his thighs and poured into the steerage room, momentarily blinding the men at the helm—for in those old ships they stood with their faces on a level with the quarter-deck—and, following whip-staff and tiller, spilled into the main deck and hold.

Philip Marsham, as the water washed him off his feet, made shift to lay hands on the shrouds, and though he had no footing and was washed far out over the side, his grasp was strong and he held himself against the rush of water as the ship rose like a dog shaking its head and coming up through a wave. In very truth she seemed to shake her head and struggle up to the black night above. But as Phil saved himself he saw Martin cowering by a gun and striving to reach the breeching; and as the ship rose, the lad half felt, half saw, some great body washed past him and over the side.

There was no one beside the gun: Martin was gone.

Though a man were a knave and liar, Phil Marsham had no stomach to see him drown thus; and though he held old Martin in contempt and bedevilled him night and day, yet he had a curious liking for the fellow. Overhead there hung from the maintop a loose rope. He faintly saw it swinging against the leaden-black sky. By a nimble leap there was a fair chance a man might reach it and if it did not part, an active man might by a stroke of fortune regain the ship. All this Phil saw in the falling of a single grain of sand, then the rope swung within reach of his hand and he seized it. Spared the hazard of leaping for it, he let go the shrouds and swung with all his strength out into the night.

Swinging high over the sea he saw for an instant, while he was in mid-air, the *Rose of Devon* surging away from under him. The single great lanthorn was burning on her poop, and dim lights in forecastle and cabin showed that those parts of the ship, at least, had come up through the sea unflooded. He thought he saw a cloaked figure like a shadow on the quarter-deck. Then he slid down into darkness till the rope burned his hands, then he struck the water and went under, gasping at the shock, for the sea was as cold as a mountain stream. He caught a last glimpse of the great ship, now looming high above him, then clutching fast the rope with one hand and wildly kicking out, he felt with his knees what might be a man's body.

With his free hand he reached for the body. He snatched at an arm and missed it, then felt hair brushing his fingers and tangled them in it and gripped it. He went down and down; then the drag of the water, for the ship was scudding fast, raised him to the surface. The ship rolled toward him and he again went under, overshadowed by the lofty poop which leaned out so far that notwithstanding the tumble home he thought the poop would come down and crush him. The ship then rolled away from him, and the rope brought up on his arm so hard that he feared the bones would pull from their sockets; but if he died in doing it he was bound he would hold the rope and keep his man.

The ship rolled till he bumped against her side and was lifted half out of water.

"Help!" he cried. "Help or we die!"

He heard voices above and felt the rope move as if some one had seized it, then the looming bulk of the ship rolled back and drove him again down into the sea.

He had no wind left for calling when he came up as once more the ship rolled, but the man he held had come to life and was clinging like a leech to the rope, which vastly lightened the strain, and some one above was hauling on it. For a moment the two swung in air with the sea beneath them, then the ship rolled farther and their weight rested on planks, and hands from within the ship reached down and lifted them on board.

The man—and it was indeed Martin—coughed like one who is deathly sick, as well he might be, and went rolling down the deck with a boy to help him. But Phil, having kept his head and having swallowed no great quantity of salt water, was able after breathing deeply a few times to stand alone beside Will Canty whose hands had drawn him to safety, and to perceive that waist, boat, capstan, windlass and sheet anchor were washed away.

He then heard a pounding and shouting aft. "What in the fiend's name hath befallen us?" he demanded.

"'Tis even worse than doth appear," Will cried. "The sea hath a free passage into the hold between the timber heads. They are pumping with both pumps. The captain hath ordered the mizzenmast cut away, the better to keep us before the wind. Hear you not the sound of axes? And—"

Out of the darkness burst the mate. "Come, my hearts! Below there! Cram blankets and hammocks into the leak, yea, the shirts from off your backs! And then to the pumps to take your turn. And pray Almighty God to give us sight of another day."

There was running on the deck and shadows passed forward and aft.

From the quarter-deck a clear voice, so sharp that it pierced the noise of the storm, was calling, "Port the helm! Ease her, ease her! Now up! Hard up! Ease her, ease her!"

As the boatswain dropped through the hatch, he saw very dimly the captain crouching under the poop, his cloak drawn close about him.

There was wild confusion below, for as the ship rolled to starboard the sea burst in through the great gap along the timber heads and pushed through the gap and into the ship the blankets and rugs that were stuffed in place. Though the men leaped after them and came scrambling back to force them again into place between the timbers, and though they tore down hammocks and jammed them in with the blankets to fill the great opening, yet as the ship again rolled and the sea once more came surging against the barrier, they again fled before it, and again the sea cleared the gap and came flooding in upon the deck. It was a sight to fill a brave man with despair.

The more hands made faster work, and though the labour seemed spent in vain they stuffed the gap anew. But now when the ship again rolled to starboard an old seaman raised his hand and roared, "Every man to his place and hold against the sea! Stay! Hold fast your ground!—Come, bullies, hold hard!—Good fellows! See, we have won!"

They had perceived his meaning and braced themselves and with their hands they had held the stuffing in the gap until the pressure ceased, which was more of a feat than a man might think, since despite their every effort the sea had found passage in great strong streams, yet they held to the last; and when the ship rolled back, Boatswain Marsham cried out:

"Now, Master Carpenter, quick! Bring great nails and hammer and a plank or two. Yare, yare!"

"Yea, yea," the carpenter cried, and came running down the deck.

The men held the planking and the carpenter drove home the nails and thus they made the plank fast along the timbers behind the gap, where it would serve to brace the stuffing. Between the plank and the stuffing they forced a great mass of other wadding, and though the ship rolled ever so deeply the plank held against the sea. They left it so; but all that night, which seemed as long as any night they had ever seen, no man slept in the *Rose of Devon*, for they still feared lest the sea should batter away the plank and work their undoing.

All night long they kept the pumps going and all night long they feared their labour would be lost. But at four in the morning one of the pumps sucked, which gave them vast comfort, and at daybreak they gave thanks to God, who had kept them safe until dawn.

The storm had passed and the sky was clear, and Phil and Martin met at sunrise.

"Since thou hast haled me out of the sea by the hair of my head," quoth Martin, after the manner of one who swallows a grievance he can ill stomach, "I must e'en give thee good morrow."

CHAPTER IX

The Master's Guest

"A SAIL! A sail!"

The seas had somewhat abated and the *Rose of Devon* was standing on her course under reefed mainsail when the cry sounded.

The vessel they sighted lay low in the water; and since she had one tall mast forward and what appeared to be a lesser mast aft they thought her a ketch. But while they debated the matter the faint sound of guns fired in distress came over the sea; and loosing the reef of their mainsail and standing directly toward the stranger, the men in the *Rose of Devon* soon made her out to be, instead, a ship which had lost her mainmast and mizzenmast and was wallowing like a log. While the *Rose of Devon* was still far off her men saw that some of the strange crew were aloft in the rigging and that others were huddled on the quarter-deck; and when, in the late afternoon, she came up under the stranger's stern, the unknown master and his men got down on their knees on the deck and stretched their arms above their bare heads.

"Save us," they cried in a doleful voice, "for the Lord Jesus' sake! For our ship hath six-foot water in the hold and we can no longer keep her afloat."

In all the *Rose of Devon* there was not a heart but relented at their lamentable cry, not a man but would do his utmost to lend them aid.

"Hoist out thy boat and we will stand by to succour thee," Captain Candle called. "We can do no more, for we ha' lost our own boat in the storm."

It appeared they had but one boat, which was small, so they must needs divide the crew to leave their vessel, part at one time and part at another; and the seas still ran so high, though wind and wave had moderated, that it seemed impossible they could make the passage. With men at both her pumps the *Rose of Devon* lay by the wind, wallowing and plunging, and her own plight seemed a hard one. But the poor stranger, though ever and again she rose on the seas so that the water drained from her scupper-holes, lay for the most part with her waist a-wash and a greater sea than its fellows would rise high on the stumps of mainmast and mizzenmast. Her ropes dragged over the side and her sails were a snarl of canvas torn to shreds, and a very sad sight she presented.

Three times they tried to hoist out their boat and failed; but the fourth time they got clear, and with four men rowing and one steering and seven with hats and caps heaving out the water, they came in the twilight slowly down the wind past the *Rose of Devon* and up into her lee.

The men at the waist of the ship saw more clearly, now, the features of those in the boat, and the one in the stern who handled the great steering oar had in the eyes of Philip Marsham an oddly familiar look. Phil gazed at the man, then he turned to Martin and knew he was not mistaken, for Martin's mouth was agape and he was on the very point of crying out.

"Holla!" Martin yelled.

The man in the stern of the boat looked up and let his eyes range along the waist of the ship. Not one of all those in sight on board the *Rose of Devon* escaped his scrutiny, which was quick and sure; but he looked Martin coldly in the face without so much as a nod of recognition; and though his brief glance met Phil's gaze squarely and seemed for the moment to linger and search the lad's thoughts, it then passed to the one at Phil's side.

It was the thin man who had been Martin's companion on the road—it was Tom Jordan—it was the Old One.

Martin's face flamed, but he held his tongue.

A line thrown to the boat went out through the air in coils that straightened and sagged down between the foremost thwarts. A sailor in the boat, seizing the line, hauled upon it with might and main. The Old One hotly cursed him and bellowed, "Fend off, fend off, thou slubbering clown! Thy greed to get into the ship will be the means of drowning us all."

Some thrust out oars to fend away from the side of the ship and some held back; but two or three, hungering for safety, gave him no heed and hauled on the rope and struggled to escape out of their little boat, which was already half full of water. The Old One then rose with a look of the Fiend in his eyes and casting the steering oar at the foremost of them, knocked the man over into the sea, where he sank, leaving a blotch of red on the surface, which was a terrible sight and brought the others to observe the Old One's commands.

Some cried "Save him!" but the Old One roared, "Let the mutinous dog go!"

Perhaps he was right, for there are times when it takes death to maintain the discipline that will save many lives. At all events it was then too late to save either the man or the boat, for although they strove thereafter to do as the Old One bade them, the boat had already thumped against the side of the ship and it was each man for himself and the Devil take the last. The men above threw other ropes and bent over to give a hand to the poor fellows below, and all but the man who had sunk came scrambling safe on board.

The Old One leaned out and looked down at the boat, which lay full of water, with a great hole in her side.

"I would have given my life sooner than let this happen," he said. "There are seven men left on board our ship, who trusted me to save them. Indeed, I had not come away but these feared lest without the master you should refuse to take them. What say ye, my bawcocks, shall we venture back for our shipmates?"

Looking down at the boat and at the gaping holes the sea had stove by throwing her against the *Rose of Devon,* the men made no reply.

"Not one will venture back? Is there no one of ye?"

"'Twere madness," one began. "We should—"

"See! She hath gone adrift!"

And in truth, her gunwales under water, the boat was already drifting astern. At the end of the painter, which a *Rose of Devon's* man still held, there dangled a piece of broken board.

"Let us bring thy ship nigh under the lee of mine," the Old One cried to Captain Candle. "It may be that by passing a line we can yet save them."

"It grieves me sorely to refuse them aid, but to approach nearer, with the darkness now drawing upon us, were an act of folly that might well cost the lives of us all. Mine own ship is leaking perilously and in this sea, were the two to meet, both would most certainly go down."

The Old One looked about and nodded. "True," said he. "There is no recovering the boat and darkness is upon us.

Let us go as near to the ship as we may and bid them have courage till morning, when, God willing, we shall try to get aboard and save them."

"That we will. And I myself will con the ship."

Leaning over the rail, Tom Jordan, the Old One, called out, "Holla, my hearts! The boat hath gone adrift with her sides stove; but do you make a raft and keep abroad a light until morning, when God helping us, we will endeavor to get you aboard."

Perceiving for the first time that the boat was gone and there was no recovering her, those left on board the wreck gave a cry so sad that it pierced the hearts of all in the *Rose of Devon,* whose men saw them through the dusk doing what they could to save themselves; and presently their light appeared.

Working the *Rose of Devon* to windward of the wreck, Captain Candle lay by, but all his endeavours could not avail to help them, for about ten o'clock at night, three hours after the Old One and his ten men had got on board the *Rose of Devon,* their ship sank and their light went out and seven men lost their lives.

The Old One, standing beside Captain Candle, had watched the light to the last. "It is a bitter grief to bear," he said, "for they were seven brave men. A master could desire no better mariners. 'Tis the end of the *Blue Friggat* from Virginia, bound for Portsmouth, wanting seven weeks."

"A man can go many years to sea without meeting such a storm."

"Yea! Three days ago when the wind was increasing all night we kept only our two courses abroad. At daybreak we handed our main course, but before we had secured it the storm burst upon us so violently that I ordered the foreyard lowered away; but not with all their strength could the men get it down, and of them all not one had a knife to cut away the sail, for they wore only their drawers without pockets; so the gale drove us head into the sea and stopped our way and a mighty sea pooped us and filled us and we lay with only our masts and forecastle out of the water. I myself, being fastened to the mizzenmast with a rope, had only my head out of water. Yea, we expected to go straight down to the bottom, but God of his infinite goodness was pleased to draw us from the deep and another sea lifted up our ship. We got down our foresail and stowed it and bored holes between the decks to let the water into the hold and by dint of much pumping we kept her afloat until now. In all we have lost eight lives this day and a sad day it is."

"From Virginia, wanting seven weeks," Captain Candle mused.

Captain Jordan stole a swift glance at him but saw no suspicion in his face.

"Yea, from Virginia."

"You shall share mine own cabin but I fear you have come only from one wreck to another."

The two captains sat late that night at the table in the great cabin, one on each side, and ate and drank. There was fine linen on the table, and bread of wheat flour with butter less than two weeks from the dairy, and a fine old cheese, and a mutton stew, and canary and sack and aqua vitæ. At midnight they were still lingering over the suckets and almonds and comfits that the boy had set before them; and the boy, nodding in uncontrollable drowsiness as he stood behind his master's chair, strove to keep awake.

The murmuring voices of the men at the helm came faintly through the bulkhead, and up from below the deck came the creak of whipstaff and tiller. The moon, shining through the cabin window, added its wan light to the yellow radiance from the swinging lanthorns, and stars were to be seen. So completely had wind and weather changed in a night and a day that, save for the long rolling swell, the great gap where waist and boat and capstan had gone, the hole stuffed with blankets and rugs and hammocks, the stump of a mizzenmast, and the rescued men on board—save for these, a man might have forgotten storms and wrecks.

"You are well found," said Captain Thomas Jordan, tilting his glass and watching the wine roll toward the brim; "yea, and we are in good fortune." His thin face, as he lifted his brows and slightly smiled at his host, settled into the furrowed wrinkles that had won him the name of the Old One.

"We can give such entertainment as is set before you," his host drily replied. Francis Candle was too shrewd a man to miss his guest's searching appraisal of the cabin and its furnishings. In his heart he already distrusted the fellow.

CHAPTER X

Between Midnight and Morning

THROUGH THE main deck to the gun-room and up into the forecastle there drifted smoke from the cookroom in the hold, which was the way of those old ships. At times it set choking the men at the pumps; it eddied about the water cask before the mainmast and about the riding butts by the heel of the bowsprit, and went curling out of the hawse pipes. It crept insidiously into the forecastle, and the men cursed fluently when their eyes began to smart and their noses to sting.

There were seven men in the forecastle and Martin Barwick was one of the seven, although his watch was on deck and he had no right to be there. Philip Marsham, whose watch was below, had stayed because he suspected there was some strange thing in the wind and was determined to learn if possible what it was. Two of the others were younkers of the *Rose of Devon*, who suspected nothing, and the remaining three were of the rescued men.

There was a step above and a round head appeared in the hatch. The dim smoky light gave a strange appearance to the familiar features.

"Ho, cook!" Martin cried, and thumped on the table. "Come thou down and bring us what tidings the boy hath brought thee in the cookroom. Yea, though the cook labour in the very bowels of the ship, is it not a proverb that he alone knows all that goes on?"

Slipping through the hatch, the cook drew a great breath and sat him down by the table. "She was the *Blue Friggat*, I hear, and seven weeks from Virginia—God rest the souls of them who went down in her!"

"From Virginia!" quoth Martin. "Either th'art gulled, in truth, or th'art the very prince of liars. From Virginia! Ho ho!" And Martin laughed loud and long.

Now it was for such a moment that Philip Marsham was waiting, nor had he doubted the moment would come. For although Martin had gone apart with the men who had come from the foundered ship, the fellow's head, which was larger than most heads, could never keep three ideas in flourish at the same time. To learn what game was in the wind there was need only to keep close at Martin's heels until his blunders should disclose his secrets.

"The Devil take thee, thou alehouse dog!" the cook cried in a thick, wheezy voice. "Did not the boy bring me word straight when he came down for a can of boiling water with which this Captain Jordan would prepare a wondrous drink for Captain Candle?"

"And did not I part with this Captain Jordan not—Wow-ouch!" With a yell Martin tipped back in his chair and went over. Crawling on his feet, he put on a long face and rubbed his head and hurled a flood of oaths at the sailor beside him, a small man and round like an apple, who went among his

fellows—for he was one of those the *Rose of Devon* had rescued—by the name of Harry Malcolm.

"Nay," the little round man very quietly replied, "I fear
you not, for all your bluster. Put your hand on your tongue,
fellow, and see if you cannot hold it. I had not intended to tip
you over. It was done casually."

"And why, perdy, did'st thou jam thy foot on mine till the
bones crunched? I'll have they heart's blood."

"Nay," the man replied, so quietly, so calmly that he might
have been a clerk sitting on his stool, "you have a way of talking overmuch, fellow, and I have a misliking of speech that
babbles like a brook. It can make trouble."

Martin stopped as if he had lost his voice, but continued
to glare at the stranger, who still regarded him with no concern.

"It is thy weakness, fellow," he said, "and—" he looked
very hard at Martin—"it may yet be the occasion of thine
untimely end."

For a moment Martin stood still, then, swallowing once or
twice, he went out of the dimly lighted forecastle into the
darkness of the deck.

"He appears," the little man said, addressing the others,
"to be an excitable fellow. Alas, what trouble a brisk tongue
can bring upon a man!"

The little man, Harry Malcolm, looked from one to
another and longest at Phil.

Now Phil could not say there had been a hidden meaning
in the hard look the little man had given Martin or in the
long look the little man had given Phil himself. But he knew
that whether this was so or not, there was no more to be got
that night from Martin, and he in turn, further bepuzzled by
the little man's words and after all not much enlightened by
Martin's blunder, left the forecastle to seek the main deck.

Passing the great cannon lashed in their places, and leaving behind him the high forecastle, he came into the shadow

of the towering poop on which the lantern glowed yellow in the blue moonlight, and continued aft to the hatch ladder. Already it was long past midnight.

He imagined he heard voices in the great cabin, and although he well enough knew that it was probably only imagination—for the cabin door was closed fast—the presence of the Old One on board the *Rose of Devon* was enough to make a man imagine things, who had sat in Mother Taylor's cottage and listened to talk of the gentlemen who sailed from Bideford. He paused at the head of the ladder and listened, but heard nothing more.

An hour passed. There were fewer sounds to break the silence. There is no time like the very early morning for subtle and mysterious deeds.

Boatswain Marsham was asleep below and Captain Candle was asleep aft, when Captain Jordan arose and stretched himself, and in a voice that would have been audible to Captain Candle if he had been awake but that was so low it did not disturb his sleep, vowed he must breathe fresh air ere he could bury his head in a blanket for the night.

Emerging from the great cabin, Captain Jordan climbed first to the poop, whence he looked down on the brave old ship and the wide space of sky and darkly heaving sea within the circle of the horizon. To look thus at the sea is enough to make a philosopher of a thinking man, and this Captain Thomas Jordan was by no means devoid of thought.

But whereas many a one who stands under the bright stars in the small morning hours feels himself a brother with the most trifling creatures that live and is filled with humility to consider in relation to the immeasurable powers of the universe his weakness during even his brief space of life—whereas such a one perceives himself to be, like the prophets of ancient times, in a Divine Presence, the Old One, his face strangely youthful in its repose, threw back his head and

softly laughed, as if there high on the poop he were a god of
the heathen, who could blot out with his thumb the ship and
all the souls that sailed in her. His face had again a haunting
likeness to the devils in the old wood-cuts; and indeed there
is something of the devil in the very egotism of a man who
can thus assert his vain notions at such an hour.

Presently descending from the poop and with a nod passing on the quarter-deck the officer of the watch, he paced for
a time the maintop-deck. He pretended to absorb himself in
the sea and the damage the storm had done to the waist; but
he missed nothing that happened and he observed the
whereabouts of every man in the watch.

Edging slowly forward, he stood at last beside a big man
who was leaning in the shadow of the forecastle.

"We meet sooner than you thought," he said in a low voice.

"Yea, for we were long on the road and entangled our-
selves wonderfully among those byways and highways which
cross the country in a manner perplexing beyond belief."

"Saw you your brother?"

"In all truth I saw him—and the Devil take him!"

The Old One laughed softly.

"It is plain thy brother hath little love for a shipwrecked
mariner," quoth he, "yet there is a most memorable antiquity
about the use of ships, and even greater gluttons than thy
brother have supped light that worthy seamen might not go
hungry to bed. We will speak of him another time. What
think you of this pretty pup we have met by the way?—Ah,
thine eye darkens! Methinks thou hast more than once felt
the rough side of his tongue."

"He bears himself somewhat struttingly—" Martin hesitated, but added perforce, since he had received a friendly
turn he could not soon forget, "yet he hath his good points."

"He was one too many for thee! Nay, confess it!"

"Th'art a filthy rascal!" Martin's face burned with anger.

"I knew he would be too cunning for thy woolgathering wits. Truly I believe he is a lad after my own heart. I have marked him well."

"But hast thou plumbed his inclination with thy sounding lead?"

"Why, no. At worst, he can disappear. It has happened to taller men than he, and in a land where there are men at arms to come asking questions."

"Hgh!"

"This for thy whining, though: we shall play upon him lightly. Some are not worth troubling over, but this lad is a cunning rogue and hath book learning."

"Came you in search of this ship?"

"It was chance alone that brought us across her course. Chance alone, Martin, that brought your old captain back to you."

Watching Martin, as he spoke, the Old One again laughed softly.

"Yea, Martin, it touches the heart of your old captain to see with what pleasure you receive him."

"Th'art a cunning devil," Martin muttered, and babbled oaths and curses.

"We must sleep, Martin—sleep and eat, for we are spent with much labour and many hardships, and it is well for them to sail our ship for us a while longer. But the hour will come, and do you then stand by."

The Old One went aft. The ship rolled drowsily and the watch nodded. Surveying her aloft and alow, as a man does who is used to command, and not as a guest on board might do, the Old One left the deck.

CHAPTER XI

Head Winds and a Rough Sea

"Lacking the mizzen she labours by the wind, which hath veered sadly during the night," quoth Captain Jordan in a sleepy voice, as with his host he came upon deck betimes.

"I like it little," the master replied.

"It would be well to lay a new course and sail on a new voyage. There is small gain to be got from these fisheries. A southern voyage, now, promises returns worth the labour."

To this Captain Candle made no reply. He studied the sore damage done to the ship, upon which already the carpenter was at work.

"With a breadth of canvas and hoops to batten the edges fast, and over all a coating of tar, a man might make her as tight and dry as you please," said the Old One. He smiled when he spoke and his manner galled his host.

"It was in my own mind," Captain Candle replied, with an angry lift of his head. There are few things more grievously harassing than the importunity and easy assurance of a guest of whom there is no riddance. It puts a man where he is peculiarly helpless to defend himself, and already Captain Candle's patience had ebbed far. "Bid the boatswain overhaul his canvas, mate, and the carpenter prepare such material as be needful. Aye, and bid the 'liar' stand ready to go over the side. 'Twill cool his hot pride, of which it seems he hath full measure."

"Yea, yea!"

As the master paced the deck, back and forth and back and forth, the Old One walked at his side—for he was a shrewd schemer and had calculated his part well—until the master's gorge rose. "I must return to the cabin," he said at last, "and overhaul my journal."

"I will bear you company."

"No, no!"

The Old One smiled as if in deprecation; but as the master turned away, the smile broadened to a grin.

Boatswain Marsham and the one-eyed carpenter who wore a beard like a goat's were on their way to the forehold. The cook and his mate were far down in the cookroom. Ten men in the watch below were sound asleep—but Martin Barwick, the eleventh man in the watch, was on deck, *and of the eleven rescued men not one was below.* With Captain Candle safe in his cabin and busied over his journal, there were left from the company of the *Rose of Devon* eight men and the mate, and one man of the eight was at the helm. These the Old One counted as he took a turn on the quarter-deck.

The Old One and his men were refreshed by a night of sleep and restored by good food. To all appearances, without care or thought to trouble them, they ruffled about the deck.

One was standing just behind the mate; two were straying toward the steerage.

"Thy boatswain is a brave lad," the Old One said to the mate, and stepping in front of him, he spread his legs and folded his arms.

The mate nodded. He had less liking for their guest, if it were possible, than the captain.

"A brave lad," the Old One repeated. "I can use him."

"You?"

"Yea, I."

The mate drew back a step, as a man does when another puts his face too near. He was on the point of speaking; but before his lips had phrased a word the Old One raised his hand and the man behind the mate drove six inches of blue steel into the mate's back, between his ribs and through his heart.

He died in the Old One's arms, for the Old One caught him before he fell, and held him thus.

"Well done," the Old One said to his man.

"Not so well as one could wish," the man replied, wiping his knife on the mate's coat. "He perished quietly enough, but the knife bit into a rib and the feeling of a sharp knife dragging upon bone sets my teeth on edge."

The Old One laughed. "Thy stomach is exceeding queasy," he said. "Come, let us heave him over the side."

All this, remember, had happened quickly and very quietly. There were the three men standing by the quarter-deck ladder—the Old One and his man and the mate—and by all appearances the Old One merely put out his hands in a friendly manner to the other, for the knife thrust was hidden by a cloak. But now the mate's head fell forward in a queer, lackadaisical way and four of the Old One's men, perceiving what they looked for, slipped past him through the door to the steerage room, where they clapped down the hatch to the main deck. One stood on the hatch; two stood by the door of the great cabin; and the fourth, stepping up to the man at the helm, flashed a knife from his sleeve and cut the fellow down.

It was a deft blow, but not so sure as the thrust that had killed the mate. The helmsman dropped the whipstaff and, falling, gave forth a yell and struck at his assailant, who again let drive at him with the knife and finished the work, so that the fellow lay with bloody froth at his lips and with fingers that twitched a little and then were still.

The man who had killed him took the whipstaff and called softly, "Holla, master! We hold the helm!" then from his place he heard a sailor cry out, "The mate is falling! Lend him aid!"

Then the Old One's voice, rising to a yell, called, "Stand back! Stand off! Now, my hearts!"

There came a quick tempest of voices, a shrill cry, the pounding of many feet, then a splash, then a cry wilder and more shrill than any before, "Nay, I yield—quarter! Quarter, I say! Mercy! God's mercy, I beg of you! Help—O God!"

There was at the same time a rumble of hoarse voices and a sound of great struggling, then a shriek and a second splash.

The man at the helm kicked the dead helmsman to one side and listened. In the great cabin, behind the bulkhead at his back, he heard a sudden stir. As between the mainmast and the forecastle the yells rose louder, the great cabin door burst open and out rushed Captain Francis Candle in a rich waist with broad cuffs at his wrists, his hair new oiled with jessamine butter, and gallant bows at his knees, for he was a fine gentleman who had first gone to sea as a lieutenant in the King's service. As he rushed out the door the man lying in wait on the left struck a fierce blow to stab him, but the knife point broke on a steel plate which it seemed Captain Candle wore concealed to foil just such dastardly work.

Thereupon, turning like a flash, Captain Candle spitted the scoundrel with his sword. But the man lying in wait on the right of the door saw his fellow's blow fail and perceived the reason, and leaping on the captain from behind, he seized his oiled hair with one hand and hauled back his head, and reaching forward with the other hand, drove a knife into the captain's bare throat.

Dark blood from a severed vein streamed out over Captain Candle's collar and his gay waist. He coughed and his eyes grew dull. He let go his sword, which remained stuck through the body of the man who had first struck at him, clapped his hand to his neck, and went down in a heap.

The yells on deck had ceased and the man who had killed Francis Candle, after glancing into the great cabin where the captain's cloak lay spread over the chair from which he rose to step out of his door and die—where the captain's pen lay across the pages of the open journal and a bottle of the captain's wine, which he had that morning shared with his guest, Captain Thomas Jordan, stood beside the unstoppered bottle of ink—walked forth upon the deck and nodded to the Old One, who stood with his hand on the after swivel gun.

There were a few splotches of blood on the deck and three men of the *Rose of Devon*'s crew lay huddled in a heap; there were left standing three other men of the *Rose of Devon,* and sick enough they looked; Martin Barwick was stationed by the ladder to the forecastle, where he stood like a pigeon cock with his head haughtily in the air and his chest thrust out; and the little round apple of a man, Harry Malcolm, who had broken in upon Martin the night before, bearing now a new and bloody gash across his forehead, was prowling among the guns and tapping the breech rings with a knowing air.

The Old One from the quarter-deck looked down at the newcomer.

"Rab took the steel," the fellow said.

"Rab!" the Old One cried. "Not Rab, you say?"

"Yea, he struck first but the master wore an iron shirt which turned the point and he was then at him with his sword."

"We have lost nine good men by this devil-begotten storm, but of them all Rab is the one I am most loath to see go to the sharks." The Old One paced the deck a while and the others talked in undertones. "Yea, Martin," he called at last, "nine good men. But we have got us a ship and I have great hopes of our boatswain, who may yet make us two of Rab. At all events, my bullies, we must lay us a new course, for I have no liking of these northern fisheries. Hark! They are pounding on the hatch."

The sound of knocking and a muffled calling came from the main hatch, whereat the men on deck looked at one another and some of them smiled.

"It were well—" the little round man began. He glanced at the huddled bodies and shrugged.

"True, true!" the Old One replied, for he needed no words to complete the meaning. "You men of the *Rose of Devon*, heave them into the sea."

The three looked at one another and hesitated, and the youngest of the three turned away his face and put his hand on his belly, and sick enough he looked, at which a great laugh went up.

"Go, Harry," the Old One cried to the little round man, "and tell them at the hatch to be still, for that we shall presently have them on deck. We must learn our brave recruits a lesson."

Again a roar of laughter rose, and as the little man went in to the hatch, the others drew about the three who cowered against the forecastle ladder, as well they might.

"Come, silly dogs," said the Old One, "in faith, you must earn your foolish lives. Lay hands on those carcasses and heave them to the fishes."

They looked into the faces of the men about them, but got small comfort as they edged toward their unwelcome task.

"It is hard to use thus a shipmate of three voyages," the oldest of them muttered.

"True," replied the Old One, "but so shall you buy your way into a goodlier company of shipmates, who traffic in richer cargoes than pickled codfish and New England herrings."

The three picked up the bodies, one at a time, each with its arms and legs dragging, and carried them to the waist and pushed them over. But the youngest of the three was trembling like a dead weed in November when they had finished, and the Old One chuckled to see the fellow's white face.

"Have courage, bawcock," the Old One cried; "there shall soon be a round of aqua vitæ to warm thy shaking limbs and send the blood coursing through thy veins. Now, Mate Harry, lift off the hatch and summon our good boatswain and carpenter."

"As you please, as you please," came the quick, gentle voice of the little round man. "But there are two of 'em left still—Rab and the captain—and there's a deal of blood hereabouts."

They heard the hatch creak as the little man pried it off. They heard his quick sentences pattering out one after another: "Hasten out on deck—nay, linger not. The master would have speech of thee. Nay, linger not. Ask me no questions! There's no time for lingering."

Then out burst Phil Marsham with the older carpenter puffing at his heels.

"What's afoot?" cried Phil. "Where's the master?—what—where—"

So speedily had they hurried from the hatch (and so cleverly had the little round man interposed himself between the hatch and the two bodies at the cabin door) that in the dim light of the steerage room the two had perceived nothing amiss. But now, looking about for the source of the fierce cries and yells they had heard, they saw red stains on the deck, and men with scared white faces.

All looked toward the Old One as if awaiting his reply; and when Phil Marsham, too, looked toward him, he met such another quizzing, searching, understanding gaze as he had long ago met when he had taken the words from Martin's lips on the little hill beside the road.

"Why, I am master now, good boatswain."

"But Captain Candle—"

"His flame is out."

The lad glanced about him at the circle of hard old sea dogs—for they were all of them that, were their years few or many—and drew away till he stood with the waist at his back. Laying hands on his dirk, he said in a voice that slightly trembled, "And now?"

"Why," quoth the Old One, "you have sat in Mother Taylor's kitchen and heard talk of the gentlemen. You know too many secrets. Unless you are one of us—" He finished with a shrug.

"You ask me, then, to join you?"

"Yea."

"I refuse." He looked the Old One in the eye.

"Why, then," said the Old One, "you are the greater fool." The circle drew closer.

"What then?"

"'Tis but another candle to be snuffed."

With hand on dirk and with back against the waist, the boatswain looked one and another and then another in the eye. "Why, then," said he, "I must even join you, as you say. But I call upon you all to witness I am a forced man." And he looked longest and hardest at the three men from the old crew of the *Rose of Devon*.

The Old One looked back at the lad and there was, for the first time, doubt in his glance. He stood for a while pondering in silence all that had taken place and studying the face of his boatswain; but his liking of the lad's spirit outweighed his doubts, for such bold independence, whether in friend or foe, was the one sure key to Tom Jordan's heart. "So be it," he said at last. "But remember, my fine young fellow, that many a cockerel hath got his neck wrung by crowing out of season." He turned to the carpenter. "And what say you? We can use a man of your craft."

"I am thy man!" the fellow cried. The stains on the deck had made him surpassingly eager, and his one eye winked and his beard wagged, so eager was he to declare his allegiance.

"Well said!" the Old One responded. "And now, Master Harry, have them up from below—the sleepers, and the cook and his mate, and all! We have taken a fine ship—a fine ship she will be, at all events, once our good carpenter has done his work—and well found. We needs must sign a crew to sail and fight her."

They heard the little round man calling down the hatch and at a great distance in the ship they heard the voices of men grumbling at being summoned out of sleep. But the grumbling was stilled when one by one the men came out on deck; and of them all, not a man refused to cast his lot with the Old One and the rest. The mere sight of a little blood and of the hard faces that greeted them was enough for most. And two or three, of whom Will Canty was one, must fain perceive how futile would be present resistance. Indeed, in the years since the old Queen had died, and the navy had gone to the dogs, and merchantmen had come to sail from the Downs knowing they were likely enough to meet a squadron of galleys lying in wait fifty leagues off the Lizard, many a sailor had taken his fling at buccaneering; and those that had not, had heard such great tales of galleons laden with treasures of the Indies and with beautiful dames of Spain that their palates were whetted for a taste of the life.

The cook smiled broadly and clapped the boy on the back and cried out that as a little lad he had sailed with John Jennings that time John Jennings's wench had turned his luck, and that having begun life in such brave company, he would gladly end it in a proper voyage if it was written that his time was near. They all laughed to see the boy turn white and tremble, and they huzzaed the cook for his gallant words. But Will Canty met Phil's eyes and there passed between them a look that made the Old One frown, for he was a man who saw everything.

The *Rose of Devon*, although close-hauled by the wind, rolled heavily, which was the way of those old tall ships; but the adverse winds and high seas she had encountered were of fancy as well as of fact. The sun was shining brightly and sky and sea were a clear blue; but despite sun and sky and sea no weatherwise man could have believed the dark days of the *Rose of Devon* were at an end. Like so many iron bars the shadows of the ropes fell blue on the sails, and the red blotches on the deck matched the dull red paint of the stanchions and the waist. The carpenter, who had come up with his plane in his hand, fingered the steel blade. The boy turned his back on the bloody deck and looked away at the sea, for he was a little fellow and not hardened by experience of the world.

"Come, my hearts," cried the Old One, and gaily enough he spoke. "We are banded together for the good of all. There is no company of merchants to profit by our labour and our blood. God hath placed in our keeping this brave ship, which will be staunch and seaworthy when our carpenter hath done his work. Harry Malcolm is our mate and master gunner as of old, and Phil Marsham shall continue as our boatswain—nay, grumble not! He came with Martin Barwick and he hath sat in Mother Taylor's kitchen, where may we all sit soon and raise our cans and drink thanks for a rich voyage. There is work to be done, for all must be made clean and tight—yea, and Rab is to be buried."

The little round man was still wandering from gun to gun and smiling because the guns pleased him. They were demiculverins of brass, bored for a twelve-pound ball and fit to fight the King's battles; but alas! they had shown themselves powerless against a foe from within the ship. And as the *Rose of Devon* rolled along in the bright sun, alone in a blue sea, the body of Francis Candle lay forgotten in the steerage room.

CHAPTER XII

The *Porcupine* Ketch

L OOKING DOWN from the quarter-deck the Old One spied the cook, who had come up to warm his bald head and fat face in the sun and to clear the smoke from his nostrils. "Ho, cook," quoth he, "I have a task for thee. Break out from the cabin stores rice and currants and cinnamon and the finest of thy wheaten flour. Seek you also a few races of green ginger. It may chance there is even a little marchpane, for this man Candle had a gentle palate. Spare not your old cheese, and if you unearth a cask of fine wine fail not to tell of it. In a word, draw forth an abundance of the best and make us such a feast as a man may remember in his old age."

The cook smiled and rubbed his round paunch (yet cringed a little), for he was of a mind, being never slow in such matters, to filch from the cabin table whatever he might desire and his heart warmed to hear the good victuals named. "Yea, master," he cried, "for thee and for Mate Malcolm?"

"Nay, thou parsimonious dog! Think you that such are the manners of gentlemen mariners? Times have changed. Though I be master, there is no salt at my board. One man is as good as another and any man may rub his shoulder with mine."

The Old One's own men chuckled at the cook's blank face and the boy shivered when he thought that he must wait on them all, of whom one was as likely as another to fetch him a blow on the head. But the cook went down below and they heard him bawling to his mate to come and help break out the cabin stores, and word went through the ship of what was afoot. And though Will Canty and the boatswain, meeting, glanced dubiously each at the other, as did others of the *Rose of Devon's* old company—for matters are in a sad way in a ship when the master feasts the men—all the foolish fellows were clapping one another on the back and crying that here was a proper captain, and there was none quite so mad as to dispute them in so many words.

The smoke grew thick between the decks, and after a while there rose the smell of baking and roasting, and the foolish ones patted their bellies and smacked their lips. They whispered about that the boy was spreading with a linen cloth the table in the great cabin and that the cook's mate was staggering under weight of rich food; and when the cook called for men to hoist out a cask of such nectar as poor sailors know not the like of, a great cheer went up and there were more hands to haul than there was room on the rope.

The Old One, leaning on the poop, smiled and Harry Malcolm, coming to join him, smiled too; for they knew well the hearts of sailormen and did nothing without a purpose.

So the table was laid and the feast was spread and in came the men. Only one remained at the helm, for the wind was light, which made light his task; six remained on deck to watch and stand by, with Harry Malcolm curled against the light gun on the quarter-deck to command them; and the cook and his mate, resting from their labours far down in the hold, gorged themselves on good food and drank themselves drunk on nappy liquor from a cask they had cannily marked for their own among the cabin stores. Of the rest, all that could find room crowded into the great cabin, and all that could find no room in the cabin squatted on the deck outside the door on the very spot where Francis Candle had fallen dead. They sat with their backs against bulkheads and stanchions, where they, too, could join in the feast and the council; and the boy, when all were fed, gathered meat from under the table like old King Adoni-bezek of unhappy memory.

It was a sight to remember, for very merry they were and save as they were rough, hard-featured men, a man would never have dreamed they bore blood on their hands and murder on their hearts. The Old One sat at the head of the table and took care that neither food nor wine was stinted. The carpenter, his one eye twinkling with pleasure and his beard waggling in his haste lest another should get ahead of him at trencher work, sat on the Old One's right, which was accorded him as a mark of honour since he had accomplished marvels in restoring the planking the storm had torn asunder. A stout seaman of the rescued men, Paul Craig by name—it was he who had needed two blows to kill the helmsman—sat at the Old One's left and squared his big shoulders over his meat and ate like a hog till he could hold no more, for he was an ox of great girth and short temper and little wit, who ate by custom more than did him good. Another of gaunt frame, Joseph Kirk by name, sat smiling at a man here and a man there and tippled till his head wagged; and off in a corner there sat a keen little man with a hooked nose, who was older than most of those in the cabin yet had scarcely a wrinkle to mar the smoothness of his shaven face save above and behind his eyes, where a few deep lines gave him the wild look of a hawk.

When he spoke, which was seldom, thick gutturals con-
fused his words, and always he sat in corners. Does not a
man looking out of a corner, with a wall on two sides of him
and no one behind him, see more than another? His
Christian name was Jacob and most of them knew him by no
other; but mocking him they called it "Yacob." Further than
that, which he took with a wry smile, they refrained from
mocking him, for though he spoke little, his silence said
much.

The Old One rose and very sober he was as he held high
a brimming can, and so steady was his hand that not a drop
spilled. For a space he paused and looked around at the
rough company seated at the long table and crouching in the
mellow shadows beyond the door, then, "To the King!" he
cried.

Those not knowing him well, who stared in perplexity at
such a toast in such a place and time, saw his eyes twinkle
and perceived he was looking at old Jacob in the corner.
Then old Jacob, smiling as at a familiar jest, rose in turn and
raised his can likewise, and pausing to look about him, cried
back at the Old One in his thick foreign voice, "The King and
his ships—be damned!"

A yell of laughter and derision shook the cabin. The one-
eyed carpenter leaped up first, then such of the rescued men
as were not too drunk to stand, then here and there men of
the *Rose of Devon*'s company, some eagerly in all earnestness, others having a mind to keep their throats in one piece,
for they perceived that like enough the unholy toast was but
to try their allegiance.

The Old One's eyes leaped from man to man and his cold
voice cut through the noisy riot of drunken mirth. "I had
said Will Canty was a man of spirit, but his can hugs the
table when these tall fellows are drinking confusion to
the King."

"A hand-napper, a hand-napper! Have him away, my hearts, to the Halifax engine," Joe Kirk bawled with a drunken leer.

"Why," said Will Canty, and his face was white, but with a red spot on either cheek, "my can, since you say what you say, was dry; and for the matter of that, I am no prating Puritan who wishes ill to the King."

Over the rumble of voices the Old One's voice rose loudest: "See you, then, religious cobblers or preaching buttonmakers among us?"

"And there are others yet besides prating Puritans, mine friend, that drink our toast!" cried Jacob.

The Old One then smiled, for he was no man to drive a nail with a two-hand sledge. But although he changed his manner as fast and often as light flickers on running water, under the surface there flowed a strong, even current of liking or ill will, as sooner or later all men that had dealings with him must learn, some to their wonder and some to their sorrow. "Enough, enough!" said he. "Will's a good lad and he'll serve us well when there's powder smoke to snuff. Be you not offended, Will. In all faith our ship is a king's ship and more, for are we not thirty kings, to fight our own battles and heave out our own flag before the world and take such treasures as will buy us, each and all, a king's palace and all the wives a king could wish? Nay, God helping us, my hearts, we shall carry home to good Mother Taylor riches that will serve for a sponge to wipe the chalk from every black post in Cornwall and in Devon, and Will Canty shall drink with us there."

There rose a thunder of fists beating the board and a rumble of "Yea's," and the Old One made no end of smiling, but there were some whom his smile failed to deceive.

"Come, boy, with thy pitcher of sack! Pour sack for all!" he cried. "Come, ply thy task and let no man go wanting. Fill you Will Canty's pot." He gulped down a mighty draught and wiped his moustaches with thumb and forefinger. "And now, brave lads, let us have our heads together: though we lie but a hundred leagues off these banks of Newfoundland, what say you? Shall we turn our backs on them and take a fling at a braver trade? Or shall we taste of fat lobsters and great cod, and perchance pluck the feathers from some of these New England towns concerning which there hath lately been such a buzz of talk in old England—at Cape Ann, let us say at venture, or Naumkeag, or Plymouth Colony?"

"Yea, yea! I am for Cape Ann," cried Joe Kirk, and his head rolled drunkenly above his great shoulders as he bolstered his opinion with curses. "Did not my brother go thither, years and years agone, for the company of Dorchester merchants? Yea, and told rare tales of succulent great fish, which are a marvelous diet."

"Nay, thy brother was as great a sot as thou," a voice put in, and Joe rose in anger, but a general clamour drowned his retort and he lapsed back into a sodden lethargy.

"As for me," bellowed Martin with bluster and bravado, "I say go we to Plymouth and rap the horns of these schismatic Puritans. Tell me not but that they've mines of rich gold hid away. Did'st ever see a Roundhead knave would brave the wild lions of America unless he thought there was gold in't?"

"Thou thyself art fool as well as knave," quoth the Old One. "Did'st thou not once cry the whole ship's company out of sleep to see a mermaid that would entice thee to thy peril? And when sober men had come on deck there was nought there but a seal-fish at play. Lions forsooth! In Africa even I have heard a lion roar, but not in America. Much searching of tracts hath stuffed thy head."

The drunken Joe roused sleepily up. "My brother saw a lion at Cape Ann plantation. My brother—" He drew a knife and wildly flourished it, but fell back in a stupor before the laughter died.

Martin's bluster, as was its way when a man boldly confronted it, broke like a pricked bubble, but his sullen glare caught the Old One's eye.

Leaning over the table, the Old One said in a low, taunting voice, "And did you never see a man dance on air? Ah, there's a sight to catch the breath in your throat and make an emptiness in a man's belly!"

As often happens when there has been a great noise and a man speaks in a low voice, there was a quick lull and the words came out as clear as the ringing of a half crown. Phil Marsham, looking across the table into the Old One's cold blue eyes, which were fixed on Martin, saw in them a flicker of calculating amusement; then he saw that Martin was swallowing as if he had a fishbone in his throat.

In truth Martin wore the sickly smile that a man affects when he is cornered and wishes to appear braver than he is. He tried to speak but succeeded only in running his tongue over his lips, which needed it if they were as dry as they were blue.

"Come, come, we get no place!"

"Yacob! Yacob!" they cried at the sound of his voice, "Up on thy feet, Yacob!"

He rose and stood in his corner. His long hair was brushed back from a forehead so high that it reached to a great lump on the crown of his head. His brows were knit with intense earnestness. His big nose and curled lips and small chin were set in what might have seemed in another place and another time scholarly intentness. They did him honour by waiting in silence for his words.

"This bickering and jangling brings us no place. Shall we go on or shall we go back? Shall we go north or shall we go south? Those are questions we must answer. Now I will tell you. If we go on, we shall find little fishing ships, with fish and no chinks, and we shall get tired of eating fish. If we go back in this fine ship that God in his goodness hath given us, we shall hang. We may yet go back to Mother Taylor, but we must go back in another ship. You know why. Now, brave hearts, if we go on to New England it shall profit us nothing. For the New-English are poor. They live in little huts. The savages come down out of the woods and kill. Whether there be lions I do not know and I do not care; those savages I have seen and they are a very ugly sight. The English plantations are cold in winter like the devil. They are poor. The English, they play with poverty.

"And if we go south? Ah-h-h! There are the Spains! They have sun and warmth and fruits and spices! They have mines of gold and silver and stones of great price. While the English play with poverty, the Spains play with empires! In New England we shall eat salt cods or starve—which is much the same, for salt cods are a poor diet. But in the South we shall maybe catch a galleon with a vast treasure." And with that, very serious and sure of his rightness, he sat down.

"Yea, Yacob! Yea, Yacob!" they bawled and delighting in the alliteration cried it again, over and over.

Paul Craig, heavy with sated gluttony, piped a shrill "Yea, Yacob," and the Old One pounded the table and grinned, for he had sailed many seas in Jacob's company. Phil Marsham— nay, and even Will Canty, too!—pricked ears at the sound of Spanish galleons; for the blue Caribbean and the blue hills of the main were fabled, as all knew, to hold such wealth as according to the tales of the old travellers was to be found in Cathay or along the banks of the first of the four rivers out of Paradise. And was not a Spanish ship fair prey for the most law-abiding of English mariners?

There was a hubbub of talk as they sat there, and there was no doubt but they were of one mind to turn their backs on the bleak northern coast and seek a golden fortune in the south. But the council arrived suddenly at an end when down from the deck came the lingering call, "A sa-i-l! A sa-i-l!"

Up, then, the Old One leaped, and he raised his hand. "A sail is cried. What say you?"

"Let us not cast away what God hath offered us!"

"Yea, Yacob!"

"Up, you dogs in the steerage! A hall, a hall!"

One fell over on the table in drunken torpor. Another rushed out the door and tumbled over a sleeper at the threshold.

"Up, you dogs! How stands he?"

They poured out of the cabin to the deck.

"He stands on the lee bow!"

"Bear up the helm! A fresh man at the helm!" the Old One thundered. He squinted across the sea. "Come, Harry—here on the poop—and tell me if she be not a ketch. Now she lifts—now she falls. 'Twill be a chase, I take it."

The round little mate came nimbly up the ladder.

"Helm a-luff!" said he in his light, quick voice, which at first the helmsman failed to hear. "Helm a-luff! A-luff, man! Art deaf? The courses hide her. There she lifts! Yea, a ketch. Let us see. It is now an hour to sunset. If we stand across her bows and bear a sharp watch we shall come up with her in early evening and a very proper moment it will be."

His light, incisive speech, so unlike the boisterous ranting of the Old One, in its own way curiously influenced even the Old One himself. A man who has a trick of getting at sound reasons, unmoved by bluster or emotion, can hold his own in any company; and many a quiet voice can fire a ship's crew to action as a slow match fires a cannon.

"Now, young men," Martin roared, "up aloft and loose fore and main topsails. And oh that our stout mizzenmast were standing yet!"

"No, no, no!" cried Harry Malcolm and he almost raised his voice. "Thy haste, thou pop-eyed fool, would work the end of us all. Think you, if they see us fling every sail to the wind, they will abide our coming without charging their guns and stationing every gunner with linstock and lighted match? Nay, though she be but a ketch, let us go limping across her bows as lame as a pipped hen."

"True, and with every man lying by the side of his gun, where they shall not see him until we haul up the ports and show the teeth of the good ship." It was Jacob who spoke thus as he climbed to Harry Malcolm's side.

The Old One, looking down at the deck below, touched his mate's arm.

"Yea, I see them. What do you want?"

"It seems," said the Old One, "that our boatswain hath a liking for the fellow."

"And that the fellow hath a liking for our boatswain, think you?"

"Well?"

Jacob thrust his long nose between them. "'Well,' you say, by which you mean 'not well.' It proves nothing that a man will not drink damnation to a king."

The three heads met, high on the poop, and now and again they glanced down at the two lads who stood by the waist and watched the distant sail, which grew black as the sun set behind it.

The sun set and the sea darkened and a light flamed up on board the chase, which appeared to show her good faith by standing toward the *Rose of Devon*.

There was a rumble of laughter among the men when they perceived she had changed her course. The sober wrung oaths from the drunk by dashing bucketfuls of cold water in their faces. The gunners moved like shadows among the guns. And high on the poop, three shadows again merged into one.

"Master Boatswain," the Old One called, but softly, "do thou take it upon thyself, although it lies outside thine own province, to make sure that powder and balls and sponges and ladles and rammers are laid ready."

Hunching his bent shoulders, Mate Malcolm came nimbly down the ladder and from the chest of arms drew forth muskets and pistols.

"Come, my bullies below there, knock open your ports!" It was the Old One's voice, but so softly and briskly did he speak that it might have been Harry Malcolm.

As the dim figures on deck moved cautiously about, the subdued voice again floated down to them:

"Let all the guns be loose in tackles and stand by to run them out when the word is given. Port your helm! Every man to his quarters. Now, my hearts, be ready to show your courage and we'll have this wandering ketch for a consort to our good *Rose of Devon.*"

Then Harry Malcolm came in haste along the deck. "Who's to this gun? And who to this? Nay, you've a man too many there. Here, fellow, come hither! Here a man is lacking. You there, who are playing the part of gunner, have you ever heard these bulldogs bark? And understand you the business? Good, good!" And he passed on up the deck. Nought escaped him. In the silence they heard the sound of his voice and the quick pattering of his feet when they could see no more than that he was still moving among the guns.

They had come so near the stranger that they must soon hail or be hailed, when a figure emerging from the steerage room in the darkness came upon Phil Marsham by the quarter-deck ladder and gave a great start. As Phil turned, the fellow whispered, "God be thanked it is thou! I thought it was another. Come with me to the side—here by the shrouds."

The two stepped lightly under the shadow of the quarter-deck to the waist, where the carpenter had nailed in place new planks not twelve hours since, and together they raised a bundle. It was on the larboard side, and since all had gathered for the moment to starboard to watch the strange ketch, there was no man to observe them. Some one moved above them and they hesitated, then they heard slow steps receding and thick undertones that they recognized as Jacob's. When he had gone, the one who had brought the bundle whispered, "Heave it far out," and together they hove it.

Still in the shadow of the quarter-deck, the two slipped silently back, unseen, and when Harry Malcolm came hurrying from one side, and Jacob from the other, to see what had made the splash, there was no one there nor could any man answer their questions.

"Have you done as you said?" Phil asked in a breathless whisper.

"That I have." And it was Will Canty who spoke.

"Then we shall like enough be hanged; but thou art a tall fellow and I love thee for it."

There came over the water a voice distinctly calling, "Whence your ship?"

"Back to your guns, ye dogs!" cried Mate Malcolm in a voice that could be heard the length of the deck, yet that was not loud enough to be heard on board the stranger.

"Of England," the Old One called from the quarterdeck. "And whence is yours?"

There was a space of silence, in which the two vessels came nearer each other, and I would have you know that hearts ever so courageous were thumping at a lively pace.

"And yours?" the Old One cried the second time.

There came voices and a hoarse laugh from the stranger, then, "Are you merchants or men of war?"

"Of the sea," cried the Old One in a voice so like thunder that a man would not think it could have come from his lean throat. "Run out your guns, O my hearts! Let him have the chase guns first. The chase guns—the chase guns!"

Now one bawled down the main hatch, and another below echoed his cry, then there sounded the quick *boom-boom* from the bows. The guns had spoken and the fight was on.

"Up your helm—up your helm! Hold your fire now, my hearts, and have at them!" the Old One cried.

And now the voice came again over the restless sea. "Our ship is the *Porcupine* ketch and our quills are set."

The dark sea tossed and rolled between the vessels and little that happened on board either was visible to the other, so black was the night; but the light of the sky, which the water reflected, made of each a black shape clear-cut as of jet but finer than the most cunning hand could carve, in which a man might trace every line and rope.

And now from on board the ketch jets of flame burst out and after them came smartly the crack of muskets.

"Now, lads," the Old One thundered, "give fire and make an end of this petty galling. Give fire!"

A gun on the maintop-deck boomed and another followed; but there was confusion and stumbling and all were slow for want of practice together, and there was time lost ere the third gun spoke. Then, while Mate Malcolm was storming up the deck and the Old One was storming down, they heard the strange master calling to his gunners; then, to the vast amazement of the men of the *Rose of Devon,* who had cherished the delusion that their chase was a weak craft and an easy prize, on board the ketch as many as a dozen guns belched flame. Their thunder shook the sea and their balls sang through the rigging, and a lucky shot struck the *Rose of Devon* in the forecastle and went crashing through the bulkhead.

The ketch then tacked as if to give fire with her other broadside but deftly swung back again and before the Old One or Harry Malcolm had fathomed the meaning of it there rose from on board her, the cries of "Bear up and close with him!"—"Board him on his quarter!" "Have ready your graplins!"

"Sheer off, sheer off!" old Jacob roared. "Our powder is good for nought. Yea, she is in all truth a prickly porcupine."

"If we foul, cut anything to get clear!" cried the Old One. "Put down your helm! Veer out your sheets! Cast off weather sheets and braces! Aloft, there, and clear the main yard where the cut tacklings foul it! Good lad, boatswain, good lad!"

For on the yardarm Phil had drawn dirk and cut at the snarl of ropes, where a chance ball had wrought much mischief. Then, as the two vessels swung side by side he looked squarely into the eyes of a bearded man in the rigging of the ketch.

The Old One—give the Devil his due!—was handling his ship in a proper manner and by luffing he had kept abreast of those guns in the ketch which had spent their charges. But it was plain that the *Rose of Devon* had caught a tartar. In all truth, she had run upon a porcupine with quills set, for though a smaller vessel, the ketch, it now appeared, carried as many men or more, and every man knew his place and duty. Looking down on her deck, Phil saw her gun crews toiling with sponges and rammers to load anew.

She was herself, it seemed, a sea rover athirst for blood and in those wild, remote seas there was no fraternity among thieves. As the main yardarm of the *Rose of Devon* swung toward her rigging when the ship rolled, the bearded man ran a rope about the spar and in a moment the vessels were locked abeam and were drifting together till their sides should touch.

Philip Marsham again drew the dirk that Colin Samson had wrought for him and leaning far out struck at the fellow's breast, who swung back to avoid the thrust, which pricked him but did no more. Then the fellow sprang to the attack with his own knife in hand, for he had thrown a knot in the rope, which creaked and tightened; and with a yell of triumph he struck at the lad, who swung to one side and struck back.

It was a brave fight in the empty air, and the two were like warring spiders as they circled and swung in the darkness and thrust each at the other. But the lad was many years the younger, and by so much the more nimble, and his dirk—for which all thanks to Colin Samson!—smote the fellow a slashing blow in the thigh. And while the fellow clung to the shrouds, weak with pain, a second *Rose of Devon*'s man came crawling over Phil who hung below from the yard, and slashed the rope.

"We are clear! We are clear! God be thanked!" the Old One yelled.

Meanwhile the men of the *Rose of Devon* had succeeded in firing three guns of the larboard broadside, which by the grace of Divine Providence wrought such ruin in the stranger's running gear that the one crew of rascals was enabled to escape fit retribution at the hands of the other. The peak of her great foresail fell and in a moment her cut halyards were swept into a snarl that needed time and daylight for untangling.

So the *Rose of Devon* slipped past the ketch, whose men were striving to clear the rigging and come about in pursuit, and having once evaded her erstwhile chase, the old ship ran away in the night. With her lights out and all the sail spread that she could carry, and favoured by clouds and fog, she made good her escape; but there was grumbling forward and grumbling aft, and there was a dead man to heave over the side.

It served Philip Marsham better than he knew that he had fought a duel on the yardarm; for dark though the night had been, there had happened little that escaped the Old One's eye; and bitter though Tom Jordan's temper and angry his mood, he was always one to give credit where he believed it due.

When he wiped the blood from the dirk, Phil remembered with gratitude the good smith, Colin Samson. Then he thought of the old lady and gentleman at the inn, and of Nell Entick, and bluff Sir John. He would have been glad enough to be out of the *Rose of Devon* and away, but for better or worse he had cast his lot in the ship, and though he little liked the lawless turn her affairs had taken, a man cannot run away by night from a ship on the high seas.

All hands stood watch till dawn as a tribute to the war of one pirate upon another, and not until the sun had risen and shown no sail in sight did the Old One himself go into the great cabin.

CHAPTER XIII

A Bird to Be Limed

A LAD BEING called into council by such a man as Tom Jordan might well think himself a fine fellow, and rare enough were lads whom Tom Jordan would thus have summoned. But although Philip Marsham, it seemed, had taken the Old One's eye and won his heart long before on the little hill beside the road, when Phil had drawn the wind from Martin's sails, and although it had not escaped Tom Jordan that Phil's hand moved easily toward his weapon, the old proverb has it "a man that flattereth his neighbor, spreadeth a net for his steps"; and "he that whistleth merrily, spreadeth his nets cunningly and hunteth after his prey greedily."

So, "Come, boatswain, and lend us thy wits," cried Tom. "Four heads shall provide more wisdom than three." And with that, he clapped Phil on the back and drew him into the cabin where Jacob and the mate sat deep in talk of the night's adventures.

"A hawk, when she is first dressed and ready to fly," said Jacob, "is sharp set and hath a great will upon her. If the falconer do not then follow it, she will be dulled for ever after. So, master, a man! Yea, and a ship."

"A great will, sayest thou?" quoth the Old One, and his voice revealed his sullen anger. "Why then, in God's name, did ye not rake them with a broadside or twain?" With which he turned on Harry Malcolm, thus to include him in the charge.

"For one thing," replied Malcolm, and testily, for ill temper prevailed both aft and forward, "we gave the gunners no firing to learn them their guns. For another thing, the powder failed us. For yet another, since you say what you say, and be cursed for it, 'twere a mad, foolish notion to run afoul a strange ship, for we have but a half the company we need to work a ship and fight. And finally, to cap our woeful proverbs, we know what we know—yea," and he shot a dark glance from under bent brows, "we know what we know; there be those who come toward us with their feet, but go from us with their hearts." His voice, as always, was light and quick, but there was a rumble in it, such as one may sometimes hear in a dog's throat.

As the three men looked first at one and then at another, there came to Boatswain Marsham, sitting as it were outside their circle, the uneasy throbbing of their suspicion.

"Of the powder," said Jacob coolly, "I have taken a little from each barrel." He laid on the table seven packages wrapped in leaves from an old book. Regarding closely the notes he had written on each package, he opened them one by one and placed them in a row.

"This," said he, "is from the barrel that good Harry Malcolm served out to the men and that doubtless this man Candle hath used from in old days. It hath lost its strength by long lying. Press it with thy fingers and thou shalt feel it soft to the touch. Here upon this white sheet of paper I lay four corns of this powder. This other powder"—and he chose a second package—"is from a barrel new opened. Press it and thou shalt see how firm and hard is each corn. And this, too, is firm and of a fair azure. And so, also, this. But this—"and he first put his eyes close to the notes on each remaining packet, then held them far off, for his sight, although good at a great distance, made out with difficulty things near at hand, "this is from a barrel that hath lost its strength by moisture; and this hath a fault I shall tell you of."

Taking a pinch of each, as he spoke, he had laid the corns, each some three fingers distant from the next, in a circle on the paper. He then struck tinder, and lighting a match made of twisted cords of tow boiled in strong lye-ashes and saltpetre, he held it over a corn of the good powder. There was a flash and puff, and the ring of powder was gone. The corns of good powder had fired speedily and left only a chalky whiteness in their place, nor had they burned the paper or given off smoke; but the corns of poor powder had burned slowly, and some had scorched the paper and some had given forth smoke.

The Old One softly swore. "And have we, then," asked he, "but three barrels of good powder?"

"Nay, there are more than three. This last is weak because they have neglected to turn the barrels upside down, so the petre has settled from top to bottom, as is its way. We shall find the bottom as strong as the top is weak, and by turning the barrel we shall renew its strength evenly."

"As for the powder that hath spoiled by long lying," cried Philip Marsham, "I will undertake to make it as good as new."

"Do you, boatswain, mind your sails and cordage," said old Jacob, with a wry smile. "An you wish to grind it in the mortar, that you may; but it is I who will measure the petre. Nay, I will make you, if you wish it for a wonder to show friends, a powder of any colour you please—white, red, blue, or green."

Of the three who leaned over the packets of powder, old Jacob was the only one who bore with even temper the sad reverse of the night before; for master and mate glared at each other in such wrath as had thrown a shadow over every soul in the ship.

Some had waked with aching heads, for which they had their own folly to thank; some were like men who dream they have got a great treasure but wake to find pebblestones or worse under the pillow: since the *Porcupine* ketch had yielded them no gold and had stung them instead with her quills. In all truth the ship was by the ears, for in extremities your sea sharks are uncertain friends, as a touch of foul weather will manifest to any man's satisfaction.

"Enough of this," said the Old One, and he pushed aside the packets and folded his arms. "We lose time. There is a thief amongst us."

"A thief, you say?" And the hot red of anger burned its way across the boatswain's face, for the three had turned and locked hard at him.

The Old One and Harry Malcolm then exchanged quick glances, and Jacob shut his small mouth tight and knotted his brows.

"Well," cried Phil, "would you charge me with theft?"

"Some one," said the Old One, lingering over each word, "hath wrought a clever plot against us."

"Say on, say on!"

"He is a man, I make no doubt, whose buttons are breaking with venom."

There was heavy silence in the cabin. Jacob, pursing his lips and knotting his brows, looked from one of them to another, and Phil, vaguely on the defensive, drew back and gave them a gaze as steady as they sent.

"He is doubtless a very cunning rascal," Harry Malcolm put in, "who hath cut his cloth by his wits; but he is making a suit that will throttle him by its narrowness about the neck."

The master and mate once more exchanged glances and the Old One then smiled lightly, as if again there were sunlight rippling over dark water.

"Nay, Philip, we think no ill of thee. But do thou have care to thy company. A foul trick hath been done with a mind to render us helpless at sea, so that we must crawl to the nearest land, where some base dung-hill spirit is doubtless of a mind to leave our company. But we have resources; yea, and of thee, Philip, we think no ill."

Despite their fair words, though, they were watching Philip Marsham like three old tomcats watching a sparrow, and he, being no fool, knew the reason why.

Three hard faces they showed: the one, handsome in a devilish way and keen; the second, unassuming, yet deeply astute and marked by a deeper rooted, if less frank, selfishness; the third, older, wiser, more self-centred.

The eyes of master and mate were coldly cruel; but old Jacob was too intent on his own thoughts to be cruel save by indifference.

All that day Jacob squatted on the deck and toiled with tools and wood. From the wood he chose certain long pieces, fine-grained and straight and dry and free from knots, and certain shorter and broader pieces that were suited to his purpose, and bade the carpenter plane them smooth. He laid out scales, working with a small square and a pair of compasses, and engraved them with utmost care. He wrought brass into curious shapes by a plan he made, and from morning till night he kept at the task, frowning and ciphering and sitting deep in thought. He called for charcoal and a mortar, and beat the charcoal to a fine powder and tempered it with linseed oil This he rubbed into the wood he had shaped to his liking, and watched it a long while, now and again touching it to try it; then with oil from a phial he had found in a chest in the great cabin he rubbed the wood clean, and there were left in the wood, set off neatly in black, the gradations and figures he had so exactly etched.

Taking his work into the great cabin, he toiled on by lanthorn light until a late hour, and there through the open door men as they passed might see him hunched over the table with his medley of tools about him. But when at last he leaned back and drew a long breath of relief, very serious and very wise, his work was done, and curiously and deftly contrived it was.

On the table before him there lay a cross-staff, a nocturnal and a Gunter's scale, "with which," said he, to the Old One, who sat opposite him quietly taking tobacco and sipping wine, "and with what instruments the thief hath left us, a man can navigate a ship where he will."

Examining closely the nocturnal, which was intricately carved and engraved, the Old One muttered, as if ignoring Jacob's words, "I will yet lime that bird."

"Though he be never so mad a callant, I misdoubt he will put his head into a noose," said Jacob in his thick, serious voice.

"Be he the one we think or not the one we think, I will set him such a trap," said the Old One, "as will take the cunningest fox that ever doubled on the hounds." And the thin face smiled in a way that was not pleasant to see.

CHAPTER XIV

A Wonderful Excellent Cook

I F AN astrologer or an Arabian enchanter could say to a man, "Beware of this or that, for it is a thing conceived of the Devil to work thy ruin," there would be reason for studying the stars or smiting the sand. And this, indeed, they do, according to the old tales. But if a sailor seek out an astrologer to learn things that shall profit him, he is more likely to find a man grown foolish by much study, who will stroke his chin sagely and say, "Come, let us look into this matter. Under Capricorn are all diseases in the knees and hams, leprosies, itches and scales and schirrous tumors, fallow grounds and barren fields, ox-houses and cow-houses, low dark places near the ground, and places where sails and materials for ships be laid." And while he talks of fixed angles and of the Lord of the Ascendant being in the fourth week, some small unsuspected thing may be the very egg on which the Devil is sitting like an old black hen to hatch forth a general calamity.

Thus certain incidents that shortly thereafter happened are to the point, for although they appeared of little moment at the time, they turned the tide of men's lives and made a stir that has to do with the current of my tale.

Now the men of the *Rose of Devon* sighted a sail at high noon when they were a week on their way south, and though she showed her heels and ran, and though the *Rose of Devon* lacked her mizzenmast, the strange vessel was but a small pink and so slow that they laid her aboard two hours before dark. In her crew she had only a dozen men, and sorely frightened they were, as they tossed in the lee of the dark frigate. So to save themselves from a more cruel fate there was scarcely one of them but leaped at the chance to join the *Rose of Devon's* crew. They tumbled up their small cargo of salt fish for Bilbao and hoisted it on board the ship, together with their shallop, and casting their pink adrift, they forbore from complaining when their new master and his men stole whatever pleased them, from the new men's rings and knives to the very clothes on their backs. So, with her plunder and her recruits, the *Rose of Devon* again squared her yards and continued on her course.

There was, to be sure, one fellow of mean spirit who whined dolefully, upon conceiving his present extremity to be distasteful. But another got comfort by knocking him on the head when no one was looking; and finding him dead, the Old One hove him overboard and there was no further trouble from the fishermen.

Yet it was no secret that there was grumbling and complaining forward among the gentlemen of the *Rose of Devon*, so the Old One sent the boatswain to summon them aft when the watches were changing.

He leaned against the swivel gun on the quarter-deck, and looking down into their faces, smiled disagreeably. "It hath come to my ears," said he, "that one hath a sad tale to tell because we failed to take the *Porcupine*, which, though a mere ketch, outnumbered us in guns and men. And another hath a sad tale to tell because this pink that late became our prize is small and of little worth, though we got from her eleven brave fellows who shall be worth a store of fine gold." He looked from one of his men to another, for they were all there—Martin and the cook, and Philip Marsham and Will Canty, and Paul Craig and Joe Kirk, the one-eyed carpenter and the rest—and his thin face settled into the many wrinkles that had got him his name. There was none of them, unless it might be Harry Malcolm or Old Jacob, who could say surely at one time or another what thoughts were uppermost in Tom Jordan's shrewd head.

"Come, now, my hearts of gold," he cried, "let us have an end of such folly. Said I not that these northern fisheries were meat for crows? And that we must go south to find prey for eagles? We will choose a fine harbour by some green island where there's rich fruit for the picking and fat fish for the catching, and we will build there a town of our own. We will take toll from the King of Spain's ships; we will take us wives and women and gold and wine from the dons of the islands and the main. Yea, we will lay up a great store of riches and live in fullness of bread and abundance of idleness."

Some were pleased, but some doubted still, which the Old One perceiving, for he read their faces, cried, "Nay, speak up, speak up! Let us have no fair-protesting friends with hollow and undermining hearts."

"Yea, it is a fair tale," cried one, in a surly voice, "but thus far we have blows to show for our pains—blows and a kettle of fish."

"And methinks," another growled, "we shall see more of salt fish and buccaned meat, than of fine wines and gold and handsome women."

"'Tis a swinish thought," the Old One retorted; but he smiled when he said it, so that they took no offense, for of such grumbling he had no fear. He was set to catch a bird of quite another feather.

Then old Jacob rose and they were silent to hear him. "Let us make an end of talk," said he slowly. "We are on our way south and to stop or turn aside would be nothing but foolishness." And with that, although they had expected him to say more, he turned away.

Then, of a sudden, "Come, Will," the Old One cried, singling out his man from all the rest, "what say you?"

If Will Canty's face changed at all, it was a whit the paler as he met the Old One's eyes. "I say," he replied, "that since we have fish on board, we are sure of fish and would do well to eat fish ere we lose it."

"There is sooth in thy words," quoth the Old One, and he smiled in friendly wise. (But despite his smile, he liked the words little, as any shrewd man might have known by his eyes, and Will Canty was no fool.) "Come, cook, and boil us a great kettle of fish."

The rumble of low voices changed to laughter and the cook boldly cried, "Yea, yea, master!"

"For our much voyaging and many pains," cried the men, as they went about their work, "we have got a kettle of fish." And they laughed mightily, for though it was the very thing that before had made them grumble, now they saw it as a droll affair and made of it many jests, of which a few were good and more bad, after the manner of jests.

As for the cook, he called his mate and bade him break out a drum of fish and set a kettle to boil, and cuffed him this way and that, till the poor fellow's ears were swollen.

And the Old One said to Harry Malcolm, "Saw you not how deftly the fellow twisted out of the corner, and with a sly remark that no one can take amiss? Oh, he is a slippery dog and I am minded to cut his throat out of hand!"

"Now, that would be very foolish, for where there's one of them, there's always two, and the one will toll the other on until there are two dogs by the heels instead of one."

At that the Old One laughed harshly, and the two, who were after a left-handed fashion uncommonly congenial, went off well pleased with their conceit.

Down in the hold the kettle boiled right merrily, and the cook swelled with pride that he had a mate to carry and fetch. He cuffed the poor fellow this way, and he cuffed him that. He threw a pan at him when the fire smoked worse than common, and he thrust a fistful of flour into his face and down his neck when he let the fire lag. He flung him his length on the floor for spilling a pint of water; and when in despair the lad fled for his life, the cook seized him by the hair and haled him back and put a long knife at his breast and swore to have his heart's blood. Oh, the cook was in a rare and merry mood, for he had drunk more sack than was good for him from the cask he had marked as his own; but as he had waxed exceeding gay and haughty, the sack had dulled his wits and he was drunker than he knew.

"Come, thou pig! Thou son of a swine!" he yelled. "Ladle out the fish and choose of the best for the cabin. Yea, choose in abundance and summon the master's boy and bid him haste. And do thou bestir thyself and carry to the men." And with that, he fetched the poor fellow a blow on his head, which knocked him off his feet.

The fellow ran to do the work and the cook, in vast satisfaction at having so well acquitted himself, sat down with a goblet of sack and tippled and nodded, and kept an ill-tempered eye on the master's boy and his own, as with shrewd fear of broken heads they scurried back and forth.

"It is most wonderful excellent sack," quoth the cook, and with his sleeve he mopped his fiery bald head. "It was by a happy stroke I marked it for my own. Truly, I had rather be cook than master, for here I sit with mine eye upon the cabin stores, from which I can choose and eat at will, and the captain, nay, the Lord High Admiral of England, is himself none the wiser. Fish, sayest thou? Nay, fish is at best a poor man's food. I will have none of it." And thus he ran on foolishly, forgetting as he drank sack, that there was no one to hear him, not even his mate. "Truly, I am a wonderful excellent cook. I may in time become a captain. I may even become the governor of a plantation and take for a wife some handsome Spanish woman with a wonderful rich dowry. She must have an exceeding rich dowry if she will marry me, though. Yea, I am a wonderful excellent cook." And the more he drank the more foolish he became.

After a while, he cocked his head upon one side; and quoth he, "I hear them calling and shouting! It seemeth they are singing huzza for me. I hear them coming down to do me honour. Truly, I am a most wonderful excellent cook and the fish hath pleased them well. Foolish ones that they are to eat it!"

The silly fellow sat with his head on one side and smiled when they burst in upon him. "Hast come for more fish?" he cried. "Yonder stands the kettle. Nay, what's that? What's that thou sayest? Nay, fellow, th'art mad? Thou know'st not to whom thou speakest."

"Fool! Knave! Scoundrel! Swine!" they yelled. "Oh, such a beating as thy fat carcase will get. Hear you not the uproar? Think you to cozzen us?"

With that they seized him, two by the head and two by the feet, and dragged him to the ladder. They threw a rope about him and knotted it fast and tossed the ends to men at the hatch above, who hauled him, squealing and kicking like an old hog, up on deck. To the cabin they dragged him, with all the men shrieking curses at him and pelting him with chunks of fish, and in the cabin they stood him before the table where the Old One and Harry Malcolm sat, and very angry were they all.

"Dog of a cook," said the Old One, "for a relish to conclude our meal, we shall see thee eat of this fish that the boy hath brought us." And he thrust before the cook a great dish. "Eat it, every shred, bones and all," said he, "or I'll have thee butchered and boiled in place of it."

"Why, now," said the cook, somewhat sobered by rough handling and a trifle perplexed, but for all that still well pleased with himself, "as for the bones, they are liable to scrape a man's throat going down. I am reluctant to eat bones. But the meat is good. I rejoice to partake of it, for so diligently have I laboured to prepare it that I have denied myself, yea, though I hungered greatly."

"Eat," said the Old One and widely he grinned.

Looking suspiciously about him, for there was something in their manner that he failed to understand, the cook thrust his hand into the dish and took from it a great slice of fish, which he crammed into his mouth.

"Eat," said the Old One, "eat, O thou jewel among cooks!"

A curious look came over the cook's face and he raised his hand as if to take the fish out of his mouth.

"Nay, swallow it down," said the Old One. "Be not sparing. There is abundance in the dish. Yea, thou shalt stand there eating for a long time to come." And though he smiled, his look made it plain that he was in no trifling mood.

The cook turned pale and choked and gasped. "Water!" he cried thickly, for his mouth was too full for easy speech.

"Nay, much drinking hath wrought havoc with thy wits. Eat, eat on!"

Prodigious were the gulps by which the cook succeeded at last in swallowing his huge mouthful, and great was his distress, for the salt in it nearly choked him. "Water, water!" he weakly cried. "Nay, temper thine heart with mercy, master! I beg for water—I beseech for water."

"Eat on," said the Old One grimly.

Then Harry Malcolm chuckled and the men in the door roared with laughter, but the cook plunked down on his fat knees and thrust out both his hands. "Nay, master, I cannot hold it down!"

"Eat on, O jewel among cooks!"

"Nay, master—"

"Come, then, lads, and cram it down his hungry throat."

Three of them seized him, and one, when he shut tight his mouth, thrust a knife between his teeth.

"Blub-bub-blah!" he yelled. "I'll eat! I'll eat!"

They let him go and he rose and ate. Time and again he gasped for water and they laughed; time and again he lagged and the Old One cried, "Eat on!" When at last he stood miserably in front of the empty dish, the Old One said, "For a day and a night shalt thou sit in bilboes with a dry throat, which will be a lesson to learn thee two things: first, before cooking a kettle of fish, do thou bear it well in mind to soak out the salt so that the fish be fit for food; and second, by way of common prudence, do thou sample for thyself the dishes that are cooked for the cabin."

They haled him forward and locked the shackles on his feet and placed beside him a great dish of the fish, that whoever wished might pelt him with it; and there they left him to repent of his folly and forswear drunkenness and whimper for water.

As the weary hours passed, the sun tormented him in his insufferable thirst; but nightfall in a measure brought relief and he nodded in the darkness and fell asleep.

Waking, he would rub his head, which sadly throbbed and would seek by gulping to ease his parched throat; and sleeping again, he would dream of great buckets of clear water. The voices that he heard buzzed in his ears as if they were the droning of flies, and hunching himself down in his shackles at one end of the iron bar, he forgot the world and was forgotten, since his fat carcase lay inertly in a black shadow and there was nothing to make a man keep him in mind.

He heard at last a voice saying, "But nevertheless it becomes you to walk lightly and carefully," and another replying, "I fear him not, for all his subtle ways. Much that goes on escapes him."

He stirred uneasily, and opening his eyes, saw that there were two men leaning side by side against the forecastle.

"In the matter of wit, you grant him less than his due," said the first speaker. "And in another matter you charge him with a heavier burden than he needs bear."

The cook stirred and groaned and the first speaker chuckled, at which the cook's gorge rose from anger.

"O jewel among cooks!" one of the two called softly, and the unhappy man knew by the voice that the speaker was Philip Marsham.

Naming no names and talking in roundabout phrases as people do when they wish one to know their meaning and another not to, the two continued with no heed at all to the cook, whom they thought a mere drunken lout. And indeed, their undertones were scarcely audible; but anger sharpened the cook's ears and his wits, and he lay and ruminated over such chance sentences as he got.

"It puzzled me from the first," said the other, "to see how easily you bore with your comrade of the road."

"Why, he is a good soul in his way."

The other gave a grunt of disgust.

"Nay, it is a wonder to me that a lad with your nice notions ever found his way to sea," Phil retorted.

"And I might never have gone, had not Captain Francis Candle been my godfather."

"As for me, I have seen both sides of life; and, but for a certain thing that happened, I might be well enough contented where I am."

"And that?"

Phil hesitated, for though they had talked freely, as young men will, the question searched a side of Phil's life to which as yet he had given no clue. "Why," said he, lowering his voice, "for one thing, I saw for the first time my own grandfather; and for another, I saw a certain old knight who quite won my fancy from such a man as a certain one we know. Come, let us stroll together." And as they walked the deck that night, arm in arm, Phil told his companion what his life had been and what it might have been, and mentioned, in passing, the girl at the inn.

Left to his miseries and his thoughts, of which the first were little better company than the second, the woeful cook turned over and over in his fat head such fragments of their talk as he had succeeded in overhearing, and to say truth, he made little more out of it all than the speakers had intended. But his parched throat teased his wits to greater effort, and being come to such a state that he would have bartered his immortal soul for water, had chance offered, he bethought him of a plan by which, if luck held good, he might escape from his shackles.

The moment for which he waited was a long time coming and he suffered a great variety of increasing miseries before it arrived; but when the watches changed, he saw among the men newly arrived on deck his erstwhile dearest friend, and somewhat reluctantly forgiving his dear friend for belabouring him over the head with a whole salt fish, the cook softly called the man by name.

The fellow came snickering, which made it none the easier to bespeak his aid; but the cook nevertheless swallowed his wrath as well as with his dry throat he could, and whispered to the fellow that he must make haste and tell the master there was news to be imparted in secret.

At this the fellow held up his hand with thumb thrust between first and second fingers.

"Give me no fico," wailed the most excellent cook. "Nay, I have stumbled upon a black and hidden matter. Go thou, and in haste, and it will pay thee well."

For a time they bickered in the dark, but there was in the cook's despair a sincerity that finally made the fellow believe the tale; and finding, upon stealing aft, that there was still a light in the great cabin, he mustered up his courage and knocked.

"Enter," cried a hard voice.

The fellow opened the door and peeped in and found the Old One sitting alone at the table. Glancing hastily about, and the more alarmed to meet the cold eye of Harry Malcolm who lay on the great bed in the corner of the cabin, he closed the door at his back and whispered, "He swears it's true—that there's foul work afoot. 'Tis the cook who hath told me—yea, and hath bade me tell you. He would say no more—the cook, I mean."

"Oh, my good friend, our most excellent cook!" Meditating, the Old One looked the fellow up and down. "Here," said he, "strike off his shackles and send him in with the key." And he threw the fellow the key to the locks.

After a while the cook came weakly in and shut the door behind him and, throwing the key on the table, fell into a chair.

"Ah," said the Old One, "what is this tale I have heard news of?"

"Water!" gasped the cook. For though he had managed, by pausing at the butt on his way, to drink nearly a quart, he had no mind the Old One should know of it.

The Old One smiled. "Go, drink, if thy tale be worth it; but mind, if I deem thy tale not worth it, thou shalt pay with a drop of blood for every drop of water."

The cook shot a doubting glance at the Old One, but went none the less, and came back wiping his lips.

"Have at thy tale," said the Old One.

There was a quaver in the cook's voice, for he was by no means sure of how great a tale he could make, and the master's face gave him small encouragement, for from the beginning of the tale to the end the Old One never altered his cold, cruel smile.

"It was the boatswain and young Canty," he said.

"Ah!"

"They was leaning on the forecastle and walking the deck arm in arm and talking of one thing and another."

"And what did they say?"

"They talked about someone's slow wit—I could not make sure whose, for they scoffed at me bitterly—and Canty was bepuzzled by the boatswain's ways, and he wanted him to do something or other."

"Go on." The Old One, grinning coldly, leaned back and watched the labouring cook, who wracked his few brains to make a worthier story.

"Nay, but I heard little else. Yet, said I, the master must know at all costs."

"What a thick head is thine and how easily seen through and through!" The Old One laughed. "Think you all this is worth a second thought? I am of the mind to have you skinned and salted. But I forgive you, since I have a milkish heart that is easy moved to pity. Get you down to your berth and sleep."

The cook departed in haste, but with a fleeting glance at Harry Malcolm whom he feared less only than the master. He was aware that for some reason he did not understand, his broken tale had served his purpose.

When he had gone the Old One turned about. "You heard him. What think you?" said he.

From the great bed in the corner, Harry Malcolm raised his head and laughed silently. "Our able cook was hard pressed for an excuse to get out of his ankle rings. Did you hear him slopping at the butt the first time passing? As for his tale, we know what we knew, and no more."

"'Slow wits'! I wonder."

"At Baracao we shall see," said Harry Malcolm. "Neither one nor a dozen can harm us before we raise land."

"And after raising land, which by God's mercy will be soon now, we shall see whose wits will nick first when the edges crack together."

The Old One stretched and yawned and Harry Malcolm softly laughed.

CHAPTER XV

A Lonesome Little Town

A LIGHT seen in the middle watch gave warning of an unexpected landfall, and calling up the Old One, who had a store of knowledge gained by much cruising in those seas, they lay off and on until dawn, when they made out an island of the Bahamas. It seemed, since by their reckoning they were still a day's sail from land, that there was some small fault in their instruments; but to this they gave little heed, and which island it was and what occasioned the light they never knew, though some ventured one guess and some another as they bore past it and lifted isle beyond isle. For two days, with the Old One conning the ship, they worked their way among the islands, and thus at last they came to a deep bay set among hills, which offered a commodious and safe anchorage, notwithstanding that on the point that guarded the bay there was the wreck of a tall ship.

In the shallop they had taken from the fishing pink, the Old One and Jacob, with four men to row them, went out to the wreck and returned well pleased with what they had found.

"God is good to us," cried the Old One, perceiving that Harry Malcolm waited at the waist for their coming. "Though her foremast and mainmast be sprung, yet her mizzen is sound as a nut."

"And is it to be fetched out of her unharmed?"

"Yea, that it is! Come, Master Carpenter, haul out our broken old stump of a mizzen. By this time on the morrow our good *Rose of Devon* will carry in its place as stout a stick as man can wish. Faith, the ill fortune of them whose ship lies yonder shall serve us well."

There was a great bustle in the old frigate, for work was to be done that needed many hands. Some went to the wreck to save masts and spars, and others, led by the one-eyed carpenter, toiled to haul out the stump. Boatswain Marsham and his mate laid ready ropes and canvas; and the most of the company being thus busied with one task or another, Martin and the cook caught a store of fresh fish, which the cook—who had now become a chastened, careful man—boiled for supper, while Martin went on shore for fruit that grew wild in abundance and for fresh water from a sandy spring. It was three days instead of one before the work was finished; but meanwhile there was fresh food and water aft and forward, and having spent at sea many weary weeks, the men rejoiced to pass time so pleasantly in a snug haven.

Indeed, a man might have passed a long life in comfort on such an island, and there were many who cried yea, when Joseph Kirk declared himself for building a town there, to which they might return with a store of wives and wines, and from which they could sally forth when their supplies of either got low, and get for themselves others out of the King of Spain's ships and plantations. But the Old One laughed and cried nay. "I shall show you a town," said he, "in a land as fair as this, but with houses built and ready for us, and with gold piled up and waiting, and with great cellars of wine and warehouses filled with food."

So they sailed from the island one morning at dawn and for a week they picked their way down the windward passages. At times they lay hidden in deep harbours of which the Old One knew the secret; and again they stood boldly out to sea and put behind them many leagues of their journey. And thus progressing, one night, as they worked south against a warm breeze scented with the odour of flowers, they sighted on the horizon a dark low land above which rose dimly the shape of a distant mountain.

The men gathered about master and mate and Jacob, then Harry Malcolm went swarming up the rigging and from the maintopsail yard studied the dim bulk of the mountain. After a time he cried down to them, "Douse all lights and hold her on her course!"

For an hour they stood toward the land, then Malcolm came down from aloft smiling, and there ran through the ship a great wave of talk. Though a man had never sailed those seas before, he would not have found the reason for their talk hard to guess, since there were few secrets on board. Time and distance had made less the grumbling occasioned by the disastrous brush with the *Porcupine* and by the littleness of the profit got from the pink, and they had warmed their hearts with the Old One's tales.

Bearing to the west, the *Rose of Devon* skirted the dark shore for miles; but the master and mate were growing anxious lest dawn overtake them before they should reach the hiding-place they sought; and when they rounded a certain wooded point and sailed into a deep, secluded bay where a ship might lie for a year unseen—which put an end to their fears—they let go their anchors with all good will and furled their sails: and at break of day they kedged the ship into a cove that might have been a dock, so straight were the shores and so deep the water.

"Mind you, Ned," or "Mind you, Hal, the night we landed on Hispaniola?" the men from the *Blue Friggat* were saying. And "'Twas thou at my side when we stole down through the palms and bottled the garrison in the little fort." And "Ah, what wine we got that night!"

"Yea, and how drunk we got! So that Martin Barwick was of a mind to go fight a duel with the captain of the soldiers. And then they burst out and drove us all away, and there was an end of our taking towns for a long, long while."

"I will have you know that I was no drunker than any man else," Martin snarled, and they laughed uproariously.

"Come," cried another, "since we have laid our ship in her chosen berth, let us sleep while the idlers watch. We shall be off in the cool of the afternoon."

"Nay, in the morning!"

"Afternoon or morning matters little," said old Jacob thickly, in the corner where he sat watching all the men. "The hour is near when we shall lay in the hold a goodly cargo. I know well *this* town. We need only find two more such towns to get the money to keep us the rest of our lives like so many dukes, each of us in a great house in England, with a park full of deer, and the prettiest tavern wenches from all the country round to serve us in the kitchen."

That day, while the men slept in such cool places as they could find, the cook and the carpenter stood watch; and a very good watch they kept, for they were prudent souls and feared the Old One and dared not steal a wink of sleep. But though there was much need that the men should sleep, there was small need of a watch, for the ship lay in that deep cove in the little round bay, with masses of palms on the high banks, which hid her from waterline to truck.

At mid-afternoon, as the Old One had bade them, the cook and the carpenter called the men, who came tumbling up, quickly awake and breathing heavily, since there was work to be done ere another morning broke, and, like enough, blood to be spilled.

From a chest of arms Harry Malcolm handed out muskets and pistols and pikes. "This for you," he said—"and this for you—and here's a tall gun for Paul Craig. Nay, curse not! Prayers, Paul, shall profit thee more than curses."

"I tell ye what, I'll not carry this great heavy gun," quoth he, and turned a dull red from anger.

"Blubububububub!" one cried, and all laughed.

"'Tis lucky, Paul," retorted Harry Malcolm, "that Tom Jordan is an easy, merciful man, or there's more than one back would bear a merry pattern in welts." He took up another musket—cumbersome, unwieldy weapons they were which a man must rest for firing—and handed it to another. "And this for you."

Jacob was turning over and over on his palm powder from a newly opened barrel, and the Old One was leaning on the quarter-deck rail, whence he sleepily watched the small groups that were all the time gathering and parting. Will Canty, his face a little whiter than ordinary and his hand holding his firelock upright by the barrel, stood ill at ease by the forecastle. The boys lurked in corners, keeping as much as possible out of the way, but watching with wide eyes the many preparations. And indeed it was a rare sight, for the staunch old ship, her rigging restored and her many leaks stopped, lay in her little cove where a cool breeze stirred the ropes, and the afternoon sun shone through the palms brightly on the deck, and the men moved about bare-armed and stripped to their shirts.

"It would save much labour," said the carpenter, "were we to use this fair breeze to go by sea."

"True, carpenter, but a ship coming in from sea is as easy spied by night as by day, whereas a company of men descending from the hills by night will have the fort before the watchdogs bark. And who is there will grudge labour in such a cause?" The Old One looked about and the carpenter himself nodded assent.

Only Paul Craig grumbled, and at him the others laughed as they ate and drank.

They slept again till just before dawn, then, running a plank to the shore, they gathered under the palms, for there was need of a last council before leaving the ship.

"We are forty men," said the Old One, "and forty men are all too few; but though it is little likely that any will stumble on the ship in our absence, it is a matter of only common prudence that we post a guard ere we go."

"Yea, a guard!" cried Paul Craig. "I, now, am a very watchful man."

"Nay, but think, Paul, how great a meal thou can'st eat when thou hast climbed up hill and down with thy gun, and how much thou can'st drink. 'T would be no kindness to leave thee. We must leave some lithe, supple lad who hath no need for the tramp." And the Old One chuckled. "Come, Paul and Martin, you shall lead our van."

Harry Malcolm met his eye, and he nodded.

"I name to guard our ship," said he, "the cook and Joe Kirk and Will Canty. Do you, lads, load the swivel guns and keep always at hand two loaded muskets apiece. Fire not unless the need is urgent, and keep the ship with your lives, for who knows but the lives of us all are staked upon your watchfulness and courage? You, Harry, since you know best the road, shall lead, with Paul and Martin upon either hand; the rest shall follow, and Jacob and I will guard the rear." He turned to the three who were to stay. "If there is good news, I will send men to bring the ship round to the harbour where, God willing, we shall load her to the deck with yellow chinks. If bad news—why, you may see us in one day, or three, or five—or maybe never."

He arched his brows and tossed his piece to his shoulder, and with Jacob at his side, he followed the others, who were already labouring under the weight of their weapons as they filed up the steep acclivity. The Old One and Jacob slowly climbed the wild, rough hill and paused until the marching column was out of hearing.

"You are a strange man," said Jacob. "I would wring his neck without thought."

"That were a mere brutal jest such as affordeth little joy," the Old One replied. "I will wind him in a tangle of his own working, then I will take the breath from his nostrils deliberately and he will know, when he dies, that I know what I know."

"You are a strange man."

"I can keep order among the gentlemen better than could any captain in the King's service; and such a game as this sharpens a man's wits. We shall see what we shall see."

Jacob slipped away by himself and the Old One followed his men.

All that morning, unseen and unsuspected, Jacob sat behind a rock within earshot of the ship. The palms shielded him and shaded him and he got himself into such a corner that no one could approach him from behind or see him without being seen. And all that morning he neither heard nor saw aught worthy of mark until about noon a voice in the ship cried out so that Jacob could plainly understand the words, "One should watch from land. Now a man on the hilltop could serve us well."

To which a second voice replied, "Go thou up, Will, go thou up! We are of no mind to stir."

There came the sound of steps on a plank, then a rattle of pebbles and a rustle of leaves; and Jacob rose quickly and followed at a safe distance a man who passed his corner on the way up the acclivity.

Reaching the summit of the hill, where he was safely out of sight from the ship, the fellow—and it was indeed Will Canty—searched the sea from horizon to horizon; but Jacob, hunting deliberately as was his manner, found a seat a great way off, yet so situated among the trees that he could watch without being seen. For an hour he sat thus in a niche in the rocks below and watched Will on the flat ledge above; then he saw him start up of a sudden and look around him very carefully and cautiously, and whip his shirt off his back and wave it in the air.

For a good half-hour Will waved the shirt, stopping now and then to rest; but it seemed that nothing came of his waving, for with a sad face he put on his shirt and again sat down and presently he returned to the ship.

Jacob dozed a while longer where he was, having seen all that; for he was a man who could put two and two together as well as another, and he had learned what he wished to know. Then he got up, and seeking out the place where the Old One and his men had passed, he followed after them at a serious, steady gait, which seemed not very fast yet which kept plodding so surely up hill and down hill and through gullies and over ledges and along beside the sea, that in two hours he had covered the distance the others, burdened with guns and pikes and swords, had covered in three; and before nightfall, following the marks they had left for him, he overtook them resting in a ravine.

Night, which comes so suddenly in the tropics, was about to darken the world, when Jacob gave them a great start by walking silently in upon them as they sat talking in low voices, with their guns lying by their sides and their minds on the work that was before them. He nodded at the Old One, who knew well enough what his nod meant, and sat quietly down among them.

There was but a small moon, and when at nearly midnight they bestirred themselves and ate the last of the sea bread they had brought, the light was dim. But their plans were laid and the hour was come and the Old One and Harry Malcolm and Jacob knew the ways they were to go.

They were more than thirty, and they straggled out in a long line as they climbed the precipitous hill. But those ahead waited at the top for those behind and together, marching in close array, they crossed a ridge and came into sight of a little town that lay below them among hills and mountains.

It was a dark and silent town, whose houses had a ghostly pallor in the faint light from the crescent moon, and it lay beside a harbour which shone like silver. There were no lights in the houses and in all the place nothing stirred; but in the harbour a ship lay anchored, concerning which they speculated in whispers.

"The road lies yonder under the rock," said Harry Malcolm.

"And one man has strayed," Jacob whispered. "I will fetch him."

He stepped back the way they had come, and returned with Paul Craig who dragged his gun by the muzzle.

The fellow's manner betrayed his cowardice and the Old One pushed the point of a knife against his breast. "If again you stray or loiter," he whispered, "this blade will rip you open like a hog fat for the killing."

Though the words were uttered very softly, others heard them, and Martin Barwick, whose courage was none of the staunchest, rubbed his throat and swallowed hard.

"Gold without stint is ours for the taking," said the Old One.

"I have a misliking of yonder ship."

"Nay, she is but one more prize."

They moved down the mountain path toward the town.

"There are twelve houses," said Jacob. "Two men to a house leaves ten for the fort." In the dim light he had missed his count, for the men as they approached the gate of the village had crowded together.

"No one sleeps in the fort," quoth Harry Malcolm in a low voice. "They go to the fort only when they are attacked by dogs of English or wicked pirates."

Some one laughed softly.

"Two men to a house," the Old One was saying. "Kill, plunder, and burn!" Then as they stood in the very gate a dog barked.

They jumped at the sound, but higher by far did they jump when from the ship lying in the harbour there came a loud hail in Spanish.

"Ha! The dogs are wakeful!" the Old One cried in double meaning, and with that he plunged forward through the shadows. Though for the most part he showed himself a shrewd, cautious man, he was not one to turn back when his blood was up; and quicker than thought he had raised his voice to a yell:

"Come, my hearts, and burn them in their beds!"

"Nay, nay!" cried Jacob. "Come back while there is yet time! They cannot yet know who we are or from whence we come. Another day, another month, will be best!" But they had gone. With a yell the Old One had led the way, and they had followed at his heels. Jacob was left alone in the dark, and being a rarely prudent man and of no mind to risk his neck lightly, he stayed where he was.

As the Old One stormed the first house, there came a shot from the darkness and he gave a howl of pain and rage. Turning, Phil Marsham saw a stranger cross the road behind him, but he had no time to consider the matter, since the first cries had waked the town. A dozen men were exchanging musket-shots with the fort, wherein they were folly-blind, for their shots went wild in the dark and their guns took a long time loading; and the Old One, thinking to further the attack and not considering that the light would reveal their whereabouts and their weakness, struck fire to dry grass, which blazed up and caught wood, but went out, hissing, under a bucket of water from within a house. Here a *Rose of Devon*'s man took the steel and died, and there another went down, hit by a musket-ball. In a lull in the firing—for the charges of their guns were soon spent—they heard plainly the sound of oars and saw that two boats were bringing men from the vessel in the harbour, and from the far side of the place others came charging with pikes and swords. In all truth, the town was aroused and the game was over, so they took to their heels and ran for their lives, since they were outnumbered and outfought and no other course was left them.

All who escaped gathered on the hill, for though a man might wish in his heart to leave the *Rose of Devon* for ever, he could find no refuge in the nest of hornets they had stirred to fury, since in the eyes of the enemy one must appear as guilty as another. So, leaving ten of their number behind them, dead or wounded or captured, every man who could walk started back for the *Rose of Devon* with the thought to cheer him on, that after daybreak in all likelihood the howling pack would be at his heels.

They bickered and wrangled and cursed, and one whispered to Philip Marsham that if they had an abler captain their luck would turn, which was a great folly and cost him a broken head.

"That for thy prattle," the Old One cried, for he had been walking just behind. And with a club he struck the fellow a blow that sent him to the ground. Indeed, the Old One had intended to kill him, and had he not been so weary, he would doubtless have stayed to complete his work, for his temper was torn to rags.

Uphill and down they went, through thickets and streams, over ledges and sandy slides, round dank old fallen logs and along firm beaches, back to their dark frigate, with their labour for their pains. And so, by broad daylight, weary and hungry and too angry for civil speech, they came to the *Rose of Devon*. The younkers trotted along, dog-tired, and the men tramped in as best they could. There were hard words on this side and hard words on that, and hands were clapped on knives for no cause at all.

They thought it queer, when in the grey morning they came sliding down to the ship, with a rattle of pebbles and loose earth, that they found her so still, and only the cook on her deck, and himself in a cold sweat of fear.

"I would have nought to do with it," he cried, and being still mindful of his thirsty hours in bilboes, he shook in his shoes lest they fix upon him a share of the blame for that which had occurred in their absence.

"With what and whom would'st thou have nought to do?" the Old One demanded, and he showed a face that made the cook's teeth rattle.

"With them—they've gone."

"Who hath gone?"

"Will Canty and Joe Kirk. They took the shallop and bread and beer."

"It seems," said the Old One, and in a strangely quiet voice, "that the edge that is nicked is not Will Canty's. Is it thine, Jacob, or mine?"

The cook thought that either he or the Old One had lost his wits, for he made no sense of the words; but Harry Malcolm and Jacob knew what was meant, and Philip Marsham made a sharp guess at it.

CHAPTER XVI

The Harbour of Refuge

IT WAS up anchor and away, for they needs must flee ere the hunters find them. They stood along the coast with a light breeze in the early morning, when the sun was rising over the sea and tipping with gold the branches of the dark palms; but the *Rose of Devon* was a hawk with clipped wings.

A company of twenty-nine or thirty men in a staunch ship with a goodly number of brass cannon and with powder and balls in abundance (which provident merchants had bought to defend their venture against pirates!) might have done very well on a merchant voyage or fishing. If there are not too many to share in the adventure, a man can earn his wages by the one; or if he would go to the banks of Newfoundland or to Massachusetts Bay, his lay of a fishing voyage will doubtless bring him enough golden chinks to drink in strong ale or sack the health of every fair maiden of Plymouth ere he must be off to fill his pockets anew. Though the times be ever so hard, he is a feckless sailor who cannot earn in such a company the price of drinking the three outs. But to work a ship and lay aboard a rich prize, with perhaps need to show heels to a King's cruiser or to fight her, is quite another game; and the Old One and Harry Malcolm, who had their full share of the ill-temper that prevailed throughout the ship, cursed their fortune, each in his own way, and wrangled together and quarrelled with the men.

And indeed, among all the men of the *Rose of Devon* there were only two or three who that morning remained unperturbed by their misadventures of the night. One was Jacob, who sat in this corner or that and eyed all comers coldly and as if from a distance. A second was Philip Marsham, who did not, like Jacob, appear to lose his warmer interest in the ship and her company, but whose interest had been always less as for himself alone.

Meeting in groups of three or five, the men ripped out oaths and told of how one captain or another had once taken a ship or a town with vast bloodshed and plunder, and thus they stormed about the deck at intervals until an hour after sunrise, when Phil from the forecastle and Old Jacob from his corner under the quarter-deck, having observed them for some time putting their heads together and conversing in undertones, heard them crying out, "Yea, yea! Go on, go on! We are all with you!" Four of the men then started through the steerage room to the great cabin and the rest gathered in a sullen half circle just under the quarter-deck.

Jacob raised his head and listened; his face was very thoughtful and his small mouth was puckered tight. At the sounds that issued from the cabin, Phil himself drew nearer.

"Well," cried the Old One in a voice that seemed as full of wonder as of wrath—they heard him plainly—"what in the Devil's name mean ye by this?"

"We ha' lost a dozen men and our shallop by this foolish march, and from this rich town of which you have promised much we have got only blows and balls for our labour." The speaker's voice was loud and harsh, and he larded his speech with such oaths and obscene bywords as are not fit for printing. "We are of a mind to change captains. You shall go forward and Paul Craig shall come aft. Speak up, Paul! Tell your tale of no marching to wear out a man's feet—"

There came a string of oaths in the Old One's voice and a wild stamping and crashing; then out they burst, jostling one another in their haste, and after them the Old One with a clubbed musket.

He subdued his fury, when he faced the ring of sullen men, as if he had taken it with his hands and pushed it down. But they feared him none the less, and perhaps the more. A man looking at him must perceive that his mind was keen and subtle, which made his quietness, when he was angry, more terrible than a great show of wrath.

"I have sailed before with mad, fickle crews," said he; "yea, once with a crew so mad that it would send a gentleman post unto the King with a petition of grievances because a King's ship had chased us from the South Foreland to the Lizard. But never saw I a more mad crew than this, which is enough to give a man a grievous affliction of the colic and stone by the very excess of its madness."

"As for madness," cried a man who stood at a safe distance behind the rest, "I charge thee with worse than madness. We have lost two fights and many men and have got to show for it—a kettle of fish."

Some laughed, but more muttered angrily.

"Why—we have had our ill fortunes. But what gentlemen of the sea have not? Come, make an end of this talk. Come out, you who spoke, and let us consider the matter. Nay? He will not come, though by his speech he is a bold man?"

Again some of them laughed, but in a mean way, for he had cowed them by his show of violence and they feared more than ever that subtle spirit which overleaped their understanding.

"Listen, then, my hearts of gold: we will come about and sail back. We will lie tonight by the very town that last night we stormed. We will seek it out as a harbour of refuge. We will tell them a tale of meeting pirates who captured our shallop and part of our men. We will give them such a story that they will think we have met the very men they themselves last night beat off, and will welcome us with open arms to succour our distress. Who knows but that we can then take them by assault? Or if for the time they are too strong for us, we will mark well the approaches and the defenses, and some night we will again come back."

The idea caught their fancy, and though a few cried nay and whispered that it was the sheerest madness yet, more cried yea and argued there was little risk, for if worst should come to worst, they could turn tail and run as run they had before. As they talked, they forgot their many woes and whispered about that none but the Old One would ever think of such a scheme.

Harry Malcolm and the Old One went off by themselves and put their heads together and conversed secretly, and throughout the ship there was a great buzz of voices. Only Jacob, who sat in his corner and watched now one and now another, and Philip Marsham, who watched Jacob, kept silence amidst the hubble-bubble.

So they wore ship, and returning along the palm-grown shores, came again at the end of the afternoon into sight of the flat mountain they had seen first by night; and though the wind fell away at times until the sails hung in listless folds, they gathered speed with the evening breeze and came at nightfall into a fine landlocked harbour with the town at its head, where there were lights shining from the houses and a ship still lying at anchor.

Upon their coming there was a great stir in the town. They saw lights moving and heard across the water voices calling; but though the men of the *Rose of Devon* stood by their guns, ready to lift the ports at a word and run out their pieces, they laughed in their sleeves at their own audacity whereby they hoped greatly to enrich their coffers.

The one in the fort hailed them in Spanish, and while the Old One made answer in the same tongue, those who understood it whispered to the rest that he was giving the men in the fort a sad tale of how the *Rose of Devon* had fallen in with a band of sailors of fortune who had killed part of her men and would have killed them all had not the Old One himself by a bold and clever stroke eluded them. The Old One and the man in the fort flung questions and answers back and forth; and as they talked, the men at the guns relaxed and softly laughed, and Martin whispered to Philip Marsham, "Yea, they are telling of a band of roving Englishmen who last night singed their very whiskers; and being clever men and learning that them whom we our-selves have met and fought were lawless English dogs, they perceive we needs have met the very rascals that made them so much trouble." Again Martin listened, then slapped his thigh. "They are sending us boats!" he exclaimed. "Though they perceive we are English, it seemeth they bear an Englishman no ill will because he is English. Truly, a fool shall be known by his folly!"

Most of the men were elated, but old Jacob watched and said nought. His black, bright eyes and his nose, which came out in a broad curve, made him look like an old, wise rat.

As the boats came over the dark water, with the soft splash of oars, there was hurried talking on the quarterdeck, then the Old One came swiftly. "Good boatswain," said he, "these foolish fellows have bade us ashore to break bread with them and share a bottle of wine. Now I am of a mind to go, and Harry Malcolm is of a mind to bear me company. We will take twelve men and so arrange it that they shall not surprise us. Yea, I am too old a dog to be caught by tricks. It may be we can strike them again to-night, and a telling blow. It may be not. But do you and Jacob keep watch on board, with every man at his station in case of need."

So the *Rose of Devon* let go her anchors and swung with the tide a cable's length from the unknown ship, which lay dark and silent and apparently deserted.

The strange boats came up in the shadow of the poop and the Old One and Harry, with their men mustered about them, exchanged greetings with the oarsmen below, in rough English and in rougher Spanish, as each side strove to outdo the other in civility.

The men—heavily armed—slid down into the boats and the Old One smiled as he watched them go, for he was himself well pleased with the escapade. Such harebrained adventures were his bread of life. He followed the men, the cabin lanthorn in his hand, and after him came Harry Malcolm, as cool as a man could desire, and watched very sharply all that went on while the boats rowed slowly away toward the land.

Then Jacob came out of his corner and spoke to Phil. "I will watch first," said he. "The cook hath laid a fine supper on the cabin table. Go you down and eat your fill, then come up and keep the deck and I will go down and eat in my turn."

At something in the man's manner, which puzzled him, Phil hesitated; but the thought was friendly, and he said, "I will not be long."

"Do not hurry."

When Phil turned away, old Jacob cleared his throat.

"Boatswain—"

"Yea?"

"Do not hurry."

As Phil sat at the table in the great cabin, which was so dark that he could scarcely see the plate in front of him (although he ate with no less eagerness because of the darkness), the planks and timbers and transoms and benches were merged into an indiscriminate background of olive-black, and there hung before him by chance a mirror on the forward bulkhead, in which the reflection of the yellow sky threw into sharp outline the gallery door at his back. Having no means at hand for striking a light, he was hungrily eating and paying little heed to his surroundings, when in the mirror before his eyes, against the yellow western sky the silhouette of a head wearing a sweeping hat appeared over the gallery rail.

There was not the faintest noise, and no slightest motion of the ship was perceptible in the brown stillness of the evening. The head, darkly silhouetted, appeared in the mirror as if it were a thing not of this earth, and immediately, for he was one who always kept his wits about him, Phil slipped silently off the bench, and letting himself down flat on the deck, slid back into the darkest corner of all, which lay to the starboard of the gallery door. There, without a sound, he rose to his feet.

The black silhouette reflected in the mirror grew larger until it nearly blocked the reflection of the door, then a board in the gallery gently creaked and Phil knew that the man, whoever he was, was coming into the cabin. Presently in the subdued light he could dimly see the man himself, who stood by the table with his back toward Phil and glanced about the cabin from one side to the other. Knowing only that he was a stranger and therefore had no right to enter the great cabin of the *Rose of Devon,* Phil had it in mind to jump and seize him from behind, for so far as he could appraise the man's figure, the two were a fair match in weight and height. But when Phil was gathering himself for the leap, he

saw in the mirror the reflection of a second head, and then
of a third.

Again the gallery creaked, for the newcomers, like the
first, were on their way into the cabin. By the door they stood
for a moment listening, and in the silence Phil heard a boat
gently bumping against the side of the ship. He was first of a
mind, naturally, to cry an alarm; but were he to call for help,
he would learn no more of their errand. They drew together
beside the table and conversed in whispers of which Phil
could distinguish nothing, although he was near enough to
reach out his hand and seize hold of the curls and brave hat
of the nearest of them. To attack them single-handed were
an act of plain folly, for they wore swords and doubtless other
weapons; but when he perceived that the first had got out
flint and steel, he knew that they must soon discover him.

"Whence and for what have you come?" he said in a low
voice.

They turned quickly but with admirable composure: there
were never seen three calmer men. The first struck light to
a slow match and held over it the wick of a candle drawn
from his pocket, upon which the flame took hold and blazed
up, throwing curious shadows into the corner of the cabin
and half revealing the hangings and weapons. The man
raised the candle and the three drew close about Phil and
looked at him steadily.

"So a watch is set in the cabin, I perceive," the man holding the candle said with a quiet, ironical smile.

By mien and speech Phil knew upon the instant that they
were Englishmen and it took no great discernment to see
that they were gentlemen and men of authority.

They pressed closer about him.

"Whence and for what have you come?" he repeated.

They made no reply but stood in the brown light, holding
high their candle and looking him hard in the face.

Again he heard the boat bumping against the side of the ship and now the murmur of the wind aloft. Far away he heard a faint sound of calling which was growing constantly louder. The three exchanged glances and whispering to one another, moved toward the gallery; but as they started to go, the one turned back and held the candle to Phil's face.

"Of this be assured, my fine fellow," said he, "I shall know you well if ever I see you again."

Phil was of a mind to call after them, to pursue them, to flee with them; but as it is easy to understand, there were strong reasons for his staying where he was, and there had been little welcome in their faces. He stood for a moment by the table and noticed that the sky in the mirror had turned from a clear olive to a deep grey and that the lines of the door and the gallery rail had lost their sharp decisiveness and had blurred into the dark background. Then he darted out of the cabin through the steerage and called sharply, "Jacob! Jacob!"

Then men watching at the guns stirred in suppressed excitement and turned from whispering uneasily.

"There are strange sounds yonder, boatswain," called one.

"And shall we knock out the ports and loose the tack-lings?" another asked.

"Be still! Jacob, Jacob!" Phil cried, running up on the quarter-deck.

There was no one on the quarter-deck; there was no one on the poop. The wind was blowing up into a fair breeze and small waves were licking against the dark sides of the *Rose of Devon*. But the after decks were deserted.

"Jacob!" Phil cried once more, and sent his voice out far across the water. But there was still no answer. Jacob had gone.

For a moment the lad stood by the rail and intently listened. The calling on shore had ceased, but a boat was rowing out from the town and the beat of oars was quick and irregular. Further, to swell his anxiety, there was a great bustle on board the unknown ship, which had been lying hitherto with no sign of human life.

Then Philip Marsham took the fate of the *Rose of Devon* in his hands and leaned out over the quarterdeck gun. "Holla, there!" he called, but not loudly, "Let the younkers lay quietly aloft and lie ready on the yards to let the sails fall at a word."

Seeming encouraged and reassured by a summons to action, the younger men went swarming up the rigging, and as quietly as one could wish; but even the low sound of their subdued voices drummed loud in the ears of the lad on the quarter-deck.

Jacob had gone! The boatswain, for one, remembered old tales of rats leaving ships of ill fortune.

CHAPTER XVII

Will Canty

THEY SAW a boat coming a long way off, with her men row-ing furiously, but by that time there were all manner of sounds on the shore whence the boat had launched forth. Shouts and yells in English and Spanish, with ever the boom-ing of guns, echoed across the harbour. Beacons flamed up and for a while danced fitfully, only to die away when those who tended the fires left them unwatched and with flaming brands joined in the cry; and in the wake of the furiously rowing boat came others that strove with a great thresh of oars to overhaul the fugitive.

The activity and tumult were very small and faint under the bright stars in that harbour girdled about with palms. Though the rugged slopes of wild mountains, rising like escarpments above the harbour, by day completely dwarfed it, yet the stars made the mountains seem by night mere pigmy hills, and even the many sounds, which a great echoing redoubled, seemed smaller and fainter in the presence of the vast spaces that such a night suggests.

Although the men in the foremost boat rowed out of time and clumsily, their fierce efforts kept them their lead, and they were still far in advance of their pursuers when they tossed up their oars and crouched panting on the thwarts in the shadow of the ship.

"Ropes, you fools!" the Old One called. "Cast us ropes! Ropes! Bind fast this bird we've caught and trice him up! Now, my hearts, swing him aloft—there he swings and up he goes! Well done! I'll keep him though I risk my neck in doing it. Make fast a rope at bow and at stern! Good! Every man for himself! Up, thou! And thou! Up go we all! Come, tally on and hoist the boat on board! And the men are aloft? Well done, Jacob! Haul up the anchor and let fall the courses!"

It was plain from their manner that those who came swarming up the sides had a story to tell, but there was little time then for story-telling. The pursuing boats lifted their oars and swung at a distance with the tide, since it was plain for all to see that they were too late to overhaul the fugitives. Although on board the stranger ship there were signs and sounds of warlike activity, she too refrained from aggression; and the Old One, having no mind to traffic with them further, paced the deck with a rumble of oaths and drove the men alow and aloft to make sail and be gone.

It was "Haul, you swine!"

And "Heave, you drunken dogs!"

And "Slacken off the weather braces! Leap for your lives!"

And "Haul, there, haul! A touch of the rope's end, boatswain, to stir their spirits!"

And "Come, clear the main topsail! Up aloft to the topsail yard, young men! A knife, you dog, a knife! Slash the gaskets clear! A touch of the helm, there! Harder! Harder! There she holds! Steady!"

Then Harry Malcolm called from the quarter-deck in his quiet, quick voice, "The swivel gun is loaden, Tom. I'll chance a shot upon the advantage."

"Good, say I!" quoth the Old One. "And if the first shot prove ill, amend it with a second."

They saw moving on the forecastle the light of a match, and after such brief space of time as a spark takes to go from brace-ring to touchhole the gun, which was charged with small shot for sweeping the deck if an enemy should board the ship, showered the distant boats with metal. They saw by the splashing that the charge had carried well and that Malcolm's aim was true, and a yell and a volley of curses told them as well as did the splash, which was dimly seen by starlight, that the shot had scored a hit.

While a sailor sponged the gun, Harry Malcolm gave a shog to the full ladle of powder, and keeping his body clear of the muzzle, put the ladle home to the chamber, where he turned it till his thumb on the ladle-staff was down, and gave it a shake to clear out the powder, and haled it forth again. Then with the rammer he put the powder home and drove after it a good wad and in anger and haste called for a shot.

Then the Old One laughed through his teeth. "Go thou down, Jacob," cried he, "and give them a ball from the stern chaser. To sink one of those water snakes, now, would be a message worthy of our parting. Jacob! Jacob, I say!"

There was no answer from old Jacob.

It was Boatswain Marsham who cried back, "He hath gone."

"Gone?" quoth the Old One. His face, as the starlight revealed it, was not for the reading, but despite him there was something in his voice that caught the attention of the men.

"Gone?" the Old One repeated, and leaned down in the darkness. The shadows quite concealed his face when he was bent over so far that no light from above could fall on it, but he raised his hand and beckoned to the boatswain in a way there was no mistaking.

In response to the summons of the long forefinger, Phil climbed the ladder to his side.

"You say he hath gone," the Old One quietly repeated. "When did he go?"

"I do not know. He kept the deck when I went below for supper."

"How did he go?"

"Nor do I know that. But three men came into the cabin by way of the gallery while I was there—"

"Three men, say you? Speak on." The Old One leaned back and folded his arms, and though he smiled, he listened very carefully to the story the boatswain told.

"And when you came on deck he was gone." The Old One tapped the rail. "You have book-learning. Can you navigate a ship?"

"I can."

"Yea, it may well be that now we shall have need of such learning. It was an odd day when you and I met beside the road. I shall not soon forget that ranting fool with the book, who was as good as a bear-baiting to while away an afternoon when time hung heavy. Oft ha' we left him fallen at the crest, in the old days when he dwelt in Bideford, but Jacob saw no sport in it, nor could he abide the fellow." The Old One looked Phil frankly in the eye and smiled. "In faith, I had a rare game that day with Martin, whose wits are but a slubbering matter at best. But that's all done and away with. And Jacob hath gone! Let him go. Betide it what may, there is one score I shall settle before my hour comes. Go forward, boatswain, and bear a sharp watch at sea, and mind you come not abaft the mainmast until I give you leave."

The Old One spoke again when Phil was on the ladder. "Mind you, boatswain: come not abaft the mainmast until I

give you leave. I bear you nought but love, but I will have you
know that in what I have to do I will brook no interruption."

Though Tom Jordan had spoken him kindly, the lad was
not so blunt of wit that he failed to detect suspicion in the
man's manner. He stopped by the forecastle, and looking
back saw that the Old One was giving the helmsman orders,
for the ship had cleared the harbour, to all appearances
unpursued, and was again bearing up the coast. The Old
One then came down from the quarterdeck, and, having
spoken to several of the men in turn, called, "Come, Martin;
come, Paul, bring the fellow in."

And with that, he went into the great cabin, where they
heard him speaking to Harry Malcolm.

As for Martin Barwick and Paul Craig, they went over to
where the one had all this time been lying whom they had
trussed up in ropes and hoisted on board. All the time he had
been in the ship he had neither moved nor spoken, nor did
he speak now as they picked him up, one at his head and one
at his feet, and carried him into the cabin. The door shut and
for a long time there was silence.

There were some to whom the matter was a mystery, and
the boatswain was among them; but the whispering and nodding showed that more knew the secret than were ignorant
of it. The ship thrust her nose into a heavy swell and pitched
until her yards knocked on the masts; the breeze blew up
and whipped the tops off the waves and showered the decks
with spray; the sky darkened with clouds and threatened
rain. But in the ship there was such a deep silence as stifles
a man, which endured and seemed—were it possible—to
grow minute by minute more intense until a low cry burst
from the cabin.

The men sitting here and there on deck stirred and looked
at one another; but Philip Marsham leaped to his feet.

"Sit down, lad," said the carpenter.

"Drop your hand!"

"Nay, it is better that I keep my hand on your arm."

"Drop your hand! Hinder me not!"

"Nay, I am obeying orders."

There came a second cry from the cabin, and Phil laid his free hand on his dirk.

"Have care, boatswain, lest thy folly cost thee dear. There are others set to watch the deck as well as I."

And now three men who had been sitting by the mainmast rose. They were looking toward Phil and the carpenter, and one of them slowly walked thither.

Though Philip Marsham had no fear of hard fighting, neither was he an arrant fool, and instantly he perceived that he was one man against many under circumstances that doubled the odds. His heart beat fast and a cold sweat sprang out on his forehead.

"What are they doing to him?" he demanded.

"Nothing that he hath not richly earned," said the man who had come near the two.

Scarcely conscious of his own thought, Phil glanced toward the dark and distant shore; but, slight though his motion, the carpenter's one eye saw it and his none too nimble wit understood it.

"Nay," said he, "it is a mad conceit."

The carpenter thrust his fingers through his beard, and, being a kindly soul in his own way and having a liking for the boatswain, he wished himself rid of his responsibilities. But since there was no escape from the situation he drew a deep breath and squared his shoulders to make the best of it. "I heard of a man once, when I was a little lad," he said, "who was cast ashore on the main, in Mexico or some such place. Miles Philips was his name and the manner of his suffering at the hands of the Indians and the Spaniards may serve as a warning. For they flung him into prison where he was like to have starved; and they tortured him in the Inquisition where he was like to have perished miserably; and many of his companions they beat and killed or sent to the galleys; and himself and certain others they sold for slaves. So grievous was his suffering, he was nigh death when he heard news of Sir Francis Drake being in those seas and ran away to join him. Yet again they caught him—caught this Miles Philips and clapped him into prison with a great pair of bolts on his legs; and yet once more did he escape, for God willed it, and filed off his irons and got him away and so betook him back to England after such further suffering from the Indians and the mosquitoes and the Spaniards and the dogs of the Inquisition as few men have lived to tell the tale of. All this, I have heard from an old man who knew him, is told in Master Hakluyt's book, where any scholar of reading may find it for himself. Though not a man of reading, yet have I taken it to heart to beware of straying from a ship into a strange land."

Of all the fellow had said Philip Marsham had heard no more than half, for the cry that had twice sounded still rang in his ears, although since it had died away the second time there was only silence on the deck save for the carpenter's rambling talk. The lad's mind leaped nimbly from one occurrence to another in search for an explanation of the cry.

"Tell me," said he, "what happened on shore?"

At this the carpenter laughed, pleased with believing he had got the boatswain's thoughts off the affair of the moment. "Why, little enough. They would have persuaded us to leave our weapons at the door, but the Old One was too wise a horse to be caught by the rattle of oats. And whilst he was ducking and smiling and waving hands with the Spaniards, I myself, my ears being keen, heard one cry in Spanish, for I have a proper understanding of Spanish which I got by many pains and much listening—as I was saying, I heard one cry in Spanish, 'Yea, that is he.' And said I to myself, 'Now Heaven keep us! Where have I heard that voice?' And then it came upon me and I cried in English, 'Who of us knew the dog,

Will Canty, could talk Spanish?' Whereat the Old One, hearing me, turned and caught a glimpse of Will in the darkness. You know his way—a shrewd blade, but hot-tempered. 'There,' cries he, 'is my man! Seize him!' And with that I, being nearest, made a leap. And they, being at the moment all oil to soothe our feelings and hood our eyes, were off their guard. So the Old One, who likely enough had heard for himself Will Canty's saying, since he too hath a curious knowledge of Spanish, cries, 'Back to the boat, my lads!' For seest thou, if Will Canty was pointing out this one or that, there was treacherous work in the wind. So down through them we rushed, all together, bearing Will with us by the suddenness and audacity of our act, and so away in a boat before they knew our thought."

"And who were the other Englishmen?"

The carpenter gave the lad a blank look. "Why, there were none."

Rising, Phil paced the deck while the carpenter and the others watched him. Some scowled and whispered suspicions, and others denied them, until Phil himself heard one crying, "Nay, nay, he's a true lad. 'Tis only he hath a liking for the fellow."

The carpenter neither smiled nor frowned, for though he knew no loyalty deeper than his selfish interests, and though he felt no qualm regarding that which was going on in the cabin (since he had little love for the poor wretch who was the victim), he had a very kindly feeling toward those who got his liking; and it sorely troubled him that Philip Marsham should suffer thus, though it were at second hand.

"Come, lad," said he, "sit down here and take comfort in the fine night."

Laying his elbows on the rail, Phil thrust his hands through his hair and bit his two lips and stared at the distant shore of Cuba. He feared neither Indians nor insects nor the

Inquisition. There were other things, to his mind, more fearful than these.

The gasping sound that then came from the cabin was one thing more than he could abide. He turned with the drawn dirk in his hand, but the carpenter was on him from behind, whispering, "Come, lad, come!" And because he could not but be aware of the carpenter's honest good will, he could not bring himself to use the dirk, yet only by using the dirk could he have got out of the long arms that held him fast. For a moment they swayed back and forth; then, when others were hurrying to aid the carpenter, the door of the great cabin opened.

A rumble of laughter issued, then the Old One's voice, "Lay him here in the steerage and shackle him fast to the mizzen. He may well be thankful that I am a merciful man."

CHAPTER XVIII

Tom Jordan's Mercy

THEY ANCHORED that noon in a great bay surrounded by forests and mountains, which formed a harbour wherein a thousand sail of tall ships might have lain. Through the long afternoon, while the *Rose of Devon* swung at her anchor, the wind stirred the palms and a wild stream, plunging in a succession of falls down a mountainside, shone like a silver thread. But Paul Craig sat guard over Will Canty, who lay in the steerage chained to the mizzenmast, and there was no chance for any one of the men to speak with Will. And on deck the carpenter measured and sawed and planed for his purpose; and having shaped his stock he wrought a coffin.

First he threw nails in a little heap on the deck, then, kneeling, he drove them home into the planed boards. It was rap-rap-rap, and rap-rap-rap. The noise went through the ship, while the men looked at one another; and some

chuckled and said that the Old One was a rare bird; but the
Old One, coming out of the great cabin without so much as
a glance at the lad who lay chained to the mast, stood a long
time beside the carpenter. He kept a grave face while he
watched him work, and very serious he looked when he
turned away and came and stood beside Philip Marsham.

"There are men that would slit the fellow's throat," he said,
"or burn him at stake, or flay him alive; but I have a tender
heart and am by nature merciful. Though he broke faith and
dipped his hands in black treachery, I bear him no ill will. I
must needs twist his thumbs to wring his secrets out of him
and I can no longer keep him about me; yet, as I have said,
I bear him no ill will. Saw you ever a finer coffin than the one
I have ordered made for him?"

What could a man reply? Although there had been complaining and revolt before, the Old One again held the ship
in the palm of his hand, for they feared his irony more than
his anger.

Darkness came and they lowered the coffin into the boat,
whither man after man slid down.

"Come, boatswain," said the Old One, in a quiet, solemn
voice. "There is an oar to pull."

And what could a man do but slide with the others down
into the boat and rest on the loom of an oar? Phil shared a
thwart with the carpenter, and raised his oar and held it
upright between his knees.

The coffin lay across the boat amidships, and there were
four oars, two on the one side and two on the other; but a
man sat beside each oarsman, two more crowded into the
bow, and two sat in the stern sheets with the Old One. Then
they lowered Will Canty to the bottom in front of the Old
One, where he lay bound hand and foot.

Shoving off from the ship, the oarsmen bent to their task
and the Old One steered with a sweep; but the boat was
crowded and deep in the water, and they made slow progress.

Mosquitoes swarmed about them and droned interminably. The water licked at the boat and lapped on the white beach. The wind stirred in the palms. The great bay with its mountains and its starry sky was as fair a piece of land and sea as a man might wish to look upon in his last hour; but there are few men whose philosophy will stand by them at such a moment, and there is an odd quirk in human nature whereby a mere droning mosquito can drive out of mind the beauty of sea and land—nay, even thoughts of an immeasurable universe.

The men beat at mosquitoes and swore wickedly until the Old One bade them be silent and row on, for although they had come near the shore the water was still deep under the boat, which tossed gently in the starlight.

A time followed in which the only sounds were of the wind and the waves and the heavy breathing of the men. Some were turning their heads to see the shore and the Old One had already risen to choose a landing-place, when Will Canty—who, although bound hand and foot, had all the while been edging about in the stern unknown to the others till he had braced his feet in such a way that he could get purchase for a leap—gave a great spring from where he lay, and thus threw himself up and fell with his back across the gunwale, whence, wriggling like a worm, he strove to push himself over the side.

The Old One sprang forward in fury to seize and hold him, and caught him by the wrist; but one of the men in zeal to have a hand in the affair drove the butt of his gun against Will Canty's chin, and in recovering the piece he stumbled and pushed the Old One off his balance. So the Old One lost his hold on Will Canty's wrist and before the rest knew what was happening Will had slipped into the deep water and had sunk. That he never rose was doubtless the best fortune that could have befallen him, and likely enough it was the blow of the gun that killed him. But the Old One was roused to such a pitch of wrath at being balked of his revenge that he was like a wild beast in his fury.

Quicker than thought, he turned on the man who had pushed against him, and reaching for the coffin that was made to Will's measure—a great, heavy box it was!—raised it high and flung it at the fellow.

It gashed the man's forehead and fell over the side and floated away, and the man himself, with a string of oaths, clapped his hand to the wound, whence the blood trickled out between his fingers.

"Swine! Ass!" the Old One snarled. "I was of a mind to lay thee in Will Canty's bed. But let the coffin go. Th'art not worthy of it." The boat grated on white sand, and leaping to his feet the Old One cried with a high laugh as he marked his victim's fear, "Get thee gone! If ever I see thy face again, I will slit thy throat from ear to ear."

"Nay, nay, do not send me away! Do not send me away!" the man wailed. "O God! No, not that! I shall perish of Indians and Spaniards! The wild beasts will devour me. Nay! Nay!"

The Old One smiled and reached for a musket, and the poor fellow, his face streaked with gore, was overcome by the greater terror and fled away under the palms. No shot was fired and neither knife nor sword was drawn ere the echo of the fellow's wailing died into silence; but the Old One then fired a single shot after him, which evoked a last scream.

"Come, Martin, take the scoundrel's oar," quoth the Old One, and he turned the head of the boat to sea.

They said little and were glad to row briskly out to the ship. Action is ever welcome at the time when a man desires most of all to get away from memory and thought.

That night, when they were all asleep, Martin leaped out on the deck and woke them by shrieking like a lunatic, until it seemed they were all transported into Bedlam. He then himself awoke, but he would say only, "My God, what a dream! Oh, what a dream!" And he would rub his hands across his eyes.

The grumblers continued quietly to grumble, for that is a joy no power on earth can take away, but there was no more talk of another captain. Some said that now the luck would change and told of prizes they had taken and would take, and recalled to mind the strong liquors of Bideford and the pasties that Mother Taylor would make for them. Others, although they said little, shook their heads and appeared to wish themselves far away. But whether a man felt thus or otherwise, there was small profit of their talking.

For another day and night they lay at anchor and ate and drank and sprawled out in the sun. The *Rose of Devon,* as they had earlier had occasion to remark, was richly found, and they had still no need to bestir themselves for food and drink. But any man with a head on his shoulders must perceive that with old Jacob, who had gone so wisely about his duties and had so well held his own counsel in many things, the ship had lost something of stability and firm purpose even in her lawless pursuits.

And Will Canty, too, was gone! As the old writer has it, "One is choked with a fly, another with a hair, a third pushing his foot against the trestle, another against the threshold, falls down dead: So many kind of ways are chalked out for man, to draw towards his last home, and wean him from the love of earth." Though Will Canty had died a hard death, he had escaped worse; and as Priam, numbering more days than Troilus, shed more tears, so Philip Marsham, outliving his friend, faced such times as the other was spared knowing.

Of all this he thought at length, and fearing his own conscience more than all the familiars of the Inquisition, in which he was singularly heartened by remembering the stout old knight in the scarlet cloak, he contrived a plan and bode his time.

In the darkness of the second night, when the Old One had somewhat relaxed his watchfulness, Boatswain Marsham slipped over the bow and lowered himself silently on a rope he had procured for the purpose, and very carefully, lest the noise be heard on board the ship, seated himself in Tom Jordan's boat and rowed for shore. An honest man can go so far in a company of rogues and no farther.

Reaching the land and hauling the boat up on the beach in plain sight of those left in the *Rose of Devon*, where they might swim for it if they would, he set off across the hills and under the palms. Upon reaching the height he looked back and for a moment watched the old ship as she swung with the tide on the still, clear water. He hoped he should never see her again. Then he looked down at the tremulous and shimmering bay where Will Canty lay dead, and was glad to plunge over the hill and leave the bay behind him.

CHAPTER XIX

A Man Seen Before

THERE WAS sullen anger and worse in the *Rose of Devon* when day broke, for the boatswain, too, had gone and the boat lay in sight upon the beach whereby all might know the means of his going.

One watching from the mountain would have seen the *Rose of Devon* spread her sails and put to sea like a great bird with white wings. But there was no one on the mountain to watch, and when the ship had sailed, no human being remained to interrupt the placid calm that overspread the bay that summer morning. The sun blazed from a clear sky, and the green palms rustled and swayed beside the blue water, and in all the marvelously fair prospect of land and sea no sign or mark of violence remained.

Phil Marsham had gone in the night over the hills and across the narrow peninsula between two bays. Though the way was rough, the land was high and—for the tropics—

open, and he had put the peninsula behind him by sunrise. He had then plunged down into a swampy region, but, finding the tangle of vines and canes well nigh impassable in the dark, he had struggled round it and had again come to the shore.

There, finding once more a place where a man could walk easily, he had pressed on at dawn through a forest of tall trees in infinite number and variety, with flowers and fruits in abundance, and past a plain of high grass of wonderful greenness.

A short time after sunrise he drank from a spring of water and ate ship's bread from the small store with which he had provided himself. But he dared not linger, and resuming his journey he came upon two huts where nets and fishing-tackle were spread in the sun to dry. The heat, which seemed to swell from the very earth, by then so sorely oppressed him that he stopped for a while in a shady place to rest. But still he dared not stay, and although upon again arising he saw that dark clouds were covering the sky, he once more stepped forth with such a stout heart as had carried him out of London and all the long way to Bideford in Devon.

It gave him a queer feeling to be tramping through an unknown land with no destination to his mind, yet he vowed to himself that, come what might, he would never go back to the *Rose of Devon*. There is a time when patience and for-bearance are enough to earn a man a hempen halter, and thinking thus, he faced the storm and renewed his determination.

The wind rose to a furious gale; the clouds overswept the sky and thunder shook the earth and heavens. The rain, sweeping down in slanting lines, cut through the palm leaves like hundreds upon hundreds of thrusting swords; and lightning flamed and flashed, and leaped from horizon to horizon, and hung in a sort of continual cloud of deathly blue in the zenith, blazing and quivering with appalling reverberations that went booming off through the mountains and came rolling back in ponderous echoes. It was enough to make a brave man think the black angels were marshalling for the last great battle; it was such a storm as a boy born in England and taught his seamanship in northern waters knew only by sailors' tales. The rain beat through the poor shelter that he found and drenched him to the skin, and the roaring and thundering to the tempest filled him with awe. And when the storm had passed, for it lasted not above three quarters of an hour, the sun came out again and filled the air with a steamy warmth that was oppressive beyond description.

Then the woods came to life and insects stirred and droned, and mosquitoes, issuing from among the leaves and grasses, plagued him to the verge of madness.

One who has lived always in a land where mosquitoes return each year in summer is likely to have no conception of the venomous strength with which their poison can work upon one who has not, by much experience of their bites, built up a measure of resistance against it. Phil's hands swelled until he could not shut them, and the swelling of his face so nearly closed his eyes that he could hardly see. When two hours later, all but blinded, and thirsting and hungry, he came again to the shore and made out in the offing, by squinting between swollen eyelids, the same *Rose of Devon* from which he had run away and to which he had vowed he would never return, his misery was such that he would have been glad enough to be on board her and away from such torment, though they ended the day by hanging him. But the *Rose of Devon* sailed away over the blue sea on which the sun shone as calmly and steadily as if there had been no tempest, and Philip Marsham sat down on a rock and gave himself up as a man already dead.

There two natives of the country found him, and by grace of God, who tempered their hearts with mercy, carried him to their poor hut and tended him with their simple remedies until he was in such measure recovered of the poison that he could see as well as ever. He then set out once more upon his way to he knew not where, having rubbed himself with an ointment of vile odour, which they gave him in goodly quantity to keep off all pestiferous insects, and on the day when he ate the last morsel of the food with which the natives had provided him he saw from the side of a high hill a strange ship at anchor in a cove beneath.

Now a ship might mean one thing or she might mean another; and a man's life might depend on the difference.

Drinking deeply from a stream that ran over the rocks and through the forest, and so at last into the cove, Philip Marsham returned into the wood and sat upon a fallen tree. He saw a boat put out from the ship and touch on the shore a long way off, where some men left her and went out of sight. After an hour or two they came back, and, entering the boat, returned to the ship. He saw men working on deck and in the rigging; he heard the piping of a whistle, and now and again, as the wind changed, he heard more faintly than the drone of insects the voices of the men.

Being high above the shore, he found the mosquitoes fewer and the wind helped drive them away; yet they plagued him continually, despite his ointment, of which little was left, and made him miserable while he stayed. He would have hurried off had he dared; but the chance that the ship would be the means of saving his life withheld him from pursuing his journey, while doubt concerning the manner of craft she was withheld him from making known his presence.

In mid-afternoon he saw far away a sail, which came slowly in across the blue plain of the sea; and having clear eyes, trained by long practice, he descried even at that great distance the motion of a heavily rolling ship. From his seat high on the hill he could see a long way farther than the men in the ship in the cove, and a point of land shut off from them an arc of the sea that was visible from the hill; so when night fell they were still unaware of the sail.

Though he had watched for hours the ship in the cove, the runaway boatswain of the *Rose of Devon* had discovered no sign of what nation had sent her out or what trade her men followed; but there came a time when his patience could endure suspense no longer. He picked his way down to the shore, following the stream from which he had been drinking during his long watch, and cautiously moved along the edge of the water till he came to the point of land nearest the anchored ship, whence he could very plainly hear voices on board her. There were lights on the stern and on deck, and through an open port he got sight of hammocks swinging above the guns on the main deck.

At last he took off the greater part of his clothes and piled them on a rock; then, strapping his dirk to his waist, he waded silently into the water. Reaching his depth, he momentarily hesitated, but fortifying his resolution with such philosophy as he could muster, he began deliberately and silently to swim. Letting himself lie deep in the water and moving so slowly that he raised no wake, he came into the shadow of the ship. It was good to feel her rough planking. He swam aft under the quarter, and coming to the rudder laid hands on it and rested. Above him he could see, upon looking up, a lighted cabin window.

His own body seemed ponderous as he slowly lifted himself out of water. He raised one hand from the tip of the rudder just above the tiller to the carving overhead and got grip on a scroll wrought in tough oak. He put his foot on the rudder, and feeling above him with his other hand seized fast the leg of a carved dragon. Very thankful for the brave ornaments with which the builder had bedecked the ship, he next got hold of the dragon's snout, and clinging like a fly, unseen and unsuspected, above the black water that gurgled about the rudder and the hull, he crawled silently up the stern.

Coming thus to the lighted cabin window, he peeked in and found the place deserted. On the table a cloth was laid, and on the cloth such a dinner service as he could scarce have dreamed of. There were glasses of rare tints, with a few drops of wine left in them, which glowed like garnets under the bright candles. There were goblets of silver, and even, he believed, of gold. There were wonderfully delicate plates crusted with gold about the edges. There was an abundance of silver to eat with and a great decanter, wrought about with gold and precious stones, such as simple folk might not expect to see this side of Heaven.

At the sound of steps, Phil drew back and hung over the water on the great stern of the ship.

A boy came into the cabin and stepped briskly about clearing the table. Voices came down from above—and they were speaking in English! What a prize she would have made for the *Rose of Devon,* Phil thought, and grimly smiled.

"Boy!" a voice bellowed from somewhere in the bowels of the ship.

"Yea, yea, master," cried the boy, and with that he scurried from the cabin like a startled chick.

Phil raised his head and renewed his hold, for he could not cling there forever; yet how to introduce himself on board the ship was a question that sorely puzzled him. He threw a bare leg over the sill, the more easily to rest, and revolved the problem in his mind. They were plainly honest Englishmen, and right glad would he have been to get himself in among them. Yet if he came like a thief in the night, they must suspect him of evil intentions without end. While he thus attacked the problem from one side and from the other, it occurred to him that the best way was to crawl down again into the water and swim back to the shore from whence he had come. There, having donned his clothes, he would call for help. Surely there was no one so hard of heart as to refuse a lad help in escaping from the pirates.

He raised his leg to swing it out of the window again and put his scheme into practice, when he felt—and it startled him nearly out of his skin—a hand lay hold on his ankle.

If you will balance yourself on the outside of any window with one foot over the sill you will find it exceedingly difficult to pull your foot away from some one inside the window without throwing yourself off the wall, and Phil for the moment was reluctant to make the plunge. Slowly at first he twisted and pulled, but to no purpose. With waxing vigour he struggled and yanked and kicked and jerked, but completely failed to get his ankle out of the hand that held it.

It seemed that a gentleman who had been sitting at a little desk, so placed that Phil could not have seen it without thrusting his head all the way into the cabin, had looked up, and, perceiving to his mild surprise a naked foot thrust in through the window, had nimbly arisen, and stepping lightly toward the foot, had seized the ankle firmly at the moment when Phil was about to withdraw it.

The gentleman marvelled much at what he had discovered and purposed to get at the reason for it. Not only did he succeed with ease in holding the ankle fast against his captive's somewhat cautious first kicks; he anticipated a more desperate effort by getting firm hold with both hands, so that when his captive decided to risk all, so to speak, and tried with might and main to fling himself free and into the water by a great leap, the gentleman kept fast his hold and held the lad by his one leg, who dangled below like a trapped monkey.

Very likely it was foolish of Philip Marsham to attempt escaping, but as I have said he was of no mind to be caught thus like a thief entering in the night, and he was so completely surprised that he had no time at all to collect his wits before he acted. Yet caught he was, and, for a bad bargain, hung by the heels to boot.

"Boy," the gentleman said, and his voice indicated that he had a droll humour, "call Captain Winterton."

The boy, further sounds revealed, who had come silently and in leisure, departed noisily and in haste.

Heavy steps then approached, and a gruff voice cried, "What devilish sort of game is this?"

"Take his other leg, Charles, and we shall soon have him safe on board. I am not yet prepared to say what sort of game it is, beyond saying that it is a rare and curious game."

Thereupon a second pair of hands closed on Philip Marsham's other ankle, and, would he or would he not, he was hauled speedily through the cabin window.

"Young man," said the gentleman who had first seized him, "who and what are you, and from whence have you come?"

"I am Philip Marsham, late boatswain of the *Rose of Devon* frigate. I came to learn from what country this ship had sailed and to ask for help. I myself sailed from Bideford long since in the *Rose of Devon,* but, falling into the hands of certain sailors of fortune who killed our master and took our ship, I have served them for weary months as a forced man. Having at last succeeded in running away from them, I have come hither by land, as you can see, suffering much on the way, and I ask you now to have compassion on me, in God's name, and take me home to England."

"Truly," said the gentleman, "those devilish flies have wrought their worst upon him. His face is swelled till it is as thick-lipped as a Guinea slave's." He spoke lightly and with little thought of Phil's words, for his humour was uppermost in him. He was in every way the fine gentleman with an eye for the comical, accustomed to having all things done for him and as little likely to feel pity for this nearly naked youth as to think it wrong that the little cabin boy should stand till morning behind his chair, lest by chance, desiring one thing or another, he must compromise his dignity by fetching it for himself.

But now the other, Captain Winterton, a tall, grave man, with cold face and hard cold eyes, stepped forward, and speaking for the first time said: "Do you remember me?"

Phil looked him in the eye and felt his heart sink, but he was no coward. "I do," he replied.

Captain Winterton smiled. He was the first of the three men who had come on board the *Rose of Devon* by way of her gallery, and had entered the great cabin the night when Phil Marsham sat there at supper.

It then burst upon Phil that in the whole plain truth lay his only hope.

"I ran away from them—they had forced me into their service!—a week since. Nay, it is true! I am no liar! And it will pay you well to keep a sharp watch this night, for a vessel like enough to the *Rose of Devon* to be her twin is this minute lying behind yonder point."

"Ah! And you sailed, I believe you said, from Bideford. Doubtless you have kept the day in mind?"

"Why, 'twas in early May. Or—stay! 'Twas—"

"Enough! Enough! The master of—"

"But though I marked neither the day of the week nor the day of the month, I remember the sailing well."

"Doubtless," quoth the captain dryly, "but it will save time and serve thy cause to speak only when I bid thee. Interrupt me not, but tell me next the name of the lawful master in whose charge thy most excellent ship sailed from Bideford."

This keen and quiet captain in the King's service was of no mind that his prisoner should tell with impunity such a story as he might make up on the moment. Accordingly he proceeded to draw forth by question after question such particular parts of the story as he himself desired to hear, now attacking the matter from one angle and now from another, watching his prisoner closely the while and all the time standing in such a place that the lad had no chance at all of escaping through the open window.

CHAPTER XX

A Prize for the Taking

"WE SHALL see," said Captain Winterton, when he had listened to all of the tale that he would hear. He turned about. "Boy," he cried, "go speedily and send Mr. Rance in to me."

The boy departed in haste and in a moment there entered a junior officer, who stared in frank curiosity at the three in the cabin.

"Mr. Rance," said the captain, "go aloft in person to the main truck and look about you sharply. Come back and report what you see."

"Yea, yea, sir," the young man replied, and with that he was gone.

The captain stood by the cabin window and frowned. Plainly he had small confidence in the good faith of the prisoner and regarded his story as at best an attempt to save himself at the expense of his friends. The gentleman of the humours, somewhat sobered by the captain's manner of grave concern, returned to his desk, but sat tapping his fingers and watching Philip Marsham.

It had instantly, of course, dawned upon the runaway boatswain that his peril was more serious than he had had reason earlier to believe. For supposing the unknown sail should in all truth be the *Rose of Devon*—and since she was cruising idly thereabouts nothing was more probable—he stood between the Devil, or at all events the Devil's own emissary, Thomas Jordan, and a deeper sea than any ship has ever sailed: the sea upon which many a man with less plain evidence of piracy against him has embarked from a yardarm with a hempen collar about his neck and a black cap over his eyes.

Who, pray, would accept for sober truth such a tale as any scoundrel would make out of whole cloth to save himself from hanging? Despite all he could do or say, he now saw plainly, he must stand convicted, in their minds, of being at the very least a spy sent to learn the state of affairs on board this tall ship in which he was now a prisoner.

Then back to the cabin came young Mr. Rance and very much excited did he appear.

"Sir," he exclaimed, and stood in the door.

"Tell your tale."

"A ship lieth two cables' lengths from land on the farther side of the point, and a boat hath set out from her and is following the shore as if to reconnoitre."

"Ah," said the captain, "it is quite as I thought. No drums, mind you, nor trumpets, Mr. Rance. Call the men to quarters by word of mouth. Make haste and put springs on the cables if there be time before the boat rounds the point. Bid the gunner make all preparations for action and order a sharp watch kept; but order also that there be no sound or appearance of unusual activity. Send me a corporal and a file of men, and the master."

The gentleman at the desk chuckled.

"Come, boy, clear the table," said the captain.

The boy jumped and returned to his work.

The master came first, but the corporal and his men were close at the master's heels.

"Take this fellow to the gun room, clap him into irons, and set a man to watch him."

"Yea, yea. Come, fellow, march along."

And thus sending before them Boatswain Marsham, erstwhile of the *Rose of Devon* frigate, the corporal and his men departed from the cabin.

There were guns on the right hand and the left—ordnance of a size to sink the *Rose of Devon* with a broadside. There were sailormen thronging between decks in numbers to appall the young prisoner who came down among them nearly naked from his swim. Though no greater of burthen than the *Rose of Devon*, the ship was better armed and better manned, and all signs told of the stern discipline of a man-of-war.

The alternatives that Phil Marsham faced, as he sat in shackles with no spirit to reply to the jibes of the sailors and watched men stripped to the waist and moving deftly among the guns, were not those a man would choose. If his old shipmates took this tall and handsome ship, a blow on the head and a burial over the side was the kindest treatment he could expect of them. And if not—the gallows loomed beyond a Court of Admiralty. For hours the hum of voices went up and down the main deck and for hours Boatswain Marsham sat with the bolts upon his legs and wrists and saw the life of the ship go on around him. The men leaped here and there at a word, or lolled by their guns waiting for orders. The night wore on, and nodding, Phil thought of the two ships lying one on each side of the point of land and by all appearances, two quiet merchantmen. Yet one, he knew to his sorrow, smelled devilishly of brimstone; and the other, in which he now sat a prisoner, though her ports were closed and her claws sheathed, was like some great tiger watching through half-shut eyes a bold, adventurous goat.

As the night wore on, he dared hope that the reconnoitring boat had returned to her ship with news that had sent her away in haste, whereby there was a chance that his tale might yet be taken for the truth that it was; and the longer he waited the higher rose his hope, and with the better reason. But an hour or more after midnight he heard men beginning to talk as if there was something new in the wind, and the nearest gunner put his ear to a cat-hole.

"The dogs are out; I hear oars," he whispered. "Yea, though they are rowing softly, I swear I can hear oars."

A hush came over the ship and those below heard faintly a hail given on deck.

Distant sounds came and went like whispers out of the sky, then somewhere outside the ship a great shouting arose and one of the men at a starboard gun cried gleefully, with a round oath, "Verily they are bent on boarding us, lads! Their foolish audacity seasons the term of all our weary waiting."

"Hark! They are hailing!" cried another.

"Come, strike your flag. Have an end of all this talk," a distant voice called. Whereat Philip Marsham, who knew the voice, thought that though their audacity cost him his life it was in its own mad way superb.

The reply was inaudible below, but a boat crashed against the ship.

There was a burst of yelling, followed by a rattle of musketry, then a voice boomed down, "Haul up your ports and run out your guns!"

At that the men beside the guns sprang up with running and calling and the ports flew open and the sounds from without became suddenly louder and clearer. On the one hand were boys handing up filled budge-barrels; on the other were gunners with linstocks ready and powder for the priming. Then, "Ho, Master Gunner," a great voice roared, "withhold your fire! The boats are under the guns and too near for a fair shot!" It was such a moment as a man remembers always, for there was the smoke of powder in the air, with a din of splashing and cursing, and overhead a great hubbub, then silence save for the quick beat of oars.

"See! See!" cried the men. "There go their boats, splintered and all but sunk! And see! There go ours! To your oars, lads, to your oars, ere their ship hath time to flee! See! There they go! Yea, and there go we!"

The Old One had made his last blunder. He had come by night, thinking to board a peaceful merchantman laden with a rich cargo, and had found himself at the head of his score of men on the deck of a man-of-war.

To all those below, but most of all to Philip Marsham chained in the gun room, it was a blind, confusing affair; but the sounds told the story; and though darkness hid the blood that was spilled, there was no mistaking the cries for quarter and the shrieks of agony.

Nor was there need for haste to reach the *Rose of Devon*, since the men left as keepers of the ship were too few to make sail. Captain Charles Winterton of the King's navy himself boarded the dark frigate by starlight, and a capital lark he found it, for behind his stern mien was a lively taste for such adventure. With lusty shouting he swept the handful of men from her deck, and having put a prize crew and his lieutenant in charge of her, he brought back a few more prisoners to join company with the luckless boarders he had sent down to be locked in irons below.

They were sad and angry gentlemen, for there are those to whom the laughter of a hundred sailors is worse than death by the sword. The first of them all to enter the gun room was Tom Jordan. His cheek was gashed and his hair was singed and blood smeared his shirt from shoulder to shoulder and one arm hung limp and broken; but though he was in great pain he smiled, and when they led him into the gun room and he saw Philip Marsham with bolts on wrists and ankles, he laughed aloud.

The fellow was a very mark and pattern of a scoundrel, but he had the courage and spirit of a hero, and had he first gone to sea under another king than James or Charles he might in some overwhelming danger have saved England. Great admirals are made of such timber—bold, resolute, utterly dauntless—and any bold man might have fallen into the same trap that had caught Tom Jordan. (Nay, had nothing warned Captain Winterton or aroused his suspicions, there was a fighting chance for Tom Jordan to have taken his ship from him even so.) But Tom Jordan had gone to sea in the days when the navy was going to the dogs, and, like many another lad of spirit who left the King's service to join the pirates, he had adventured with the Algerians before he led the gentlemen of Bideford. And at last, hazarding a final effort to retrieve his luck, he had unwittingly thrust his head into the halter.

Yet, though they had broken his body, they had failed to touch his courage; despite his pain, he could smile and even laugh. Turning his great grief into a jest, he cried, "Holla, O bravest of boatswains! This is a joy I had not looked for. It seems that, if hang I must, I shall not hang alone." And laughing again, right merrily, he swooned away, which Captain Charles Winterton, having himself come down with the others to see them all shackled, watched with quiet interest.

They brought down the carpenter, who was shaking like a man with an ague, and his beard waggled as he shook. They brought down Martin Barwick, whose face was drawn and haggard, and his hand rubbed his throat, for it itched in a prophetic manner. Then came Harry Malcolm, who stopped before Phil and spat at him and cursed him, and Paul Craig, who had neither eye nor thought for any one besides himself, and a dozen others of whom there was not one that failed to revile at their erstwhile boatswain. A hapless time of it Philip Marsham had among them, but it added little to his great burden of misery.

Nor, for the matter of that, did reviling content them; for toward morning, when the others were dozing, Harry Malcolm, whom they had locked to a longer chain, crawled over to where Phil lay and very craftily tried to kill him with bare hands. The guard cried out, but instead of stopping, the man redoubled his efforts to throttle the lad whom he had seized from behind when he was asleep; whereupon the guard struck a sharp blow with the butt of his musket, and when the corporal had come running and had felt of Harry Malcolm's wrist and had listened for his heart and had turned him over on his back, he cursed the guard with fluent oaths for robbing the gallows.

CHAPTER XXI

Ill Words Come True

To the Isle of Wight, and thence to Spithead and Dept-
ford, came in time the *Sybil* of forty-four guns, Captain
Charles Winterton, and accompanying her, in the hands of a
prize crew, the *Rose of Devon* frigate. There, bundling certain unhappy gentlemen of fortune out of the ship, they sent
them expeditiously up to London and deposited them for
safekeeping in the Marshal-sea prison, a notable hostelry
which has harboured great rogues before and since.

In the fullness of time, the Lord High Admiral of England,
"who holds his court of justice for trials of all sea causes for
life and goods," being assisted by the Judge of Admiralty and
sundry others, officers and advocates and proctors and civil-
ians, was moved to proceed against the aforesaid gentlemen
of fortune. So they heard their names cried in the High
Court of Admiralty and were arraigned for piracy and robbery on the high seas and charged with seizing the frigate

199

Rose of Devon, the property of Thomas Ball and others, and murdering her master, Francis Candle, and stealing supplies and equipment to the value of eight hundred pounds. Nor was that the whole tale of charges, for it seemed that the Lords of Admiralty laid to the discredit of those particular gentlemen of fortune numerous earlier misdeeds of great daring and wickedness and an attempt to take His Majesty's ship *Sybil,* which had cost the lives of certain of His Majesty's seamen and had occasioned His Majesty much grief and concern.

He who read the indictment spoke in a loud and solemn voice, such as might of itself make a man think of his sins and fear judgment; but they were already cowed and fearful, save only the Old One, who still held his head high and very scornfully smiled. The cook bent his head and shivered and dared not look the jury in the face. The carpenter wept and Martin Barwick was like a man struck dumb and Paul Craig kept working his mouth and biting at his lips.

There was a great concourse of people, for who would not seize upon the chance to see a band of pirates? But a very poor show the pirates made, save the Old One; for though they had talked much and often of their valour and had represented themselves as tall fellows who feared nothing in life or death, they were now and for all time revealed as cowards to the marrow of their bones.

Quietly and expeditiously the officers of the Court swore their first witness, who smelled of pitch and tar and bore himself in such wise that he was to be known for a sailor wherever he might turn.

To their questions he replied with easy assurance, for he was not one of those fellows who cope with great gales and storms at sea only to be cowed by a great person on land. "Yea, sir," quoth he, "there is among mariners common talk of a band of sea sharks that hath long resorted to His Majesty's port of Bideford. Yea, my lord—And have I met with them? That I have, and to my sorrow. This month two years I was master in a likely snow, the *Prosperous* of three hundred tons, which fell afoul of that very company, as their boasting and talk discovered to us, who took our ship and set me adrift in a boat with seven of mine own men, whereby, God being merciful unto us, we succeeded after many hardships in winning to the shore of Ireland, whence the *Grace of Bristol* bore us home to England—The fate of the others in our company? In faith, some, I am told, joined themselves with that same band of sea sharks. The rest were slaughtered out of hand—Nay, my lord, the night was black and my sight of the scoundrels was brief. I much misdoubt if I should know them again."

"Come, come," quoth His Lordship, tapping the papers spread on his great table, "look at these prisoners gathered here at the bar and tell me if there be one among them of whom you can say, 'This man was there; this man did thus and so.'"

So the witness came, with the air of a man who is pleased to be seen of many people, and looked them over, one and all; but at the end of his looking he sadly shook his head. "Nay, my lord, the night was dark and sight was uncertain; and though I should rejoice—none more than I!—to see a pirate hanged, I am most loath to swear away the life of an innocent man. There is no man here of whom I can truly say I have seen him before."

His Lordship frowned and the proctors shook their heads; the prisoners sighed and breathed more freely. The tale was at an end, and bearing away with him his smell of pitch and tar the fellow returned to his place.

Four witnesses were then summoned, one after another, and told tales like the first. One had been in a ship that was seized and sunk in Bristol Channel; the second had received a gaping wound in the shoulder off St. David's Head, and had known no more until he found himself alone on the deck of a plundered flyboat; the third had fallen into evil company in Plymouth, which beat him and robbed him and left him for dead, and from the talk of his murderous companions he had learned, before they set upon him, that they were certain gentry of Bideford; and the last of the four told of the murderous attack of a boarding party, which had taken a brig and tumbled him over the side into a boat. "Yea, my lord," he cried, "and I fear to think upon what befell our captain's little son, for of all our crew only three men were left alive and as they sailed away from us three we heard the boy shrieking pitifully." One by one the witnesses wove with their tales a black net of wickedness, but they could not or would not say they knew this prisoner or that.

The Judge frowned darkly from his bench and the people in the seats opened their mouths in wonder and excitement at the stories of robbery and murder. But the net was woven loosely and without knots, for thus far there had been no one to pick out this man or that and say, "It was he who did it." So the cook and the carpenter took heart; and the colour returned to Martin Barwick's face; and the Old One, leaning back, still smiled scornfully. Yet the Judge and the advocates seemed in no way discouraged, from which the men of the *Rose of Devon* might have drawn certain conclusions; for as all the world knows, judges and advocates with a band of pirates under the thumb are, for the honour of the law, set upon making an example of them.

There was long counselling in whispers, then a bustle and stir, and an officer cried loudly, "Come, make haste and lead her in."

A murmur passed over the court and the people turned their heads to look for the meaning of the cry. Then a door opened and an officer appeared, leading by the arm a very old woman.

Phil Marsham felt his heart leap up; he saw Martin raise his hand to his throat with a look of horror. But when he stole a glance at the Old One, he saw, to his wonder, that the Old One was smiling as calmly as before: truly the man was a marvel of unconcern and a very cool and desperate rascal.

"Is this the woman?" quoth my Lord the Judge, who raised his head and lifted his brows to see her the better.

"Yea, my lord."

"Hm! Let us look into this matter!" There was silence in the room except for the sound of shuffling papers. "This woman, commonly known as Mother Taylor, is to be hanged this day sennight, I believe."

"Yea, my lord."

"And it hath been suggested that if she can lay before us such evidence as is needful, she will be commended to the King's mercy and doubtless reprieved from the gallows. Hath all this been made plain and clear to her?"

"Yea, my lord."

"Hm! It appears by these papers, woman, that keeping a house to which rogues of all descriptions have resorted is the least of your crimes."

A strange, cracked old voice burst shrilly upon the still court. "'Tis a lie, my lord! Alas, my lord, that wicked lies should take away my good name, and I tottering on the edge of the grave!"

There were cries of "Silence!" And the officer at the old woman's side shook her by the arm.

"And to continue from the least to the greatest, you have disposed of all manner of stolen goods, and have prepared slow poisons to be sold at a great price and have stained your hands with murder."

"Alas, my lord, it is a wicked lie!"

They shook her into silence, but her lips continued to move, and as she stood between the officers her sharp little eyes ranged about the court.

There was further counselling among the proctors, then one cried sharply, "Come, old woman, remember that the hangman is ready to don his gown, and answer me truly before it is too late: on such and such a day you were at your house in Bideford, were you not?"

"Nay, sir, I am old and my wits are not all they were once and I cannot remember as I ought."

"Come, now, on such a day, did not a certain man come to your house in Bideford and abide there the night?"

"It may be—it may be—for one who keepeth a tavern hath many guests."

"Look about you, old woman, and tell us if you see the man."

"Nay, good sir, my wits wander and I do not remember as I used."

As Philip Marsham watched her hard face, so very old and crafty, he paid little heed to the low voices of the proctors and the Judge. But the sharp command, "Look this man in the face and tell us if you have ever seen him before," came to the erstwhile boatswain of the *Rose of Devon* like the shock of cold water to a man lying asleep.

They led her before Tom Jordan—before the Old One himself—and the two looked each other full in the face, yet neither fluttered an eye. In all truth they were a cool pair; it had taken a Solomon to say which of them was now the subtler.

"Nay, my lord, how should I know this man? He hath the look of an honest fellow, my lord, but I never saw him ere this."

Thereupon the officers exchanged glances and the proctors whispered together.

They led her before Martin Barwick and again she shook her old white head. "Nay, my lord, I know him not." But Martin was swallowing hard, as if some kind of pip had beset him, and this did not escape the notice of the Court.

Down the line of accused men she came and, though she walked in the shadow of the gallows, she said of each, in her shrill, quavering old voice, "Nay, my lord, I know him not."

Of some she spoke thus in all truth; of others, though she knew it would cost her life, she craftily and stoutly lied. And at last she came to Philip Marsham, whose heart chilled when he met the sharp eyes that had looked so hard into his own in Bideford long before. "Nay, my lord, he is a handsome blade, but I never saw him ere this." Some smiled and sniggered; but the old woman shrugged, and lifted her brows, and stood before the Court, wrinkled and bent by years of wickedness. Say what you will of her sins, her courage and loyalty were worthy of a better cause.

In despair of pinning her down, they led her away at last to a bench and there she sat with officers to guard her. Now she watched one man and now she watched another. Often Philip Marsham felt a tremor, almost of fear, at seeing her eyes looking hard into his own. But though of the old woman the Court had made nothing, the exultation that showed in the faces of some of the prisoners was premature, for the Lords of Admiralty had other shafts to their bow, as any gentleman of fortune might have known they would.

Again there was a stir among the ushers, and in the door appeared one at whose coming Tom Jordan ceased to smile.

The fellow's chin sagged and his eyes were wild and he ducked to His Lordship as if someone had pulled a string; and when they called on him to give the Court his name he cried very tremulously, "Yea, yea! Joseph Kirk, an' it please you, my lord!"

"Come now, look about you at these men who are arraigned for piracy. Are there any there whom you have seen elsewhere?"

"Yea, yea, that there be! There! And there! And there!"

"Ah! Hm! Men you have seen elsewhere! Tell us who they are." And His Lordship smiled dryly.

"It is not to count against me, my lord? I have repented— yea, I have repented! 'Twill not undo the King's pardon?"

The very Judge on the bench gave a grunt as in disgust of the abject terror the fellow showed, and a murmur of impatience went through the room; but though he afforded a spectacle for contempt, they reassured him and urged him on.

"Yea, yea! That one there—he at the end—was our captain, and Tom Jordan his name. It was he who led us against a vast number of prizes, which yielded rich profit. It was he and Harry Malcolm—why, Harry Malcolm is not here. Huh! 'Tis passing strange! He hath so often stole beside them, I had thought he would hang beside them too. Yea, and as I was saying—Let us consider! Yea, yea, it was he and Harry Malcolm who contrived the plan for killing Captain Candle and taking the *Rose of Devon*. Yea, they called me apart on the forecastle and tempted me to sin and forced me with many threats. He it was—"

Tom Jordan was on his feet. "You lie in your throat, you drunken dog! It was you who struck him down with your own hand!"

"Nay, nay! I did him no harm! It was another—I swear it was another!"

"It seems," said His Lordship, when they had thrust Tom Jordan back in his seat and had somewhat abated their witness's terror of his one-time chief, "it seems this fellow's words have touched a sore. Go on."

"And there is Martin Barwick—nay, hold him! Nay, if I am to go on, I must have protection!—and there Paul Craig and there our boatswain, Philip Marsham—" And so he continued to name the men and told a tale of shameful acts and crimes for the least of which a man is hanged. Indeed, Philip Marsham himself knew enough of their history to send them one and all to the gallows, but he had not heard a tenth part of the story of piracy and robbery and murder and black crimes unfit for the printed page that this renegade pirate told to the full Court of Admiralty. The fellow made a great story of it, yet kept within a bowshot of the truth; but he was a villain of mean spirit and, though he did for the Court the work it desired, he bought his life at cost of whatever honour he may have had left.

And then came Captain Charles Winterton, who rose, bowing in stately wise to His Lordship, and with a composed air and an assured voice very quietly drew tight the purse-strings of the net that Joe Kirk had knotted. In his grand and dignified manner he bowed now and then to His Lordship and to the proctors, who asked him questions with a defer-ence in their bearing very different from their way with the other witnesses.

"Yea, these pirate rogues boarded His Majesty's ship *Sybil* and killed three of His Majesty's men before they perceived the blunder they had made and gave themselves up—How many lives did the boarders lose? Probably twelve or four-teen. Several bodies fell into the water and were not recov-ered. It was useless to hunt for them, my lord. Great sharks abound in those waters—Yea, this Thomas Jordan led them in person. In truth, there is little distinction between them in the matter of guilt. The man Marsham, whom the previous witness named a boatswain, was the first to board the *Sybil*. He entered the great cabin by way of the stern, apparently to spy out the situation on board. He declared himself a forced man who had run away from the pirates. Who could say? The situation in which he was taken was such, certainly, as to incriminate him; though 'twere cause for sorrow, since he was a brave lad and had given no trouble during the voy-age home."

There was a great whispering among the people, who thought it was a shame for so likely a lad to hang with a pack of pirates. But it was plain by now to the greatest dullard among those unhappy gentlemen of fortune that hang they must; and for Philip Marsham, who sat as white as death from the shame of it, there was no slightest spark of hope.

The net was woven and knotted and drawn, and the end of it all was at hand.

When, according to the custom of the time, they called on Tom Jordan for his defense, he rose and said, "Alas, my lord, the ropes are laid that shall hang me. Already my neck aches. This, though, I will say: whatever these poor men have done, it is I that compelled them into it, and I, my lord, will stand to answer for it."

Some gave one defense and some another; and meanwhile there was much legal talk, dry and long and hard to understand. And so at last they called on Philip Marsham to rise and speak for himself if he had anything to say in his own defense.

He rose and stood before them, very white of face, and though his voice trembled, which was a thing to be expected since he saw before him a shameful death, he told them his true story, beginning with the day he sailed from Bideford, very much as I have told it here. But when they asked him about affairs on board the *Rose of Devon* that concerned the others and not him, he replied that each man must tell his own tale and that though he swung for it he must leave the others to answer those questions for themselves.

"Come," quoth His Lordship, leaning forward and sharply tapping his table, "you have heard the question asked. Remember, young man, that you stand in a place exceeding slippery. It shall profit you nothing to hold your peace."

"My lord," said he, "the tale hath been told in full. There is no need that I add to it, and were I to speak further I should but carry with me to the grave the thought that I had done a treacherous thing. Though I owe these men for nought save hard usage, yet have I eaten their bread and drunk their wine, and I will not, despite their sins, help to hang them."

It was doubtless very wrong for him to reply thus, as any moralist will point out, since it is a man's duty to help enforce

the laws by bringing criminals to justice. But he answered
according to his own conscience; and after the craven talk of
Joseph Kirk, the lad's frank and honest statement pleased
perhaps even my Lord the Judge, sitting high above the
court, who frowned because his position demanded frowns.
Surely loyalty ranks high among the virtues and great credit
is due to a keen sense of personal honour. But there then
came from his talk a result that neither he nor any other had
foreseen.

Up sprang Tom Jordan. "My lord," he cried, "I pray thee
for leave to speak!"

To the frowns and chidings of the officers who forced him
down again, he paid no heed. A tumult rose in the room, for
they had hurled the Old One back and clapped hands over
his mouth; but out of the struggle came again the cry, "My
lord! My lord!" and His Lordship, calling in a loud voice for
order and silence, scowled and gave him the leave he asked.

As Martin had said long before, Tom Jordan was an ugly
customer when his temper was up and hot, but no man to
nurse a grudge.

"I thank you, my lord," said he, the while smoothing his
coat, which had wrinkled sadly in the scuffle. "Though I
must hang I desire to see justice done. It lay in the power of
this Philip Marsham to have added to the tale of our sins and
the sum of our woes; wherefore, since he hath had the spirit
to refrain from doing thus, why, my lord, I needs must say
that he hath spoken only the truth. He was a forced man, and
having a liking for him, since he is a lad of spirit, I would
have had him join us heart and soul. 'Tis true likewise that he
ran away from our ship and turned his hand against us, and
for that I would have let him hang with these other tall fellows but for the brave spirit he hath shown. But as for yonder
swine—yea, thou, Joe Kirk! Quake and stare!—he hath done
more mean, filthy tricks to earn a hanging than any other
gentleman of fortune, I believe, that ever sailed the seas."

"Not so, my lord!" Joe Kirk yelled. "He fears me for my knowledge of his deeds! Help! Hold him—hold him!"

Tom Jordan swore a great oath and Joe Kirk leaped up in his seat, white and shaking, and cried over and over that it was all a lie, and there was a merry time of it before the attendants restored peace.

And then, to the further amazement of all in the court, Captain Charles Winterton again rose.

"If I may add a word, my lord? Thank you, my lord. I observed that when the prisoners went below their manner toward this man Marsham was such as to lend a certain plausibility to his story. They took, in short, so vindictive a delight in his misfortunes that even then it seemed not beyond reason that his tale was true and that he had indeed left them without leave. That, of course, proves nothing with regard to his being a forced man; but it is a matter of common justice to say that, in consideration of all that I have seen before and of that which I have this day heard, I believe he hath told the truth both then and now. Thank you, my lord."

Such a hullabaloo of talk as then burst forth among the spectators, and such learned argument as passed between the proctors and the Lieutenant of Admiralty and His Lordship the Judge, surpass imagination. Some quoted the Latin and the Greek, while others of less learning voiced their opinions in the vulgar tongue, so that all in all there was enough disputation to fuddle the wits of a mere layman by the time they gave the case to the jury.

Then the jury, weighing all that had been said, put together its twelve heads, while such stillness prevailed in the court that a man could hear his neighbor's breathing. It seemed to those whose lives were at stake that the deliberations took as many hours as in reality they took minutes. There are times when every grain of sand in the glass seems to loiter in falling and to drift through the air like thistledown, as if unwilling to come to rest with its fellows below.

Yet the sand is falling as fast as ever, though a man whose life is weighing in the balance can scarcely believe it; so at last the jury made an end of its work, which after all had taken little enough time in consideration of the matter they must decide.

"You have reached with due and faithful care a verdict in this matter?" quoth His Lordship.

"We have, my lord."

"You will then declare your verdict to the Court."

"Of these fourteen prisoners at the bar of justice, my lord, we find one and all guilty of the felonies and piracies that are charged against them, save only one man." In the deathly silence that fell upon the room the name sounded forth like the stroke of a bell. "We acquit, my lord, Philip Marsham."

There and then Philip Marsham parted company with the men of the *Rose of Devon*. His hands shook when he rose a free man, and when many spoke to him in all friendliness he could find no voice to reply.

Never again did he see their faces, but he heard long afterward of how, a week from the day of their trial, they went down the river to Wapping in wherries, with the bright sun shining on the ships and on the shore where a great throng had assembled to see them march together up the stairs to Execution Dock.

Though they had always made themselves out to appear great and fierce men, yet on that last day they again showed themselves cravens at heart—except Tom Jordan. The Old One, stern, cold, shrewd, smiled at his fellows and said, "It is to be. May God have mercy on me!" And though he stood with the black cap over his eyes and the noose round his neck, he never flinched.

As for Martin Barwick, his face grey with fear, he strove to break away, and cried out in English and in Spanish, and called on the Virgin. Sadly, though, had he fallen from the teachings of the Church, and little did his cries avail him! He came at the last to the end he had feared from the first; and his much talk of hanging was thus revealed to have been in a manner prophecy, although it sprang from no higher oracle than his own cowardly heart.

One told Philip Marsham that Mother Taylor was hanged; another said they let her go, to die a natural death in the shadow of the gallows that stood by the crossroads in her native town of Barnstable. Either tale is likely enough, and Phil never learned which was true.

For aught I know to the contrary, she may have found an elixir of life as good as the one discovered by the famous Count de Saint-Germain, and so be living still.

Whatever the end she came to, Phil Marsham was far away when they determined her fate. For the day he stepped out in the streets of London, a free man once more and a loyal subject of the King, he took the road to the distant inn where he was of a mind to claim fulfillment of Nell Entick's promise.

CHAPTER XXII

Back to the Inn

IF THIS were a mere story to while away an idle hour, I, the scribe, would tie neatly every knot and leave no Irish pennants hanging from my work. But life, alas, is no pattern drawn to scale. The many interweaving threads are caught up in strange tangles, and over them, darkly and inscrutably, Atropos presides. Who cannot recall to mind names and faces still alive with the friendship of a few weeks or months—a friendship pleasant in memory—a friendship that promised fruitful years, but that was lost for ever when a boy or man drifted out of sight for one reason or another, and on one tide or another of the projects that go to make up life? To Philip Marsham, tramping again the high roads of England, there came, mingled with many other desires, a longing to see once more the Scottish smith who had wrought the dirk that had tasted blood for his protection in those dark adventures at sea. But when he came to the smithy beside the heath he found it open and empty. The wind blew the door on rusty hinges; brown leaves had drifted in and lay about the cold forge; the coals were dead, the bellows were broken, and the lonely man who had wrought iron on the now rusty anvil had taken his tools and gone.

The day was still young, for the wayfarer, starting early and in the fullness of his strength, had this day covered three miles in the time that one had taken him when he walked that road before. So he left the smithy and pushed on across the heath and far beyond it, marking each familiar farm and village and country house, until night had fallen and the stars had come out, when he laid him down under a hedge and slept.

He was thinking, when he fell asleep, of Nell Entick. He remembered very well her handsome face, her head held so high, her white throat and bare arms. He was going back to the inn to claim fulfillment of her promise and he pictured her as waiting for him there. In most ways he was a bold, resolute youth who had seen much of life; but in some ways, nevertheless, he was a lad of small experience, and if he thought at all that she had been a little over-bold, a little over-willing, he thought only that she was as honestly frank as he.

Waking that night upon his bed of leaves, he saw far away on a hill the dancing flames of a campfire, concerning which he greatly wondered. For, having been long out of England, he had small knowledge of the ups and downs of parliaments and kings; and in the brief time since his return, of which he had spent nearly all in prison, he had heard nothing of the tumultuous state of the kingdom, save a few words dropped here or there while he was passing through hamlets and villages, and seen nothing thereof save such show of arms as in one place or another had caught his eye but not his thought. Although he knew it not, since he was a plain lad with no gift of second-sight, he lay in a country poised on the brink of war and his bed was made in the field where a great battle was to be fought.

He went on at daylight, and going through a village at high noon saw a preacher in clipped hair and sober garb, who was calling on the people to be valiant and of good courage against those wicked men who had incited riot and rebellion among the Roman Catholics in Ireland, whereby the King might find pretext for raising a vast army to devastate and enslave England. Sorely perplexed by this talk, of which he understood little, Phil besought a sneering young fellow, who stood at no great distance, for an explanation; to which the fellow replied that it was talk for them that wore short hair and long ears, and that unless a man kept watch upon his wits his own ears would grow as long from hearing it as those of any Roundhead ass in the country. At this Phil took umbrage; but the fellow cried Nay, that he would fight no such keen blade, who was, it seemed, a better man that he looked. And with a laugh he waved the matter off and strolled away.

So to the inn Phil came in due time, having meditated much, meanwhile, on the talk of the King and war and the rights of Parliament, which was in the mouths and ears of all men. But he put such things out of his mind when at last he saw the inn, for the moment was at hand when his dreams should come true and he should find waiting for him the Nell Entick he remembered from long ago.

Surely a lad of enterprise, who had ventured the world over with pirates, could find in any English village something to which he could turn his hand. Indeed, who knew but some day he might keep the inn himself—or do better? Who knew? He remembered Little Grimsby and drew a long breath. Caught in a whirl of excitement that set the blood drumming in his ears, he strode into the house and, boldly stepping up to the public bar, called loudly, "Holla, I say! I would have speech of Mistress Nell Entick."

From a tall settle in the corner, where he sat taking tobacco, there rose a huge man with red and angry face.

"Who in the Devil's name art thou," he roared, "that comes ranting into an honest house and bawls out thus the name of Mistress Nell Entick?"

There were as usual a couple of countrymen sitting with pots of ale, who reared their heads in vast amazement, and in the noisy kitchen down the passage a perceptible hush followed the loud words. The house seemed to pause and listen; the countrymen set down their pots; there was a sound of creaking hinges and of lightly falling feet.

Very coolly, smiling slightly, Philip Marsham met the eyes of the big, red-faced man. "It seems," said he, "thou art riding for another fall."

A look of recognition, at first incredulous, then profoundly displeased, dawned on the red face and even greater anger followed.

"Thou banging, basting, broiling brogger!" he thundered. "Thou ill-contrived, filthy villain! Out the door! Begone!"

"It seems, Jamie Barwick, that thy wits are struck with years. Have care. Thy brother is already on the road to Wapping—they have signed and sealed his passage."

The fat man came to Phil with the slow gait and the low-hung head of a surly dog. He thrust his red face close to Phil's own.

"Yea, it is thou," he sneered. "I am minded to beat thee and bang thee till thou goest skulking under the hedges for cover. But it seems thou hast good news. What is this talk of the hangman's budget?"

"It is true. By now thine excellent brother hath in all likelihood donned the black cap and danced on air. As for beating and banging—scratch thy head and agitate thy memory and consider if I have given thee reason to hope for quietness and submission."

There was a flicker of doubt in the man's small eyes, whereby it seemed his memory served him well.

"And what meanest thou by saying thou would'st have speech of Mistress Nell Entick?" he asked suspiciously.

"That concerns thee not."

"Ha!" He scowled darkly. "Methinks it concerns me nearly!"

And then a high voice cried, "Who called my name?"

They turned and Phil Marsham's face lighted, for she stood in the door. She was not so fair as he had pictured her—what lad's memory will not play such tricks as that?—and he thought that when he had taken her away from the inn she need never again wear a drabbled gown. But it was she, the Nell Entick who had so lightly given him her promise and kissed him as he fled, and he had come for her.

"Back again, John? Nay, John was not thy name. Stay! No, it hath escaped me, but I remember well thy face. And shall I bring thee ale? Or sack? We have some rare fine sack."

He stared at her as if he could not believe his ears had told him right. "I have come," he said, "to claim a certain promise—"

She looked bewildered, puzzled, then laughed loudly. "Silly boy!" she cried. "I am these six months a wife."

"A wife!"

"Yea, and mine," cried Barwick. "Come, begone! I'll have no puppies sniffling at her heels."

At something in the man's manner, the full truth dawned on Philip Marsham. "I see. And you have taken the inn?"

"Yea, that I have! Must I split thy head to let in knowledge? Begone!"

She laid her hand on Barwick's wrist. "The lad means no harm," she whispered. "Come, it is folly to drive trade away." And over Barwick's shoulder she cast Phil such a glance that he knew, maid or matron, she would philander still.

But Phil had seen her with new eyes and the old charm was broken. (Perhaps if Tom Marsham had waited a year before he leaped into marriage, I would have had no story to tell!) All that was best in the father had come down to the son, and Phil turned his back on the siren with the bold, bright eyes. He turned his back on the inn, too, and all the dreams he had built around it—a boy's imaginings raised on the sands of a moment's fancy. Nay, he turned his back on all the world he had hitherto known.

With a feeling that he was rubbing from his face a spider's web of sordidness—that he was cutting the last cord that bound him to his old, wild life—stirred by a new and daring project, he went out of the inn and turned to the left and took the road in search of Sir John Bristol.

CHAPTER XXIII

And Old Sir John

SIR JOHN Bristol! There, gentlemen, was a brave, honest man! A man of spirit and of a humour! If you crossed him, if you toyed with him, his mirth was rough, his hand was hard, he was relentless as iron. But for a man who stood his ground and fought a bold fight and met squarely the old man's eyes, there was nothing Sir John would not do.

After all his weary travels by land and sea, Philip Marsham had at last come back to find a man whom he had seen but once and for a brief time. Yet in that man he had such complete confidence as he had never had in any other, and since Jamie Barwick had left the man's service and taken the inn—who knew?

Striding over the same rolling country road that he had tramped with Martin long before, and coming soon to the park, he skirted it and pressed on, keeping meanwhile his eyes and wits about him, until he perceived a gate and a porter's lodge. He went to the gate and finding it ajar slipped through and made haste up a long avenue with overarching trees. A man from the lodge came out and angrily called after the intruder, but Phil never looked back. The avenue turned to the left and he saw at a distance the great house; he was of no mind to suffer hindrance or delay.

The sunset sky threw long, still shadows across the grass, and countless wandering branches of ivy lay like a dark drapery upon the grey walls of the old house. A huge dog came bounding and roaring down the avenue, but when the lad smiled without fear and reached a friendly hand toward him, the beast stopped clamouring and came quietly to heel. Lights shone from the windows and softly on the still evening air the thin, sweet music of a virginal stole over the broad terraces and lawns.

The clamour of the dog, it seemed, had attracted the attention of those within, for a grey-haired servant met the stranger in the door. He stood there suspiciously, forbiddingly, and with a cold stare searched the young man from head to heel.

"I would have speech of Sir John Bristol," said Phil.

The servant frowned. "Nay, you have blundered," he replied haughtily. "The servants' hall—"

"I said Sir John."

"Sir John? It is—ahem!—impossible."

"I said Sir John."

The servant moved as if to shut the door.

"Come," said Phil quietly, "enough of that! I will have speech of Sir John Bristol."

For a moment the servant hesitated, then from within a great voice cried, "Come, Cobden, what's afoot?"

In haughty disapproval of the lad without, the servant turned his back, but to the man within he spoke with deference, as if apologizing. "Yea, Sir John. The fellow is insistent, but I shall soon have him off."

"Go, Cobden. Leave him to me."

The servant moved away and disappeared.

The virginalling had ceased, and on the lawns and the avenue and the park, which stretched away into the dark valley, a deep silence had come with the twilight. The sun had set and the long shadows across the grass were lost in the greater shadow of evening. As the world without had grown darker, the lights within seemed to have grown brighter.

"Come, fellow, come into the hall. So! Have I not seen thee before?"

"Yea, Sir John."

"Ha! I can remember faces. Aye, there are few that escape me. Let us consider. Why, on my life! This is the lad that gave Barwick such a tumbling that the fellow walked lame for a month. Speak up! Have I not placed thee right?"

"Though I was faint for want of food, I was quicker on my feet than he."

The old man laughed until his brave curls shook.

"In faith, and it is said with moderation. And what now, lad? What hath brought thee hither?"

"Since Barwick hath left your service—"

"That he hath, that he hath!"

"It seemed there might be a place for a keeper."

"For a keeper? Ha, ha, ha! Nay, th'art too spirited a lad to waste away as keeper. Mark my word, lad, the King will shortly have need for such courageous gallants as thou. Unless I mistake thy spirit, we shall soon see thee riding among the foremost when we chase these dogs of Roundheads into the King's kennels and slit their noses and prick their ears as a warning to all of weak mind and base spirit."

"I have a taste for such sport, and God knows I am the King's man."

"Good, say I!" Sir John's clear eyes searched the frank eyes of the lad, and the old man was pleased with what he found.

"Come, the cook shall fill thy belly and Cobden shall find thee a bed. Cobden! Cobden, I say!"

"Yea, Sir John."

"Make place for this good fellow in the servants' hall and see that he hath all that he can eat and drink."

"Yea, Sir John."

"But stay a moment. Thy name, fellow."

"Philip Marsham."

"Philip Marsham?" The heavy brows knotted and Sir John spoke musingly. "Philip Marsham! I once knew a man of that name."

Silence fell upon the hall. Grey Cobden stood a little behind his master, and when Phil looked past Sir John he saw standing in a door the tall, quiet girl he had seen with the old knight that day in the wood so long since. Doubtless it was she who had played upon the virginal. Her dark eyes and fine dignity wove a spell around the lad—a spell of the magic that has come down from the beginning of time—the magic that is always young.

Take such spells, such magic, as lightly as you please; yet they have overturned kingdoms and not once, but many times, have they launched a thousand ships.

"Did you ever hear of Dr. Marsham of Little Grimsby?" Sir John asked, and he watched the lad very closely.

"Yea."

"And what have you heard of him?"

"He is my grandfather."

"So!" The old knight stepped back and bent his brows. "Verily," he said, "I believe the lad hath spoken truth. Go, Cobden. There is no place in the hall for this lad."

The servant departed and the girl stepped nearer.

"Your father's name?" Sir John said.

"My father's name was Thomas Marsham."

"Doubtless he bred you to the sea."

"He did."

"He broke the hearts of his father and his mother."

Phil stood silent in the hall and looked Sir John in the eye. Since there seemed to be no reply, he waited for the knight to speak again.

"Tom Marsham's father and mother are dead, but within the year, lad, they stood where you are standing now. It was the last time I saw them."

What could a young man say? Phil Marsham remembered well the one time he had himself seen them. Who knew what might have happened had he spoken? But the chance was gone, and for ever.

"There is no place for Philip Marsham in my servants' hall," said Sir John. "His father—but no! Let the dead lie. There is no place for Philip Marsham in my servants' hall. Under my roof he is my guest."

CHAPTER XXIV

And Again the *Rose of Devon*

THE STORY of Philip Marsham and of Sir John Bristol, and of the fortune left by the good Doctor Marsham of Little Grimsby—how it came to his grandson and was lost in the war that brought ruin to many a noble family—is a tale that may some day be worth the telling. Of that, I make no promises.

The years that followed were wild and turbulent, but during their passage Phil chanced upon one reminder and another of his earlier days of adventuring. He saw once again the long, ranting madman who had carried the great book. He might not have known the fellow, who was in a company of Brownists or Anabaptists, or some such people, had he not heard him crying out in his voice like a cracked trumpet, to the great wonder and admiration of his fellows, "Never was a man beset with such diversity of thoughts." There was Jacob, too, who had sneaked away like a rat on the eve of the

day when Tom Jordan's schemes fell about his ears: Phil once
came upon him face to face, but when their eyes met Jacob
slipped round a corner and was gone. He was a subtle man
and wise, and of no intention to be reminded of his days as a
pirate.

Philip Marsham went to the war with Sir John Bristol, and
fought for the King, and rose to be a captain; and with the
story of Philip Marsham is interwoven inseparably the story
of Anne Bristol and of her father, Sir John. For Sir John
Bristol died at the second battle of Newbury with his head
on Philip Marsham's knees; and in his grief at losing the
brave knight who had befriended him, the lad prayed God
for vengeance on the Roundhead armies.

And yet, though his grief was bitter, he had too just a mind
to see only one side of a great war. Once, when they sent him
from the King's camp on a secret mission, the enemy ran him
to cover, and he escaped them only by doubling back and
hiding in the garret of a cottage where he lay high under the
thatch and watched through a dusty little window the street
from the Red Boar Inn down the hill to the distant meadows,
without being himself seen. He heard far away a murmur as
of droning bees. Minutes passed and he heard the drone
settle into a hollow rumble, from which there emerged after
a time the remote sound of rattling drums and the occasional
voices of shouting men. Then, of a sudden, there broke on
the air a sound as of distant thunder, in which he made out a
chorus:

> *His staff and rod shall comfort me,*
> *His mantle e'er shall be my shield;*
> *My brimming cup I hold in fee*
> *Of him who rules the battlefield.*

The voices of the singing men came booming over the
meadows. They were deep, strong voices and there was that

in their volume and fierce earnestness which made a man shiver.

Phil heard a dog barking; he saw a woman standing in the door of a cottage; he saw a cloud of dust rise above the meadow; then they came.

First a band of men on foot in steel caps, with their fire-locks shouldered, swinging out in long, firm strides. Then a little group of kettledrums, hammering away in a fierce rhythm. Then a number of horsemen, with never a glint of gold on their bridles and never a curl from under their iron helms. Then, rank behind rank, a solid column of foot that flowed along the dusty road over hillock and hollow, dark and sombre, undulating like a torpid stream of something thick and slow that mightily forces a passage over every obstacle in its way.

They came up the hill, turning neither to right nor to left, up the hill and over it, and away to the north, where King Charles and all his armies lay.

It was a fearful sight, for they were stern, determined men. There was no gallant flippancy in their carriage; there was no lordly show of ribbands and linen and gold and silver lace. They frowned as they marched, and looked about them little. They bore so steadily on, they made one feel they were men of tempered metal, men of no blood and no flesh, men with no love for the brave adventures of life, but with a streak of iron in their very souls.

Philip Marsham had heard the men of the *Rose of Devon* go into battle with cries and shouting, and laugh when they killed; he had seen old Sir John Bristol throw back his head proudly and jest with the girls of the towns on their march; but these were men of another pattern.

He became aware, as he watched them go by—and he then knew the meaning of fear, safely hidden though he was, behind the dirty and small window in the gable; for had one man of those thousands found him there, it would have

ended the fighting days of Philip Marsham—he became
aware that here was a courage so stubborn there was no mas-
tering it; that here was a purposeful strength such as all the
wild blades in his master's camp could never match. Their
faces showed it; the marching rhythm of the never-ending
column was alive with it.

Behind the first regiments of infantry, horsemen came,
and, at an interval in the ranks of the cavalry, five men rode
together. The eyes of one, who led the four by a span or two,
were bent on the road, and his face was stern and strong and
thoughtful. As Phil watched him, the first hesitating surmisal
became conviction, and long afterward he learned that he
had been right. From his gable window he had seen Oliver
Cromwell go by.

All that afternoon the column streamed on, and in the
early darkness Philip fell asleep to the sound of men marching. In the morning they were gone, and he went on his way
and fulfilled his mission; but though the King's men fought
with a gallantry that never lessened, the cause of the King
was lost, and the day broke when Philip Marsham was ready
to turn his back on England.

So he came a second time to the harbour of Bideford, in
Devon, and had it in his mind to take ship for some distant
land where he could forget the years of his youth and early
manhood. He was in the mood, then, to envy Sir John Bristol
and all the gallant company that had died on the fields of
Naseby and Newbury, and of many another great battle; for
he was the King's man, and great houses of the country had
fallen, and many lords and gentlemen whose estates had
gone to pay the cost of Cromwell's wars had as much reason
as he, and more, to wonder, at the sight of deep water,
whether it were better to die by one's own hand or to seek
new fortunes beyond the sea.

There were many vessels in the harbour and his gaze wan-
dered over them, ships and pinks and ketches and a single

galliot from the Low Countries, until his eyes came at last to one of singularly familiar aspect. He looked at her a long time, then strolled down to the quay and accosted an aged man who was warming his rheumatic limbs in the sun.

"What ship is that," said Captain Marsham, "which lies yonder, in line with the house on the farther shore to the right of the three trees?"

The aged man squinted over the harbour to pick up the bearings his questioner had given him and cleared his throat with a husky cough.

"Why, that," he said, "be the frigate they call *Rose of Devon*."

"The *Rose of Devon*—nay, she cannot be the *Rose of Devon*!"

"Can and be. Why does 'ee look so queer, sir?"

"Not the *Rose of Devon!*"

"Art 'ee addled?" He laughed like a cackling hen. "Aye, an' yon's her master."

The master turned when the young captain accosted him, and replied, with reasonable civility, "Yea, the *Rose of Devon,* Captain Hosmer, at your service, sir. Passage? Yea, we can take you, but you're a queer sort to ask passage ere you know whither she sails. Is it murder or theft?"

"Neither. The old order is changing and I would go abroad."

"To the colonies?"

"They tell me all the colonies are of a piece with these Roundheads here, and that as many psalms are whined in Boston in New England as in all the conventicles in London."

He laughed in good humour. "You are rash," said he. "Were I of the other side, your words might cost you your head. But we're going south to Barbados, and there you'll find men to your own taste."

Captain Philip Marsham wished no more than that. So he struck a bargain for passage, and paid with gold, and sailed from England for the second time in the old *Rose of Devon*, the dark frigate that by God's grace had come back to Bideford in the hour when he most needed her.